THE HALLOWED HUNT

A Wild Hunt Novel, Book 5

YASMINE GALENORN

A Nightqueen Enterprises LLC Publication

Published by Yasmine Galenorn

PO Box 2037, Kirkland WA 98083-2037

THE HALLOWED HUNT

A Wild Hunt Novel

Copyright © 2019 by Yasmine Galenorn

First Electronic Printing: 2019 Nightqueen Enterprises LLC

First Print Edition: 2019 Nightqueen Enterprises

Cover Art & Design: Ravven

Art Copyright: Yasmine Galenorn

Editor: Elizabeth Flynn

ALL RIGHTS RESERVED No part of this book may be reproduced or distributed in any format, be it print or electronic or audio, without permission. Please prevent piracy by purchasing only authorized versions of this book.

This is a work of fiction. Any resemblance to actual persons, living or dead, businesses, or places is entirely coincidental and not to be construed as representative or an endorsement of any living/ existing group, person, place, or business.

A Nightqueen Enterprises LLC Publication

Published in the United States of America

❦ Created with Vellum

ACKNOWLEDGMENTS

Welcome back into my world of the Wild Hunt. This series has taken full hold with me and the world is expanding in wonderful and mysterious ways. Ember and Herne's world is expanding with each passing day and I'm so grateful that my readers have taken it into their hearts. I'm loving writing this like nothing else that I've written in a long, long time. I'm also planning to introduce a spinoff series, alongside the original, this year.

Thanks to my usual crew: Samwise, my husband, Andria and Jennifer—without their help, I'd be swamped. To the women who have helped me find my way in indie, you're all great, and to the Wild Hunt, which runs deep in my magick, as well as in my fiction.

Also, my love to my furbles, who keep me happy. And most reverent devotion to Mielikki, Tapio, Ukko, Rauni, and Brighid, my spiritual guardians and guides. And to the spirit of the Wild Hunt, Herne, and Cernunnos, who still rule the wild places of this world.

If you wish to reach me, you can find me through my

website at Galenorn.com and be sure to sign up for my newsletter to keep updated on all my latest releases!

Brightest Blessings,
~The Painted Panther~
~Yasmine Galenorn~

WELCOME TO THE HALLOWED HUNT

Life isn't easy when you bear the mark of the Silver Stag.

It's October, and with Samhain approaching, Ember must enter the Cruharach to face the darkest night of her life. As she gives herself over to the Autumn Stalkers and the Leannan Sidhe, she is plunged deep into the shadows of Annwn to face Cernunnos and the test of the Hallowed Hunt.

Meanwhile, the Wild Hunt is trying to contain collateral damage throughout the city. A Fae hate group is terrorizing Seattle, going after shifters and humans alike. In the middle of investigating the deadly cult, Herne takes on a new case.

A frantic wolf-shifter mother begs the Wild Hunt Agency for help. Her three-year-old daughter has been abducted. With three other young girls already dead at the hands of a serial killer dubbed the Angel of Mercy, Herne and Ember find themselves in a desperate race to find the girl before the Angel of Mercy claims another victim.

Reading Order for the Wild Hunt Series:

- Book 1: The Silver Stag
- Book 2: Oak & Thorns
- Book 3: Iron Bones
- Book 4: A Shadow of Crows
- Book 5: The Hallowed Hunt

CHAPTER ONE

"You have got to be kidding me," Viktor said, shaking his head as he grabbed another cookie from the tray in the center of the table. "Everybody knows that Skyler has the best record. He's gonna take it."

"Oh hell no." I practically jumped out of my seat, unable to believe that Viktor was siding with the enemy. "If *anybody's* going to win the title, it will be Balentine. You wait and see. He's come so far in the past few months, and there's no way he's going to let Skyler beat him now. I don't care what his record is, Skyler is done. Over. *O-V-E-R*."

"Put your money where your mouth is, Kearney?" Viktor held out his hand, rubbing his fingers together. "Bet you a hundred on it."

"Make it a hundred and you're on." I snorted. "Balentine managed a backside 1260 off the heels—that little trick that helped Sage Kotsenberg win the Olympics. Even now, only a handful of snowboarders can do it." We had been arguing for the past fifteen minutes, and by now we were reduced to *He said–she said* tactics.

"A hundred it is. Prepare to lose your money." Viktor flashed his phone my way. "Skyler landed that same jump two days ago in Aspen."

Angel leaned between us, her hands firmly planted on the table.

"Will the two of you *please* shut up? Nobody else gives a damn about the match. Make your bet. Buy nachos and beer for the games. But if you don't stop this incessant squabbling, I'll break the TV so you won't be able to watch the race. And since it's on a weekday afternoon, there's no chance in hell you'll be able to sneak out. *Do you understand me?*"

Viktor cleared his throat. I stared at my hands. Nobody was safe when Angel got into a snit and there was no doubt, she was well into one now.

"Well? Are you going to answer me?" She folded her arms across her chest.

"Fine, we'll keep it for after hours." I narrowed my eyes at Viktor, sticking my tongue out.

"Adulting *really well*, Kearney," Viktor snorted, but he stopped when Angel turned to him.

"What did I say?" She tapped her foot on the floor, her boot making a definitive *I'm waiting* statement.

"All right, all right. I'm good. Ember and I were just having some fun." Viktor shrugged, giving me a guilty smile.

I sighed. "We're good. We weren't really fighting. We're just…passionate…about snowboarding." I turned back to Viktor. "This winter, want to head up to the slopes for some practice? I'm not very good, but I've tried it a few times and love it."

He picked up a cookie and tossed it to me. I caught it mid-air.

"Sure thing. I'm not sure how I'll fare, given my size, but I'm willing to give it a go." He laughed in that gentle-giant sort of way. "Sheila might want to come along, too. Maybe we should get up an agency-wide outing. What about it, Talia? You willing to hop on a snowboard?"

Talia choked on her cola. "*Me*? On a snowboard? Even when I had my full powers, I don't think I would have been interested in risking my neck, barreling down the side of a hill at what…thirty, forty miles per hour or more?" She glanced at the door. "When's Herne supposed to get here?"

"He was supposed to have been here by now," I said, glancing at the clock. Herne had texted everybody in the Wild Hunt at around seven o'clock with a note that we needed to make sure we were at work on time. He hinted that something big had happened. We were all waiting in the break room. It was now eight-fifteen and he was late.

"Well, he'd better get here soon, because we have a client coming in to talk to him about billing at nine. Dwarf who thinks Herne overcharged him."

I rolled my eyes. "Dwarves *always* think they're being overcharged. Even Ginty's a pain in the ass about money, and I *like* him."

Dwarves were notorious for hoarding treasure and money, and they didn't like giving any of it up. While Ginty McClintock kept his prices at his bar low enough, he was good at nickel-and-diming his customers to death.

"*Who* do you like? Better not be talking about another

beau." Herne entered the break room. Stopping to give me a quick kiss, he tossed his messenger bag on the counter and headed to the coffeepot, where he poured himself a tall mug of black coffee. He set it down next to his bag, then shrugged off his leather jacket. His hair was hanging loose today, long and golden blond, grazing the back of his shoulder blades. His eyes were cornflower blue, and the slight scruff of a beard made him look just unkempt enough to be super-sexy. He was wearing a pair of black jeans with a silver belt, and a V-neck T-shirt.

"If I had another beau, I'd be exhausted. You're man—or rather *god*—enough for any woman," I said, winking at him. "I was saying that I like Ginty, even if he's cheap."

"He may be cheap, but he's generous to a fault when it counts," Herne said, sliding into his chair. "But we can talk about him another day. We've got a problem."

I sighed. It seemed every time we turned around, we had a problem.

Yutani looked up from his laptop and brushed his hair back from his face. He was pensive today, and had barely spoken since Angel and I arrived. Now, his dark eyes flashed and he cleared his throat. "Need me to take notes?"

"No, let Talia do it. I want you to check on a few things as I go along." Herne glanced around the room, the smile fading from his lips, replaced by a somber look. Something must have happened to make him so pensive so early in the day. "Everybody ready?"

I pulled out my tablet. Angel, Viktor, and Talia did the same. Yutani was poised with his fingers ready to play across the keys as Herne needed information.

"Ready, boss," Talia said.

"These were found at the scene of an assault last night." He pulled a sheath of papers out of his bag and tossed them on the table in front of Angel. They were flyers, advertising something. "I made photocopies so you can all look at them. Pass them around, please."

Angel took one, then handed out the rest.

As I picked up the flyer I stared at the words emblazoned on it. They were printed in brilliant yellow lettering, outlined with black.

"What the hell is this?" I wasn't sure what I was looking at.

FAE BRETHREN OF SEATTLE
THE TUATHAN BROTHERHOOD NEEDS YOU!
Tired of catering to shifters and humans? Do you long for the days when our great cities spread across a nation rather than a few thousand acres? Tired of being "kept in line" by rules and regulations meant to benefit the mundanes of the world?

Join us, and take back the streets of Seattle. Drive out the filthy pelt-changers and head-blind humans, and reclaim this land for those who tended to it in the first place—the Fae.

UNITE NOW AND JOIN US! For information on joining the TUATHAN BROTHERHOOD, email: fae-supremacy@faemail.com

---

Herne shook his head. "I have no clue, at this point. But the flier was found at the scene of a nasty brawl. Three wolf shifters and two humans were beat up pretty bad outside the LaLeeq Nightclub last night. They were there, celebrating the fact that one of the shifters just got a big promotion at work. They were all a little tipsy—well, more than a little, they were plastered. They were standing outside the club, near an alley, waiting for a LUD."

LUD stood for "Let-Us-Drive," a rideshare company who had become the hit of Seattle, boasting excellent customer service and moderate prices. They catered to their customers and had practically put all the other rideshares and taxis out of business.

"Let me guess, they were jumped by some thugs from the alley?" It happened all too often, and always made me wonder why people thought they were safe in the middle of the night, standing near a dark alley. Especially when they were drunk.

"Oh, they were jumped, all right. By a gang of at least six or seven Fae. And they meant business. Two of the shifters are in serious condition, and the third is stable, but pretty bruised up. The humans are both in critical condition." He shook his head. "The gang meant business. This wasn't just a 'rough them up' session. And the only reason they stopped was because the LUD driver happened to pull in at that moment and he called the cops. He started honking his horn and the thugs ran."

I stared at the flier, my mind whirling. "A *Fae hate group*? The Fae Courts hate *each other*, and they're arrogant...well, *we* tend to be arrogant, and impulsive. But the Fae don't usually expand their dislike to include humans or shifters. And right now, both Courts are working as a unified front because of the Fomorians and the Cryptozoid Association."

Recently, the United Coalition that ruled the country had welcomed in a fifth group. Now, instead of the four groups that normally governed the country in joint agreement—the Human League, the Fae Courts, the Shifter Alliance, and the Vampire Nation—the United Coalition had five governing groups.

"I know. It boggles the mind," Herne said.

"Have you talked to Cernunnos?" Viktor asked.

Cernunnos was Herne's father, and he was Lord of the Forest. Herne was Lord of the Hunt. Cernunnos and Morgana—a goddess of Fae, and Herne's mother—were responsible for the Wild Hunt Agency. Our primary mission was to keep the animosity from between the Light and the Dark Fae from spilling over into the human community. My people, like it or not, scored low on impulse control. The Courts had waged war against one another since time began.

As for me, neither side liked admitting I even existed. I was half Light, half Dark, and my parents had paid the ultimate price for their love. The distinction between the two Courts was a misnomer. Neither side was either fully good or bad—both Light and Dark Fae were about evenly matched as far as morality—or amorality—went. But as for a hate group? I had never seen them go this far.

"I talked to my father this morning before I came to work. He and Mother want us to look into this immediately. It's a code red situation, because this could go very bad, very fast. We need to talk to Saílle and Névé as soon as possible. I put in a call and am waiting for both sides to get back to me." Herne paused, leaning back.

"Is this localized, I hope?" Talia asked.

Herne stared at the flier, then a dark cloud passed over

his face and he crumpled it into a ball and threw it in the garbage can. "That, I'm also waiting on. I have calls to the other agencies around the world to see if any of them have heard any rumors about this, or if they're having problems, too. So far, this is the only blip that's crossed my radar, so I'm hoping it's a small group of nutjobs trying to get some attention."

The Wild Hunt was monitored by Cernunnos and Morgana, but other variants of our agency existed throughout the world. There was Odin's Chase in Norway, Mielikki's Arrow in Finland. Diana's Hounds watched over Italy, and Artemis's Huntresses—Greece. I wasn't sure how many more there were, but all of them worked the way we did, and all were loosely grouped together under a governing cloud of gods from the various pantheons.

"Are we sure there's a connection between the flier and the thugs? Could the flyer have been there before the assault?" Talia asked.

Viktor frowned. "That seems like it would be an unlikely coincidence."

"Yes, it would be, but coincidence does happen and we can't discount the possibility." Talia turned to Yutani. "Can you find anything on this Tuathan Brotherhood?"

"Already on it," Yutani muttered, tapping away at the keys. "I'm drawing a blank so far, but let me keep digging. They could be a new organization, or they could just have their info buried so deeply that it's hard to find. It might be part of the Dark Web."

"That's a scary thought," Talia said.

"What's the Dark Web?" I asked.

Yutani looked up from his keyboard. "You've heard of

the sites where unlicensed guns are sold, and illegal drugs, and far worse things, like human trafficking?"

I nodded. "Yeah."

"Those are primarily found on the Dark Web. You have to download a specific tool in order to access it, and it's a dangerous place to delve. But hate groups? I can see them using the Dark Web." He frowned, shaking his head. "I'll search for them on my other laptop—I keep one that's locked down to the point of being the armored tank of computers. We *never* want anybody headquartered on the Dark Web to know we're looking for them."

"Thanks," Herne said. "Let me know if you find out anything. Maybe shoot them an email from there, too? From a hidden account? Express interest, see what you can find out."

"Will do, if I can find an opening." Yutani pushed the laptop away. "Though most hate groups tend to be pretty vocal about their activities."

"I dunno. They may claim responsibility for attacks, but you won't find them planning them out in the open, or a convenient address to send the SWAT team to." Viktor turned to Herne. "Want me to ask Erica at the station if she knows anything about the group? If they've struck before, or if anybody has reported their propaganda before now?"

Erica was Viktor's source for information at the police station. Most of the police worked under the jurisdiction of the Fae by this point, and sometimes matters were skewed to the Fae Queens' advantage.

"Good idea," Herne said. "Meanwhile, we have to keep a close eye on the response to this. It's bound to stir some blowback." He let out a loud sigh. "Some days, I hate coming to work. Especially when it involves crap like this."

"Anything else?" Angel asked. "You have an appointment with Curnzey Duggath at nine. He's coming in to talk to you about his bill."

Herne wiped his hand across his face as he stood up. "Spare me from cheapskates. So that's why you were talking about Ginty when I arrived." He pointed to the fliers. "Keep one of those for research, each of you, but keep them out of sight. They are in no way, shape, or form, to be seen by anybody outside of this room. I mean it. My mother was appalled, by the way. She wants this nipped in the bud as of yesterday, which means we'd better find out who's behind it."

As everybody headed toward their private offices, I tapped him on the shoulder. "Do you need me there when Curnzey comes in?"

"Nope. I'll deal with him myself and spare you his angst."

"Thanks." I started for my office, then paused, glancing over my shoulder. "Do you mind if we reschedule tonight? Angel and I want to stop by a hamburger joint on the way home. They make lime milkshakes and pizza burgers."

Herne grimaced. "That sounds terrible. At least the milkshake." He didn't care for citrus-flavored desserts.

"To you, maybe, but it's an annual tradition for us. And tonight's the season premiere of *Rudding Place Northwest*. I thought you might want to skip the invitation to watch it with us."

"What's that?" Herne frowned, staring at me.

"A period drama set at the turn of the twentieth century. It's basically an historical soap opera set in 1915, around a woman—Emma Smyth—who's struggling to make it as a dressmaker after her husband dies. Most of his assets go to his brother, leaving her without a penny. The brother's a cad and offers to set her up as his mistress, but she refuses, determined to make it on her own. We've gotten hooked on it."

Herne coughed, smiling as he covered his mouth. "You thought right. Of course we can reschedule. I've got plenty of chores I need to get done at home. Enjoy your soap and your lime shake." With a shudder, he went into his office and closed the door.

As I entered my office, a glint of sunlight peeked through the window. The room was small but cozy, and the window looked out into First Avenue, the street where the Wild Hunt Agency was located. Against the wall the window was located on was a second desk. On my left stood a filing cabinet and a bookshelf, flanked by an oversized armchair. To the right was my desk, with both a desktop and my office laptop.

I had painted the room sage, and added green velvet curtains that I could close when we were working late into the night and the blinds felt too stark. I had also added a vase of fresh flowers, and Herne brought me new ones every week. Several pictures by Diago—a shifter artist who had a way with a camera and cats—brightened the walls. The portraits were beautiful and haunting, and the cats looked almost luminous.

Viktor and Yutani teased me about being a "cat lady," but I just ignored the good-natured ribbing. I had one cat, and he was my buddy. Mr. Rumblebutt was a Norwegian Forest cat with silky black fur, and a purr that you could hear across the room. He had adopted

Angel when she moved in, and he kept both of us in line.

I sat my things on my desk and opened the blinds, letting the light pour through the glass. Sunshine was a rarity in Seattle, and I enjoyed it when we had it. As I glanced down at the street, I noticed a man approaching the building. Oh hell, it was Ray Fontaine, my ex-boyfriend—now stalker. He was in a wheelchair, staring up at the building. There was an access ramp he could use around the back of the building, but I didn't think he knew that.

I darted out to the reception area.

"What's up?" Angel asked from the front desk, where she was getting organized for the day.

"Ray Fontaine, outside in a wheelchair," I mouthed. I didn't want to tell Herne for fear he might just put Ray back into the hospital.

"Cripes. Want me to come with you?" Angel asked.

I nodded. "Please."

As we waited for the elevator, which opened directly into the office reception area, I rubbed my head.

Ray had gotten hooked on me thanks to my Fae glamour, a fact I hadn't realized until a month ago. Then he'd stalked me till Herne was ready to put him on ice. Finally, in a misguided attempt to warn him off, I had confronted him in a parking lot where he ended up on the wrong side of a distracted driver. He'd been lucky he hadn't been killed. After talking to my mentor, she had cast a spell to neutralize the effect my glamour had on him. I hadn't seen him since then.

"At least I'll find out whether the spell worked," I said to Angel as we headed out the front door.

"Ten to one, he's still an asshole. You might end the stalkerish behavior with magic, but nothing can fix stupid or mean."

I motioned for her to wait as I dashed down the front steps to where he was waiting, glaring up at the building.

"Nice accommodation policy, Kearney." He glared at me.

"What do you want, Ray?" I hoped to hell he wouldn't start spouting off about being in love with me again. *Please, please, let Marilee's spell work*, I thought.

"Not much from you, *bitch*. You thought I wouldn't find out, didn't you?" He leaned forward. He seemed to be out of his casts, but I had the feeling it would be awhile before he was up and walking again. The driver had almost killed him, she'd been so wrapped up with her cell phone.

I rubbed my forehead. That wasn't exactly the greeting of a love-struck suitor. "Just what are you talking about?"

"Oh come off it, Ember. You know very well what I'm talking about. Don't play innocent with me, because in no way are you innocent of *anything*." The expression on his face was dark enough to shadow the sunlight.

I let out a long sigh. "I don't have time to play games, Ray. Tell me what you're talking about or get the fuck out of here."

He sputtered, grabbing the arms of his wheelchair as he leaned forward.

"You know! You know! How you trapped me and then blamed me for being a stalker! You bitch. You really like your head games, don't you? Well, I'm not your sucker anymore. In fact, you better watch your step because you just made yourself one hell of an enemy." His eyes flashed, and his voice held a veiled threat.

I leaned back against the stone railing that bordered the stairs. "Are you talking about my Fae glamour?"

"What the fuck did you think I was talking about? You put me under a spell, then jerked my heart around. Now, you're bored so you set me free after mowing me down in a parking lot?" He was shouting, loud enough to be heard by the handful of streeps—the street people—who were hanging out, hoping against rain.

I narrowed my eyes. "You listen to me, Ray Fontaine. I didn't do it on purpose. I didn't even *realize* that I *have* a Fae glamour. I don't know how you found out about it, but yes, I had a friend cast a counterspell, just in case you had been caught up by it. Apparently, you were, but what's also apparent is that you're an asshole *either way*."

He tried to stand, but then fell back in his seat. "Wait till I'm out of this chair. I'll teach you what it's like to be a puppet. Oh, and if you sic your watchdog fuck-toy on me, tell him that I'll call the cops and have him busted. I don't care if he's a god or not."

That was it. I'd had enough.

"Go ahead and do that! I'll prosecute you for stalking me. I felt sorry for you, thinking my glamour spurred it on, but now, I see no matter what, you're just a jerk who's looking for a fight." I turned, stomping up the stairs.

"Ember, get the fuck back here and talk to me!" Ray bellowed.

I spun around and held out my arm. "Talk to the hand, dude. Because *I'm* not listening." Before he could say another word, I slammed through the front door, followed by Angel, leaving Ray on the front walk screaming as he cursed me out soundly.

BACK INSIDE, I said to Angel, "I wish the driver had broken his jaw when she hit him, so he couldn't speak."

"He's just pissed, I guess. But how did he find out? Who told him? Marilee wouldn't, would she?" Angel's forehead creased as she followed me to my office, peeking out the window to see if he was still there. I glanced over her shoulder.

Ray was wheeling himself into a van, so I guessed that he had either bought or rented an accessible vehicle. As the van pulled away from the curb, I breathed a sigh of relief.

"It was bad enough dealing with him when he was obsessed with me. Dealing with him now that he hates me is going to be a nightmare."

"Maybe he's got it out of his system and will just stay away." Angel glanced at me, a hopeful look on her face. "Mind you, I realize that's not exactly how these things work, but there's always hope."

"Yeah, well, at least he's not mobile enough to chase me down the street." I shook my head and turned back to my desk. "Herne said no problem on rescheduling, so we're on for tonight."

"Rafé's busy too, so I'm good." She paused. "What do you think about the whole hate group thing?" Her voice quivered. "I don't mind telling you, it makes me nervous. I see enough of that aimed at people my color. I know that the Fae and shifters have been targets as well. But now…"

I stared at the flier. "I don't know what to think. It doesn't make sense. Even though I've seen disdain for humans and shifters from the Fae, I've never seen or heard outright hatred. The Dark and Light Courts are too busy hating each other. A hate group from one Court against the other? That would make sense."

"There's a lot of hidden prejudice, Ember. I can believe it exists, to be honest. Sometimes all you have to do is look under the nearest rock for it. I guess we'll find out when Yutani finishes his searching. Better him than me. The Dark Web?" She shivered. "That's another place that I sure wouldn't want to hang out."

A sudden burst of cursing hit the air as Herne's door to his office opened and Curnzey Duggath came storming out, waving his fists. "You're a cheat, Master Herne! You're a cur! You and your whole agency will be the death of my wallet. It's robbery, that's what it is, and I'm going to tell all of my friends what a thief and a scoundrel you are!"

Herne's eyes were narrowed. "You go right ahead, Duggath, and see how far it gets you next time there's a goblin rustling your sheep. You hired us for the job and we did it, and we managed to find two of your sheep for you before they were slaughtered. You just can't stand paying a good wage for a good job. You and your father have always been the cheapest bastards on the planet." Herne held his hand out in front of him, palm facing his face, and jerked it up in the time-honored expression that basically meant, at least among the dwarves, "Fuck you."

"Ach, what are you doing, insulting my family? Herne, I would challenge you here and now if this weren't a place of business with womenfolk watching. But lad, is this the way you treat your loyal customers?"

"What are they doing? Are we going to see an actual fistfight?" Angel whispered to me.

I turned to Angel, suppressing a grin. "No, just watch. Herne knows what he's doing."

"*Loyalty*? You know nothing of the sort. You agree to pay a set-upon price, and then renege after we do an excellent job! Did we, or did we not, stop that piece of shit sheep rustler?" Herne crossed his arms, planting his feet firmly on the floor.

Curnzey let out an exasperated sigh. "Well, yes, there I can't fault you."

"And did we, or did we not, round up the two missing sheep that were still alive?"

"I cannot deny that you did that as well," the dwarf said, frowning.

"And did you not sign the contract to seal the deal?" Herne leaned forward, glaring at Curnzey.

Finally, after a long pause, Curnzey relented.

"Aye, I did. But you charge too much! Never let it be said the Duggaths don't pay their debts. But next time, son of Cernunnos, I expect a discount. Mind you, you'd better not raise your rates on me." Curnzey turned to Angel. "Come along, lass, and I'll settle up with you." He glanced back at Herne. "You're a cagey one, Lord of the Hunt. I've got my eye on you."

And with that, Herne held out his hand and Curnzey stared at it for a moment, then gave him a hearty handclasp.

"Good doing business with you, Duggath. Tell your wife I send my regards."

"She'll be happy enough to have the mutton back where it belongs. Next time you're out our way, drop in and have a cup of tea. Aletha makes the most excellent gingersnaps." And with that, Curnzey followed Angel to the reception desk to settle his account.

Herne snorted, then held out his arm. I slipped into the offered embrace, and he snuggled me close to him. "Come on." He led me into his office and shut the door behind us.

"One of these days, I'd like to skip the testosterone battle, but what can I say? That's the Duggaths for you. They keep their wallets close."

"What would happen if you refused to play the game?"

Herne shrugged. "He'd probably take offense and refuse to pay me at all. Or maybe he'd actually try to call me out, though that would be a stupid move, considering I'm a god and he's mortal, dwarf though he may be." He leaned down and nuzzled my neck, trailing light kisses on the skin. "Mmm, it's been too long."

I grinned as he began to slide his hands along my back, toward my butt. "Two days, lover boy. Two days. Granted, I could go for a quickie, but we have too much to do today, given this new situation. So you're going to have to wait till tomorrow night, unless you want to come by and watch the show with us, and stay the night."

Herne's lips were buried in my neck, and in a muffled voice he said, "You make me so hard. I go crazy thinking about fucking you."

I caught my breath, swept up in his desire. One thing I had learned over the past six months: having a god for a boyfriend meant a never-ending smorgasbord of carnal delights. The sex was great, and unlike most mortals, his stamina was amazing. In fact, sometimes it was too much and I'd have to beg off because I was a wee bit too sore to play.

"When?" he whispered.

"Tomorrow night. I'll come to your place. I think Rafé's coming over and he and Angel will want some privacy." Before I pulled away, I grabbed his chin, bringing his lips to mine, and kissed him so deep that I almost came right there. We came up for air when someone knocked on the door.

"There. That will have to keep you," I said.

"Damn. Well, that will have to do. Wait till I sit down to open the door," he added, grinning as he headed for his desk, his all too obvious arousal pressing against the front of his jeans.

I laughed, then opened the door as soon as he sat down. At least we women didn't have to worry about our arousal showing so obviously.

Angel peeked in, glancing at Herne, then at me. "Sorry to interrupt, guys, but I have a prospective client out here who I think you should talk to."

"We're full on cases right now—" Herne started to say, but Angel shook her head.

"Please, hear her out. I think we may want to take this one," she said. "I have a feeling about it."

That was all she had to say. Angel was human, but she was an incredible empath and we trusted her hunches.

"Show her in, then." Herne cleared his throat and took a swig of water from the bottle on his desk as Angel ushered a thin, wiry woman into the room.

"Herne, meet Amanda Skellig. Her daughter is missing."

Right away, I could tell she was a wolf shifter—the pheromones left nothing to the imagination. And right now she was desperate and afraid. A wave of emotion filled the room as she approached the desk. For a moment she stood, wringing her hands, and then she collapsed into one of the chairs in front of Herne's desk, sobbing.

"Please, please…I need you to find my daughter. She's been abducted."

Hearing the pain infused in her voice, I knew we'd be taking the case.

CHAPTER TWO

Herne slowly leaned his elbows on the desk, then gave a nod to Angel, who vanished out the door. He jerked his head at me, and I quietly picked up a box of tissues and then pulled a chair over to sit beside Amanda. I held out the box and she looked up. Exhaustion filled her eyes, and it poured out of every pore. She took a tissue and blew her nose, trying to dab at her eyes. They were already red, and I got the feeling she had been crying for days.

"Amanda…Ms. Skellig…would you like some herbal tea or some water?" Herne avoided offering her coffee. When clients came in who were terribly upset, we avoided offering them anything with caffeine unless they asked for it. Amanda was jittery enough as it was, and she looked so tired that caffeine would just overload her senses.

She gave a weary nod. "Water, please."

Herne punched the intercom. "Angel, please bring in some water for Ms. Skellig." He sat back, watching her for a moment. Then, after Angel brought in a bottle of cold water for her, he cleared his throat. "Do you mind if I record our meeting? It will help me to remember facts that might slip my mind. If you decide not to hire us, I'll delete the information in front of you so you know it's gone."

She paused for a moment, then warily nodded. "Sure."

"All right. Let me set up the digital recorder." After he made sure it was working, Herne recorded the date and Amanda's name, and taped her permission to record the session. "All right, now, why don't you tell us why you're here. You said your daughter is missing?"

Amanda shuddered, then set the water down on the desk. She cleared her throat and, in a strained voice, said, "Yeah. She was abducted three days ago on the twenty-second." She stared at the floor, looking bewildered. "I can't believe this is happening to us."

"First, have you talked to the police? Do you know if they're working on the case?" He gave me another nod. I didn't have my tablet with me, so he handed me his. I'd keep notes, observing her as he asked questions.

"Yeah, they're looking into it, but they don't really have many leads. The security cameras caught footage of a woman leading her away, but only her back and it's blurry. There's no way to know who she was." Amanda looked up at Herne, her eyes filling again. "Can you please help me? I can't bear to lose her. She's my heart. She's my everything."

"I can't promise anything, but we'll try. Tell me what happened, as best as you can remember." Herne leaned back in his chair, his arms open. He was always careful to use body language that invited the client to open up to him. The more information we had about cases, the better.

Amanda caught a deep breath, then slowly exhaled, wiping her eyes again. The bleak expression on her face tore at my heart.

"Saturday, I took Eleanor to the mall. She needed new shoes and a new jacket, so I thought we'd spend the afternoon at the mall and then go to dinner. I work long hours, so when I get a free day, I always spend it with her."

Herne nodded. "Does your husband work as well, and do you have a nanny?"

"No. I'm a widow. My husband died a year ago in a freak accident. My mother—Eleanor's grandmother—babysits for me. I drop her off before I go to work, then pick her up afterward. I don't earn enough to hire a nanny. Luckily, my mother's always willing to help me. Our pack—the West Seattle Wulfine Pack—is very supportive to single mothers."

"Do you have a picture of Eleanor for us?" I asked.

She opened her purse. Pulling out a small notebook, she removed a picture from the pocket divider inside, handing it to me. I glanced at it before setting it on Herne's desk. The little girl in the picture had a brilliant smile. She was fair haired, with bright blue eyes, and she was holding a stuffed panda.

"She's lovely," I said, glancing at her mother. "How old is she?"

"She turned three years old just two weeks ago. Lani's my heart," Amanda said. "That's her nickname. I don't think I would have survived after Ken died if it hadn't been for her. She gives me a reason to keep on going."

Herne stared at the picture for a moment, then asked,

"What happened to her father, if I might ask? Sometimes facts that seem to have no bearing can actually help a case."

Amanda straightened her shoulders, swallowing hard. "He worked for Puget Sound Power, Gas, & Light as a line installer. During that horrible windstorm last year—the one that knocked out power to over four hundred thousand people? He was out repairing lines when a tree that had been destabilized during a storm toppled. He was up in the bucket of the service truck when the tree came crashing down. It hit him full force, breaking his neck as it took out the upper boom. He was dead before the tree hit the ground."

"I'm so sorry," I murmured. That definitely counted as a freak accident, though I imagined more people were hurt during repair jobs than one might think.

"It was hard. We weren't prepared. There wasn't enough life insurance to cover our needs over the next few years, so I had to go back to work. And Ken…he was my high school sweetheart. We expected to grow old together." She shuddered, then shook her head. "Sometimes life doesn't work out the way you think it will."

Herne nodded. "Unfortunately true. So, on Saturday, you took Eleanor to the mall. What time was it?"

"We got to the mall right around lunch time—about twelve-thirty. I remember because we stopped at Big Ben's Burgers before we went to eat lunch. We had hamburgers and fries, and Lani had a fruit cup for dessert."

"So she wasn't hungry when you arrived at the mall, correct?"

"Right. She wanted candy, but she always wants candy. Anyway, we went to the Kingsgate Entrance, the one off the front where you walk in and find yourself facing Bon Chance, that fancy furniture store. I was holding her hand, and we headed to the Little Miss Boutique for her coat. She tried on several, but none of them were quite right, so I decided we'd find her shoes first, then look elsewhere. We went to the Shoe Bargain Barn. I bought her a pair of sneakers, a pair of Mary Janes, and a pair of bright blue rain boots. She wanted to wear the boots so we sat down outside the store, on one of those long benches, and she put them on."

"What else was she wearing?" Herne asked.

"A pink sweater with butterflies on it, and a pair of jeans—blue. They have an elastic waist to go over her pull-up pants." Amanda's voice was shaking.

"Did you notice anybody following you? Or paying attention to you?" Herne asked.

Amanda quirked her lip, a thoughtful look in her eye. "I don't recall anybody. I mean, the mall was crowded, so there were people everywhere."

"What happened next?" I asked.

"I was deciding where to go next when my phone rang. I didn't recognize the number, but sometimes I get calls from clients who really need to contact me, and so I always answer."

Herne nodded. "What do you do?"

"I run a small catering company. I serve private dinner parties, small group events, that kind of thing. So I'm always looking for new clients. I have a store front, because it's just easier than jumping through the hoops I would need to in order to get permits to work from home." Amanda handed me one of her business cards. "This has my work address on it."

"Was the call from a client?"

"Yes, a friend who knew my client from my last gig called to set up an event. Lani and I were on one of the benches in the middle of the mall. As I said, it was crowded. Lani must have slid off the bench, and somehow I didn't notice. When I got done with the call, I realized she wasn't sitting beside me. I panicked because she's always such a good girl and when I tell her to stay put, she does. There were so many people milling around. I couldn't see her anywhere and I started to scream. A security guard came over to find out what was going on. That's the last time I saw her." She came to an abrupt halt.

I glanced at my notes. It wasn't much to go on. "What happened after you talked to the security guard? What did they do?"

"He immediately called in to their control room and they enacted a Code Adam alert. They called the police, who oversaw a mall-wide search. But there are one hundred and twenty stores in that mall, and so many exits, when you count the fire doors and so forth. They searched for three solid hours. But when they were looking over the security camera footage, they found a short clip of a woman leading Lani out of the mall, through one of the side entrances." Amanda started to cry. "The woman had hold of Lani's hand, but her face was turned away from the camera. The timestamp shows that she left the mall with my daughter while the police were still on the way."

I closed my eyes, leaning back. Every investigator knew that every hour that passed after a child abduction significantly decreased the chance of the child being found alive.

Herne gave Amanda a moment, then softly asked, "Did you recognize anything about the kidnapper on the footage? Anything at all?"

Amanda thought for a moment, then gave us a resigned shrug.

"No. I couldn't see her face. And from the back? I didn't recognize her. The footage was blurry, and it didn't show much other than she appeared to have light hair, and she was short and trim. She was wearing jeans and some kind of coat. Lani didn't look like she was being dragged, so she must have trusted the woman."

"Have you received any requests for ransom?" If she had, then we had more leeway. There would be a slightly higher chance Eleanor was still alive.

"No," Amanda said, paling. "Do you think my daughter's still alive?"

I let Herne field that question. He was much more diplomatic than I was.

"There's *always* a chance. Why did you come to us?" He leaned forward. "What can we do, that the police can't?"

Amanda hung her head. "They're overwhelmed and understaffed. And when they talked to me in the mall, they seemed to… I think they blame me. But no parent can keep an eye on their children every single second. And all it takes is that one small fracture—that single time you look away for someone to strike." She paused, then whispered, "Is this my fault?"

"No," Herne said. "Abductions happen every day, and there's no way to predict when you're being targeted. What matters now is that we do everything we can to find her." He studied her face for a moment. "I'll start a file and we'll do whatever we can. I can't promise we'll find her, but we'll do our damnedest."

"I don't know if I can pay your rates," Amanda said in a hesitant tone. "I'll mortgage my house if I have to."

"No, you won't." Herne wrote something down on a piece of paper. "Give this to Angel at the front door. We'll work out something that won't strain your budget. Meanwhile, I need you to give Angel a list of everybody who has been in your house the past couple of months. *Everyone*. I'll send Ember and another one of our investigators out to your house, if you don't mind. It can help us to look through her belongings, to see if there's anything there that seems odd or out of place. We need to figure out if this woman has had contact with your daughter before. We'll also need to talk to your mother to see if she's noticed anything out of the ordinary."

I jotted down everything Herne was saying, given I'd be doing some of the investigating.

Amanda murmured a thank you, but I could tell the woman was on the edge of collapse.

"You need to get some rest. I'll bet you've barely slept since Saturday. Am I right?"

She nodded. "I've probably managed about three hours of sleep. I can barely think."

"Can your mother stay with you for a few days? So you can rest up?" Herne asked.

"No, but my best friend can," Amanda said. She lowered her eyes to the ground. "It's so hard. It makes me want to start drinking again, but I don't dare go down that route again."

Neither Herne nor I commented. She had enough to

deal with, without us prying into what sounded like an addiction. We'd have to check into it, but we could do so later.

Herne stood, pressing the intercom for Angel to come in. "Amanda, we'll do all we can. Angel," he said as she popped her head through the door. "Will you take Amanda to your desk and set up a file for her?"

As Angel led Amanda away and closed the door behind her, I turned to Herne. "What do you think? Do we really have a chance of finding her daughter? Alive?"

Herne shrugged. "To be honest, I don't know. The chances of finding her alive are probably slim, but you never know. And if Eleanor *is* still alive, we can't just walk away. We have a lot of legwork to do with this one, though, and we have to balance it along with looking into the Tuathan Brotherhood. Morgana made it clear that's our top priority."

I nodded. "Late nights and busy days, it looks like. Are you going to set a meeting this afternoon about the new case?"

He glanced at the clock. It was ten-fifteen. "Actually, give the others a heads-up that we're meeting again at ten-thirty. Then I'll assign tasks for the day and get you guys out on the street. Time is of the essence for both cases."

I gave him a quick kiss. "Thank you, for caring."

"What do you mean?" He looked bewildered.

"What I mean is that you actually give a damn about a little lost wolf shifter. And that, my love, makes you special." I drew back, holding his gaze. "I mean it. So many people would just refuse to take the case because of the odds, or because she can't pay a huge fee. But you…you don't shy away. You're a god, but you care about mortals and their heartaches."

Herne reached for my hands and I gave them to him, closing my eyes for a moment as his warm fingers closed over mine. He brought them up to his lips, kissing them gently.

"Ember, in the realm of the gods, you have two choices. Or at least, *I* believe you do. You can either ignore mortal-kind, or you can get involved. There's no real space for in-between. You meddle a little, and you chance changing the course of history, but skip the responsibility. You ignore it? Well, then you remove yourself from the realm and begin to look down on humans."

"And if you choose to get involved?"

"If you get involved, you'd damned well better care because you're going to be stirring the pot. And you can stir it for good, or for ill. My father loves mortals, as problematic as humans and the SubCult can be. My mother was mortal—one of the magic-born—who chose to become a goddess rather than enter the Force Majeure. I have her blood in my veins as well and I'm proud of it." He ducked is head, smiling. "They brought me up to respect the world of mortals as well as the world of the gods."

I nodded. "I know. And yet, your father and you...even Morgana...are so far removed from our experiences that it never fails to amaze me when you empathize with us."

"Well, we do. We may not be able to understand it from a personal point, but we've all lost people we love, and we've all experienced heartbreak and sorrow." He kissed me on the head. "We'll do our best to find Eleanor. Now go tell the others to meet in the break room while I make a few phone calls."

THE HALLOWED HUNT

ONCE AGAIN, we gathered in the break room.

"Viktor," Herne said after briefing the others on the new case while I filled in the gaps from my notes, "I want you to check with Erica on this case as well. See if there have been any other missing children in the past year that might somehow connect with this one."

Viktor jotted down Eleanor's name and a few pieces of info. "Right. Looks like I'm going to be buying Erica lunch. You guys better hope she never gets kicked off the force, because my other lines of communication aren't all that cooperative lately. At least not here."

"Just keep everything quiet, and make certain that she's down with this. I don't want to put her job in jeopardy. Especially with this mess about the Tuathan Brotherhood." Herne turned to Talia. "Talia, do some sleuthing into Amanda's family. Does she have any siblings? Are there any problematic uncles, brothers, even sisters?"

"You mean, are there any sexual predators in her family?" Talia said, leaning back in her chair. "We all know that most children are hurt by people they know. Charity begins at home and sadly, so does abuse."

"Right. I wasn't going to put it so bluntly, but that's exactly what I mean." Herne motioned to Yutani. "Yutani, you and Ember go talk to Eleanor's grandmother. See if there's anything out of the ordinary there. Also, drop by Amanda's house and just…get a feel for things. I'll go visit the victims of the beatings in the hospital. Check in with Angel if you're not going to make it back here before seven-thirty."

"Is there anything Charlie can do?" I asked. Charlie

was our recent hire. He was a vampire—a good sort, actually—and he worked remotely most of the time, doing data entry and some research for us. He was barely nineteen, turned only recently, and smart as a whip.

"Actually, I wanted to talk to you all about that," Herne said. "I'm planning on sending Charlie back to college. I've been watching his work the past few weeks, and he's brilliant with numbers. I talked to him last night about his plans before he was turned."

"Didn't he want to be an accountant or something?" Yutani asked.

"Right. But he couldn't afford to go full-time, and then when he was turned, he just assumed that was the end of his plans. The job at the VN Worldwide Bank didn't pan out, and he quit his baking job to work with us. I decided to pay his tuition to an online university so he can follow his dream job, which is accounting. In exchange, he'll work for us as a full-time accountant. That will take one big responsibility off both Angel's and my hands when he finishes with his degree. He's entering an accelerated program." Herne chuckled. "I've never seen anybody so happy about numbers. But Charlie was born to it, I think."

"So what does that mean for his work with us now?" Talia asked.

"What it means is he'll be doing mostly data entry, so that he can focus on making it through the accelerated class. If he keeps up with the work, he'll graduate in half the time."

Viktor grunted, but he was smiling. "I'm glad the runt is getting a chance to follow his passion. He's a super-geek, but he's okay. And he's trying to get a handle on the vampire thing. He's not comfortable with it, which is probably a good thing, but he'll have to find his way sooner or later. At least being around us, he can hold onto his humanity a bit better."

"Do you want us to meet back here before end of the day?" I asked. We had all afternoon, but it was amazing how long some interviews could take.

"No, we'll compare notes at the staff meeting tomorrow. So, go ahead and head out after the meeting. Keep me updated if you feel I should know about anything. And Viktor, when you talk to Erica, see if you can get a copy of the security camera footage that shows Eleanor being led out of the mall by the unknown woman."

Viktor nodded. "Will do. All right, I've set a lunch date with her, so I'm heading out." He stood and stretched. Viktor was half-ogre, half-human, and he had the frame of a massive body builder. With his bald head, tattooed on one side with a tribal design, and trim waist, he was more than impressive. He was also one of the most sensitive men I had ever met, and the dichotomy was oddly mesmerizing.

I leaned across the table and tapped Yutani's laptop. "You ready to go?"

He shook his head. "Give me fifteen minutes and I will be. Why don't you get the addresses for Amanda and the grandmother while you wait?"

Gathering up my tablet and notes, I headed toward the door. I had transferred the notes I took with Amanda to my own tablet. "Will do, but we need to stop at the Coffee Shack along the way, for caffeine and some food."

"Yeah, yeah. But you're paying," he said. "And I'm not riding in your car if you insist on drinking a quint shot mocha again. You were buzzing so loud that I wanted to smack you." He wrinkled his nose at me, but he was smiling, and I laughed back.

As I entered my office, my personal phone rang. I kept the ringtones on my work phone distinctly separate from those of my personal cell, so that I immediately knew which one to answer. I glanced at the caller ID screen and a smile flickered across my lips.

"Hey, Raven. What's up?"

Raven BoneTalker was one of the Ante-Fae who had started out a client and become a friend. Not only was she Ante-Fae, but she was also a bone witch, which meant she dealt with spirits and death and other delightful subjects like that. Unlike most of the Ante-Fae, she actually interacted with both members of the SubCult and humans alike.

"Yo, Ember. I wondered if you and Angel could come hang out Saturday night. I have a favor to ask you guys, but I want to do it in person. I'll make spaghetti, if you want to bring the wine." Her voice was husky, smooth in a lounge singer sort of way.

I pulled out my calendar and glanced at the week. "I'm good. I think Angel's free, but you might want to call her. I'd love to stay and chat, but I have interviews to conduct, and I need to get a move on."

"Pencil me in, then. I'll call Angel. See you later, babe." Raven signed off, again with a tinkle of laughter, one I was glad to hear. She had lost her fiancé to a killer recently, and she hadn't smiled or laughed all that much since we had known her.

I slid into my chair and brought up the Pages Directory, which gave address listings for everybody in the general vicinity. It was a little tool that Yutani had created, mashing up data from several sites that he had managed to hack into. It gave us a leg up, and as long as nobody realized that we were using it, we couldn't be accused of stealing data. Herne had no problem with the little hacks that Yutani pulled together—they helped us solve cases, and we never disseminated the private information we had at our fingertips.

I typed in Amanda Skellig's name and sure enough, her address popped up. Then, realizing that we had forgotten to ask for her mother's name, I called her—making sure I used my work phone. Herne was very strict about keeping our private lives out of the cases as much as possible.

"Amanda, we'd like to come over and talk to you this afternoon. I also need your mother's name and contact information."

"Let me text you her number. Her name is Molly Skellig." She sounded sleepy.

"Did I wake you? I'm sorry."

"Not a problem. I slept for an hour or so, but I need to take a bath and then try to eat something. I'm not hungry, but I get low blood sugar episodes if I don't eat regularly." She sounded so forlorn that it felt like a punch to the gut.

"Do you mind if my coworker and I come over?" We needed to talk to her but I wanted it to be her idea, so we wouldn't feel like intruders.

"No, please, anything to help. Herne said you'd need to." She paused, then added, "The house is a mess. I haven't done anything since…"

"That's fine. Don't worry about it. We'll be there within the hour. Meanwhile, you eat something and make some tea for yourself."

After I finished texting the names, numbers, and

addresses of Amanda and Molly to Yutani, I made sure I had everything I would need for the afternoon. Phone, tablet, notebook, it all went into my tote bag. For a while, I had carried everything in my purse, but it made it hard to dig through to find my wallet or brush or anything else I needed, so I had bought an all-weather tote with black polka dots on a cobalt blue background. I had come to love it.

By the time I was ready, Yutani peeked into my office. "Good to go?"

I nodded. "Come on. I'm driving."

We waved at Angel as we headed toward the elevator.

"I'll be back to pick you up when I'm done," I called to her. We had driven into work together that morning.

"Don't you dare forget me, or I'll go on strike in the kitchen!" Angel shouted after me. She was my roommate as well as my best friend.

"Trust me, with that threat, you know I'm not about to forget." As the elevator doors closed, I shook my head, thinking it seemed like forever since we had started working for the Wild Hunt, even though it had only been about six months.

So, I'm Ember Kearney, and I'm thirty years old.

To others in the Fae Courts, I'm generally known as a *tralaeth*—an epithet meaning half-breed, and usually followed by some oh so witty adjective like *slut*, or *bitch*. I've reclaimed the term and wear it as a badge of honor in memory of my parents' love. Neither gave a fuck about proper custom when they fell in love—my mother from the Light Court and my father from the Dark Court. All they knew was they wanted to spend their lives together and they weren't going to let anybody stop them.

And nobody did. At least not for sixteen years. At age fifteen, I came home one day to find them murdered, blood everywhere on the floor. They had been stabbed multiple times—talk about overkill. My paternal grandfather and maternal grandmother had been responsible for sending the assassins after them, which I had suspected, but only found out for sure this year. They would have killed me if I had been there, that much I also knew.

So I moved in with my best friend, Angel, and her mother—Mama J. I left three years later, and Angel followed me to college where we roomed again, but she had to drop out to get a job and help out at home.

Now, Mama J. was dead. About eighteen months ago, a drunk driver had slammed into her, leaving Angel and her little brother DJ orphaned. Angel took care of DJ as best as she could for a while, but now he was living with a foster family, and Angel had once again become my roommate.

Until this past May, Angel had worked at a dead-end job, while I worked as a freelance investigator, solving problems for the SubCult. I went after sub-Fae who were causing havoc—like goblins raiding hen houses, and so forth. There were a lot of sub-Fae skulking around Seattle, though they weren't officially allowed within city limits. But the laws weren't enforced and there were a lot of places to hide, so they managed to eke out a living through petty thievery and pilfering from the urban farmers who lived around the area.

Then DJ went missing, and Angel called me, begging

me to find him. That had led to meeting Herne, and *that* led to both Angel and me working for the Wild Hunt. And that's when I ended up as a god's girlfriend. A convoluted story, but that's life for you. At least we can say our lives aren't boring. Although sometimes, boring would be a nice change of pace.

Yutani rode shotgun as I eased out of the parking garage and we headed for the West Seattle area to talk to Amanda. Over the years, the area had gone from a gangsta neighborhood to the shifter-suburbs. Oh, the houses were still somewhat rundown, and there was a lot of petty crime, but the hoods had moved out of the hood, so to speak, and West Seattle now mostly housed low-to moderate-income shifters and their families.

"You think we're going to find this girl?" Yutani asked.

As I eased the car to a crawl, I stared out the window at the reminder signs to slow down near schools. Recess appeared to be in session at an elementary school as we passed by, with children running around on the playground. The kids all looked so young, and so fragile.

"I don't know. I really don't. I don't want to even speculate on it, because I don't want my mind going into the dark places I know exist out there. I can tell you this. Amanda's devastated. Angel felt the fear and heartache rolling off her, and I could smell it. Wolf pheromones," I said, giving him a grin. "You have them too, but they're slightly different given you're a coyote shifter, and you control yours better than any other shifter I've met. How do you manage that?"

"I had to learn early, given my childhood and upbringing. To say I was unwelcome among my village is an understatement." He pressed his lips together, glancing at the house numbers. When we arrived at Amanda's house, I eased into the driveway.

"I guess we'd better go in. I'm not looking forward to it. I don't deal well with crying women. I never know what to do or say."

"Sometimes, saying 'I'm sorry' is the best you can do." I unbuckled my seat belt. "I don't think I'll ever get used to interviewing victims and their families. It's all so raw."

"You never will, if you're lucky. Get too used to this and you lose your heart. The only thing you can hope for is to be able to put on a mask when you're talking to them, because the last thing they need is your pain on top of theirs." With that, he headed up the sidewalk and I followed along behind.

CHAPTER THREE

If Amanda's home was cluttered by her standards, I wondered what she considered spotless. Oh, there were a few piles of clutter here and there—toys and books, an unfinished knitting project in a basket next to the recliner. But there was no sign of dirt or squalor anywhere.

As Yutani and I sat down at the kitchen table, she carried in a tray holding a teapot, cups and saucers, and a sugar bowl and creamer.

"Would you like a cup of tea?" she asked.

I nodded. I didn't like tea all that much, but by accepting, it would put her at ease. Yutani also accepted a cup. I could smell the lavender wafting off the dark brew.

"I'm glad you got some sleep," I said, breathing in the floral scented steam from the teacup. Behind the notes of lavender were the subtle fragrances of lemon, and the smell of the tea itself. "Have you talked to a doctor who might be able to give you an aid to help you rest?"

Amanda shook her head. "I keep thinking, if I fall

asleep, I'm betraying her. Because what kind of a mother can sleep when her baby is missing?" The pain in her voice was palpable.

"You need to be clear headed to help her. You can't help her if you're exhausted and foggy." I leaned forward, shaking my head. "Promise me you'll talk to your doctor about this?"

She sniffed, wiping her eyes again. "All right."

Yutani cleared his throat. "What we'd like to do is go over this list of people who've been in your house lately, and talk to you about them. The list you gave to Angel. We'd also like to look in Eleanor's room, just in case there's anything there that either you or the police missed."

"That's fine. I want my daughter back. I'll help in whatever way I can." Amanda rubbed her brow, propping her head in her hands as she leaned her elbows on the table. "Lani is the only thing that makes my life worth living."

I glanced around. There were the usual pictures on the walls—a few landscape paintings, which shifters had a tendency to like, family photos, a wedding photo showing a beaming Amanda with a handsome young man who had his arms around her.

Yutani handed me a copy of the list. "So, your mother and cousin are here a lot?"

Amanda nodded. "They both help me with Lani. Alberta is the same age as I am, and she has two children. We get them together for play dates."

I skimmed over the list. It was pretty standard. Relatives, a couple friends. "The cable repairman was here? Did he have a badge with him?"

Amanda nodded. "I always check for badges. He was legit, or if he wasn't, his badge sure looked it. He fixed the cable without saying much. I remember his name was Chris…something. He was tall and thin, with short, dark hair and he wore glasses with round lenses. He seemed nice, and Lani wasn't home when he arrived. She was at my cousin's on a play date. We exchange play dates so that we each get a little free time. She's a single mother, too."

"Did he say anything about…oh, your family pictures?" I pointed to the pictures of Eleanor that littered the coffee table.

She thought for a moment, then shook her head. "No, he didn't. He just told me that the cable box had given out and replaced it."

I went back to the list. There didn't seem to be anybody else who might be suspicious on it. Amanda apparently either didn't have many friends, or she didn't entertain much.

"What about your friends? Are they old friends? Long term, I mean?" Yutani asked.

"Suze has been my friend since we were little, and Tawny, I've known for about seven months. I met her in…" She paused, pressing her lips together.

Both Yutani and I frowned, watching her.

"Yes?" Yutani said.

Amanda hesitated another moment, then let out a deep sigh. "Please don't tell her I told you this—we're not supposed to give out private information. I met Tawny at AN."

"What's that?" I asked.

"AlkaNon, a group for recovering alcoholics," Yutani said.

Amanda nodded. "He's right. Tawny and I are support buddies. You know, when we feel the urge to drink, we call each other and talk each other down from the cravings. Things like that."

Yutani glanced at me, and I knew his expressions well enough to read that he wanted me to take over the questioning. I might be a tad too direct at times, but Yutani could be downright rude without meaning to and he fully acknowledged the tendency.

"So you're…" I wasn't sure how to put it without sounding rude.

"Yeah, I'm an alcoholic. I always liked my wine, probably too much. But I had it under control until Ken died. The day I got the news he had been killed, though, everything spiraled. I began to sneak-drink. I just wanted to forget. Before long, I was drinking from the moment I woke up until I went to bed. My business was starting to suffer."

"What made you stop?"

She shrugged. "My mother. She stepped in and slapped me silly. She got it through my head that I was putting my daughter in danger. And then she told me she would take Lani away if I didn't shape up. That day, I joined AN and started going to the meetings. I quit drinking. I've been sober for six months as of last week. You don't know what it's taking for me to steer clear of the booze right now. Tawny's coming over this afternoon. She'll stay with me for a few days." Amanda covered her face. "I'm so embarrassed. But I wasn't drunk when Lani was abducted—I promise you, I was sober."

"I believe you." I glanced around. "May we take a look around, especially in Lani's room?"

Amanda nodded, leading us down the hall to a room fit for any little princess. It was painted purple and blue. The bed looked slept in and I glanced back at Amanda, who was leaning against the door.

"I took a nap in her bed. I can smell her on the covers, and it makes me feel closer to her." Her voice held a hollow ache.

Yutani and I sorted through the room, looking through the toys. There didn't seem to be anything out of the ordinary, and each item we asked about, either Amanda or her mother had bought for Eleanor. There was nothing hidden under the bed, or in the closet. Just the toys and clothes of a very small girl, lost in a very big world.

"Thank you. We appreciate your help. Please remember, you need to sleep. When Tawny gets here, she can keep watch for you while you rest," I added.

Amanda nodded as she saw us out the door, whispering a "Thank you" that I could barely hear.

Back in the car, I turned to Yutani. "What do you think?"

"I think she's spiraling down, and I hope to hell we can find her kid or she's going to bottom out. I've seen it a dozen times." He pulled out his phone. "Her mother lives about ten minutes from here."

The visit to Molly Skellig wasn't very helpful. The woman was obviously a matriarch of the Pack, but she was also friendly. She, too, was broken-hearted. She didn't say much about her husband, but I got the distinct impression he was a quiet man who was more interested in his work than his family. But we were able to confirm everything Amanda had told us.

On the way back to the office, Yutani said, "Amanda isn't the first person to be sucked into an alcoholic spiral by grief. I saw it a lot through my travels around the country, especially among my people. The reservations took a high toll. They're a little better now, but it took a lot of work to get them out of the dark hole from which they were first conceived."

"The Fae aren't as affected by alcohol as shifters or humans. Rather, we aren't pulled into the addiction as easy. But among my people, both Courts, there is a predilection toward addiction of certain drugs."

After a few moments, Yutani heaved out a sigh. "I don't know if Herne told you, but a dozen years ago or so, I had a close call. I had been working for the Wild Hunt for about thirty years when I ended up in a really bad relationship. I don't want to talk about it, but after she left me, I went off the rails. I left the agency and ended up living in a tent city. I started hitting the bottle. While I never quite made it to the point of being an alcoholic, I was coming close. I have Herne to thank for pulling me out of it. He tracked me down and dragged me back to his place. He sobered me up, made me talk to a counselor and get my shit straight. Then I came back to work. Now, I'll drink a bottle of beer or a glass of wine, but I limit it. I also avoid hard liquor."

I cleared my throat. Viktor had actually been the one to tell me, so I could honestly say, "Herne never said a word to me about that." I wasn't sure whether to thank him for trusting me with the information, or just let it rest.

"I understand Amanda's grief, though mine came on from other causes. That's why my aunt Celia comes up once a year. She loves me, yes, but she comes to make sure I'm still walking the talk. She practically worships Herne for helping me. Which, I suppose, makes sense since he's a god." He let out a sigh. "The rest of my family turned their back on me when I accidentally burned down the village. They sent me away and not one of them has ever contacted me. It's not easy to carry memories like that around."

I nodded. Yutani seldom opened up. I felt almost like he was talking to a sounding board, and if I said something he'd fall into silence again.

He glanced at me as I changed lanes, into a turn lane, then came to a stop at a red light. "I notice things. You've never asked about my life, though you talk to Viktor quite openly."

I licked my lips, turning left when the light changed. "You seem very…reticent. And I'm not one to pry unless it's necessary. I try to respect boundaries."

Yutani laughed. "Well, I appreciate that. Not everybody does. But I suppose eventually you'll ferret out my secrets, and I'll find yours. Those you have left, that is," he said with a sly smile. "I'm very good at finding out information."

There was something about the way he said it that made me shiver—and I wasn't sure whether it was a good shiver or a bad shiver.

"What secrets of mine have you uncovered?" I flickered a glance his way.

"Oh, enough. But they're all safe with me."

Frowning, I wondered what the hell he was talking about. As abruptly as he had confided in me, now it felt like he was playing some sort of game. And I didn't like head games and wouldn't feed into them. I turned my attention back to the road as I guided us into a parking spot in front of the building.

Before I stepped out of the car, I turned to him. "Look. If you're aiming to get a rise out of me, then I suggest you find another route. I don't play head games, and I won't let anyone else play them on me. So whatever you know about me, fine. Tell me, or don't. But I'm not going to freak out and beg you to keep quiet over whatever it is you think you know. My life is pretty much an open book, so whatever you dig up? Good for you."

I held his gaze. Among canine shifters—including wolf and coyote—that was a challenge.

Yutani grunted, returning my stare, but then he got out of the car and headed up the steps toward the office without another word. I glanced at the car clock. It was almost five-thirty, so I texted Angel to meet me when she was ready, and stayed out front.

We were on the way home before I told her what Yutani had said. "I wanted to backhand him right then and there. I don't like people trying to mess with my head."

"He's an odd one, all right." She puttered with the heater, turning it up. "How did it go with Amanda?"

I told her what we had found out. "Tell me something. You talked to her. What's your take on her? Is she telling us the truth? Is she hiding anything?"

Angel shook her head. "I don't think she's hiding anything other than shame over the booze. When she came out of the elevator, the wave of sadness and loss that came in with her almost drowned my senses. She had nothing to do with her daughter's disappearance, if that's what you're asking. I'm sure of it."

That set me at ease. I didn't like the direction my thoughts had been going. I decided it was time to change the subject.

"Did Raven contact you?"

"About dinner on Saturday? I told her sure."

"Good. I think we could use a girls' night out." I flipped on the turn signal, looking for a break in the traffic to our right so I could change lanes. Finally, I saw a narrow opening and eased the car over, wedging my way into it. A moment later and we were at the turnoff into Big Ben's Burgers. As I pulled into the drive-thru lane, I held out my hand.

"My wallet, please? And what do you want?"

Angel laughed, digging through her purse. "My turn to pay. You paid for dinner the other night at Hunan Garden. Here," she said, handing me a twenty. "I want a Big Burger Combo meal, Hawaiian style, and a lime shake."

"Fries, tots, or jojos?"

"Jojos, please. Spicy flavor." Angel loved the spiced potato wedges.

I moved ahead to the ordering screen. As I rolled down my window, the cashier's voice came out through the static.

"Welcome to Big Ben's Burgers. May I have your order please?"

"Two Big Burger combos, one Hawaiian style, and one Pizza Burger with extra cheese. We'd like an order of jojos with the Hawaiian burger, and an order of curly fries with the Pizza Burger. We also want two biggy-piggy lime shakes."

The biggy-piggy shake was pretty much the size of two milkshakes. For some reason, Big Ben's Burgers always ran a limited special on lime milkshakes from mid-October till the end of the month. They were neon green, tart and sweet at the same time, and Angel and I had made it a tradition every year to fill up on them for a couple of days.

Angel handed me the cash and I paid for our food. Handing the bags to Angel, I pulled out again. After a quick stop for cat food for Mr. Rumblebutt, we headed home.

OUR HOUSE—MY house, rather, though I always thought of it as *ours*—was on 36th Avenue, across from Discovery Park. It had been a murder house, but we had cleared out the spirits who had been lingering. Now, it was just a lovely little house, complete with enough upgrades to make it feel newish, on a double lot. We had left the paintjob on the outside. It was new enough to still be tidy, and a pretty navy blue with white trim. But inside, we had repainted every room.

I parked in front of Angel's car, wishing we had a garage. Carrying our food, we entered through the front door. To our right, the hall led to the kitchen. The hallway had a powder room on the left, beneath the stairs, and an office off to the right. Parallel to the inner hallway wall, the staircase led to the upstairs, with three bedrooms and two bathrooms. Straight ahead was the arch leading into the living room.

Angel carried the food into the living room and I

followed. An opening at the other end of the living room also led into the kitchen, and Mr. Rumblebutt was lying right across the archway, stretched out on his back with his feet in the air. He let out a purp when we entered the room, and I laughed.

"Yo, Mr. R., silly boy. Were you waiting for us, or just having fun in the…well, no sun, but…" I leaned down and scooped him up into my arms. His fur was so long that my hand disappeared as I cuddled him to me. He began to purr as I rubbed my nose against his side. "I love you, you silly little booger."

Angel snorted. "He's got you snowed, girl. He's a cagey one, aren't you, Mr. Rumblebutt?"

He sneezed and shook his head, his ears tickling my face. Then, with a glance at Angel and then back to me, he squirmed out of my arms and ran into the kitchen.

"I guess it's dinner time in the cat world." I followed him through the arch into the kitchen. As I flipped on the lights, for a second I almost thought I saw my grandfather standing there, but then, the shadow was gone. Shuddering, I tried to brush away the memory of killing him, but it had been only a few weeks back, and it wasn't all that easy to stop the images of his body lying on the floor from flickering through my thoughts.

Angel passed by me, clapping me on the shoulder. "Stop thinking about it," she whispered. "You had no choice. It was self-defense." She handed me two plates and then rummaged in the drawer for silverware.

"You always can read me," I said. "Plates, for burgers and fries?"

"Regardless of what we're eating, we deserve plates and silverware and napkins. Mama J. always told me, treat yourself like royalty and others will treat you accordingly." She paused, then added, "Girl, let me tell you something. You didn't murder him. Yes, you *killed* him, but murder's an ugly word and you had no intention of harming him until he showed up here, trying to hurt you. It was self-defense, no matter what method you used."

I nodded, trying to hold on to that thought. "I know, but it just keeps playing over and over in my head. And it didn't help that I took Saílle's damned check. I feel like it was blood money. That she paid me for assassinating him."

"No again, girl. She paid you to keep you from making a fuss about him coming here to harm you. He was a member of her court, and placed fairly highly. He didn't do any favors to her by deciding to flip out and use you for a guinea pig, and she knows it. You could have demanded much more than you accepted from her and she would have paid it."

I slowly nodded. I knew she was speaking the truth, but the fact was, I still felt like Saílle had bought me off. That she had paid me blood money because I killed him and took care of a budding problem in her court.

"Well, he inadvertently paid off a sizable chunk of my house loan. Okay." A shiver ran up my back. "I want to stop talking about him for now." My phone rang, and I set the plates on the coffee table in the living room as I answered it.

Marilee was on the phone. She was my mentor, guiding me as I approached the Cruharach—the stage in every Fae's life when they came of age. The ritual was paramount. Whether I was prepared or not, I would enter the rite of passage. But go in unprepared and there was a good chance I wouldn't come out of it sane. Or worse yet, I'd die. I had no clue what I'd be facing, but Marilee had been training me for eight weeks.

"Ember? I wanted to talk to you about our Saturday meeting."

"I needed to talk to you about changing Saturday's time as well," I said. "I promised Raven I'd come to dinner and it's likely to run late."

Marilee paused, then said, "That's fine. I was going to cancel Saturday, anyway. You need a couple of days between the last session and the Cruharach, and on Samhain Eve, the night of the thirty-first, you *will* enter the Cruharach. You'll either pass through by morning, or…" Her voice trailed off. I didn't have to ask what she meant.

"So, this is it. Next Monday, then?" My stomach felt full of butterflies, and I stared at my feet, unsure what to say.

"Yes, so Wednesday night is your last chance to train with me." She paused, then added, "I trust you. I trust in your abilities. And once the Cruharach is over, you'll be free of that worry forever."

"Yeah," I said softly. "If I live. And if I do pass through, will I still be me?"

"Trust, Ember. Trust in the process. Trust in yourself. Trust in me."

As I punched the end button, Angel joined me and arranged the food on the coffee table.

"That was Marilee? I heard something about the Cruharach."

"Yeah, it was Marilee. The ritual is set for Samhain

Eve." I turned to Angel, so nervous I wanted to throw up. "What if I fail? What if I don't make it through?"

"You will. You'll do fine, Ember. You've been trained by the best, right?"

"Right."

"Morgana chose your trainer for you, correct?"

Again, I nodded.

"Then trust Morgana. She's not going to let you down. And before you say it, you're not going to let yourself down either. Don't ask me how, I just know." She poked her finger at the food waiting on the plates. "Let's eat before it gets cold. Where's the remote?"

I handed it to her, folding my legs beneath me as I curled on the sofa and bit into my burger. It was delicious, as was the lime shake, but I could barely taste either one. Regardless of what Angel said, there was always a chance that the ritual would fail.

Angel turned on the TV and tuned into channel 1450 —Channel Q—the Quirk Channel. As *Rudding Place Northwest* flickered onto the screen, I did my best to lose myself in the garish and flamboyant show, but try as I might, the story failed to suck me in, and all I could think was, *What's the ritual going to be like*, and *Will I measure up?*

MORNING CAME FAR TOO EARLY, and I woke with the dawn. I rolled over and tried to go back to sleep, but Mr. Rumblebutt had other plans. He snuck up near my face and pounced on my nose, claws retracted, but nevertheless, it was a shock to find my mouth full of cat fluff. I sputtered and he flopped over on his side next to me, spreading his legs. I rubbed his belly and he squirmed around like he was high on catnip.

"You doofus. It's barely six."

I normally didn't rise till seven, but now that I was awake I took a quick shower and dressed in a pair of dark jeans, a periwinkle cold-shoulder top with lace sleeves, and a pair of knee-high lace-up boots. After tying them, I put on my makeup and gathered my hair into a high ponytail. Heading downstairs, I stopped to feed Mr. Rumblebutt before I slid on my leather jacket, then headed into our side yard. It was six-thirty, and I decided that some time in the garden would calm my mind.

The morning was colder than I expected, and a trail of frost glazed the grass, weaving a lace web to cover the yard. Everything seemed clear and clean, as though the frost had spread its magic across the city. I glanced into the sky. The clouds were tinged with silver, reminding me of snow-weather, though there hadn't been any forecasts predicting it.

I opened the gate leading into the extra lot that we called our side yard and stared at the barren soil. We had managed to clear through the overgrown gardens, rooting out the dead plants, dividing the bulbs and replanting them, pruning the overgrown roses and hydrangeas, trimming the lilacs and rhododendrons. We had called in an arborist to check the health of the massive cedars and firs that covered the lot, and he had pronounced them all thriving, though they needed a good pruning, which we had hired his company to do.

Now, the beds were ready for spring, and Angel and I were planning out what we wanted to do. I wanted an herb garden, and Angel wanted a kitchen garden and a pumpkin patch, and we wanted to expand the roses. But we were still designing out the beds and plotting out where we wanted them.

As I sat on the bench near the roses, bracing myself against the chill, there was a loud cawing overhead. I glanced up at the bevy of crows that were swooping in to land on the bare branches. Reaching up to my throat, I touched the crow pendant that hung around my neck. It had been a gift from Morgana, marking me as hers. She had taken me under her wing, like she had taken my mother, and I was pledged to her service as well as to Cernunnos.

One of the larger crows—not a raven, though close in size—hopped forward to stand near my feet. He stared at me with his piercing gaze as a cold gust blew past, chilling me. I could feel Morgana nearby. I glanced around but didn't see her anywhere.

Are you here? I asked silently, reaching out for her. *What do you want me to know?*

I had no sooner than formed the questions in my mind than I found myself sliding into trance. I could barely hold my eyes open, and I couldn't move. I struggled to stand, but fell back on the bench and finally, remembering Marilee's words about trusting in the process, I let myself go, sliding into the abyss that opened up before me.

I WAS STANDING on the edge of a long shore in the dark, with the moon high overhead. The water was foaming against the sand, and every incoming wave swept in a thousand sparkles to light the beach. The twinkling lights were blue and green, and they burned brightly in the darkness, swirling in the water. Mesmerized, I moved forward.

As I approached the edge of the ocean, a massive wave rose up. On it stood Morgana, her arms wide as she stepped out of the water and onto the shore. She seemed so much taller than normal. She was in her true form, unmasked. Her hair caught up in a web of silver moon drops that held the coil of curls back from her face, she tilted her head, a feral smile on her face.

"I have one last piece of advice for you, before you enter the Cruharach. Quit trying to outguess the future. Quit pitting the two sides of yourself against one another. Both make you who you are, and you must let them settle the battle for dominance."

Her words echoed around me, ricocheting off stone and wave alike. They settled in the pit of my stomach as I understood what she was saying. I had been rooting for the Autumn Stalker side of me to reign supreme because I was so afraid of my Leannan Sidhe heritage. When my mother's blood rose to protect me, I had drained the life force out of my grandfather, and the fury and joy I had felt during the act terrified me. I kept thinking, what if that side came out on top? The Autumn's Bane stalkers were just as dangerous but more reasonable.

"Your mother found a way to keep her nature in check. If that is to be your path, trust that you, too, will decipher your way through the labyrinth." She paused, holding my gaze. "Answer me this: *Do you trust me?*"

I caught my breath. "Of course I do, My Lady. I trust you with all my heart."

"Then trust me when I tell you that you will emerge

through the Cruharach exactly as you are destined to. Go in with no preconceptions or you will taint the ritual. In your words, don't try to rig the results."

The sparkling water splashed around my feet now, and I could feel the innate magic within the faerie fire that marked everything it touched.

I lowered my head. "As you will, Lady. I will step out of my own way."

"Best you do, or you'll find your journey through the ritual a difficult and terrifying one, and I will not vouch for your success." With that, she began to withdraw.

"Lady! Wait—"

She turned around. "Yes?"

"Am I ready? Have I learned enough?" The fear in my heart rose up again, overwhelming me. I tried to shake it off, but found it hard to let go. I hated situations I couldn't control, and this was about as far outside my wheelhouse as I had ever faced.

Morgana held my gaze. She shook her head. "Oh child. I ask once more, *Do you trust me?*"

I searched within my heart, finally raising my head. "I trust you, Lady, but I'm finding it hard to trust myself."

"To trust me *is* to trust yourself. *I believe in you*, Ember, and I never place my belief lightly. From where comes your doubt? Who told you that you weren't good enough? And don't play the blame game. Saílle and Névé are irrelevant to this situation."

I paused, trying to formulate an answer to her question. And then, I found it, that worm of niggling doubt skulking in my heart.

"I couldn't stop my parents' deaths. I wasn't strong

enough to stop them. If I can't protect my loved ones, how can I protect myself?"

Morgana began to laugh, her laughter resounding on the wind.

"Oh blessed child, we can *never* protect anyone one hundred percent. You cannot conquer death, and you cannot conquer destiny. You must accept your vulnerability in order to embrace your strengths. For only then will you have a true vision of your abilities. Only then can you make clear choices and decisions. Surrender yourself to a universe filled with events outside your control. Haven't you yet realized that the gods to whom you are pledged are chaos incarnate?"

She began to dance on the shore, swaying as a drumbeat rose up in the distance.

"The Lord of the Forest is wild and feral, and he will run you down in the forest, and drag you with him on the most magical and ancient Hallowed Hunt. Your boyfriend embodies unchained passion, and he will dance you into the faerie ring and ravish you until you can think no more, but merely feel the rhythm as your bodies meet. And I? I am the soul of ecstatic magic. With me, you lose yourself in the dance as we journey along the web of life. You live in chaos, Ember. You live on a planet hurtling through space, around a star in a spiraling galaxy, in the corner of the universe. *You control none of this.*"

I saw it then—the brilliant stars spread out overhead in a silver wheel surrounding a gleaming castle. And everything, from the stars to the castle to Morgana, to me, was connected by a web of glistening energy. We were *all* linked: everything and everyone. Every single movement spread out in concentric circles to ripple through the universe. Everything that happened was all a dance. It was all a prayer.

"What's that?" I whispered, pointing at the spiraling castle of stars overhead.

"That is Caer Arianrhod, home to the center of our magic, the center of our power, and the center of Annwn." And then, before I could speak again, she said, "Remember what I said. Your life depends on it. I will see you after the Cruharach."

And with that, she vanished, and I was back on the bench. As one, the crows took wing and flew away.

CHAPTER FOUR

When we got to work, Herne was waiting in the break room and he didn't look happy. Talia had come in early and she had already made coffee. I took one look at both of them and knew something had happened.

"What's up?" I asked, giving him a quick kiss.

He shook his head. "It's bad, Ember. Wait till everyone gets here. I don't want to have to go through it several times." He glanced around. "Damn it, I forgot my tablet. I'll be right back."

As he headed out of the room, Talia waited till he was out of earshot, then quickly sat down beside me.

"I'm not sure exactly what's up, but he was on the phone when I got here, and I could hear yelling on the other end. And if I'm not mistaken, I think it was Cernunnos. I don't know what he was saying, but I've never seen Herne look so pale. He just murmured a 'Yes sir' and got off the phone as fast as he could. I knew better than ask what was going down. I'm sure we'll find out in a few minutes. I called Viktor and Yutani to light a fire under their butts. They'll be on time."

Talia had known Herne a long, long time. She had been with the agency since before it had come over from England. A harpy who lost her powers, Talia had accepted Herne and Morgana's help, and she was probably Herne's oldest friend.

I decided to leave the subject alone. As Talia said, we'd find out soon enough.

"So, how are you? How are Roxy and Rema?"

Talia smiled. She loved talking about her greyhounds. "They're doing well, thank you. I took them out to the park with Viktor. He brought Anastasia—that little mutt he adopted that you found in that junkyard. We had a nice evening and a good, long walk." Her smile faded a little. "Actually, I've had a troubling letter from home."

I frowned. Talia had been slowly warming up to Angel and me, and we occasionally got together for drinks or dinner. But she had never mentioned before that she was still in connection with her family.

"I didn't realize that you had reconnected with your family."

"Oh, not my mother. No, trust me, I couldn't care less what happens to her, given she threw me out when I was injured. My sister Varia contacted me about a year ago. I've been cautious about how much I've talked to her, but I did answer her. Now, she wants to come out here to see me."

I swallowed, hard. "She's a harpy like you, right?"

Talia nodded. "Yes, indeed. And she still has her full powers. She's been rather snotty to me. I think she sees me as disabled and she's not very gracious about it. But I received a letter from her yesterday saying she wants to come visit. And get this, *she's already on the way*. I can't stop her from coming because I can't reach her."

"Lovely. So you get to see her whether or not you want to, right?"

Irritation flared in Talia's eyes. "Right. She'd better not make a scene."

I had the sudden image of a harpy shrieking, flying around the hallways, and grimaced. Herne wouldn't stand for it.

"Oh, if she shows the first sign of disrespect, she's out of here. Even if I have to hand her over to Cernunnos to use for hunting practice." She stopped as Viktor and Yutani entered the room. Angel followed them, followed by Herne, holding his tablet.

"I've locked the elevator so that we won't be interrupted," she said.

Herne motioned for us to all sit down. "Good." He tossed what looked like a police report on the table, along with what appeared to be a stack of photocopies. "I made copies for everybody. We've got serious trouble. Saílle and Névé contacted Morgana this morning, and they're both frantic. I don't blame them, this time."

"What happened?" I couldn't see what the report said from where I was sitting, but it looked long and involved, and there were pictures attached.

"Our lovely little hate group, the Tuathan Brotherhood, has struck again. Jasper Elrich, one of the Light Fae, plowed his car into a group of partygoers in the Crown Hill district, over on 13th Avenue. It's a predominantly human neighborhood that borders on a mostly shifter neighborhood. They had blocked off the streets from 85th to 87th for a neighborhood autumn block party breakfast."

Herne was right. This was bad. Viktor picked up the copies of the report and began passing them out to us.

"How many were injured?" Talia finally asked.

"Five adults injured, two dead. Both of the dead are shifters. Three children dead, one of them a shifter, two humans. He swerved to do the most damage."

"They catch him?" Viktor skimmed over the report.

"He killed himself before the cops could get him out of the car. Bullet to the head. A stack full of Tuathan Brotherhood pamphlets in the backseat." Herne's voice was strained. "Cernunnos and Morgana want this brought to a halt, *now*." He slid into a chair, his expression grim. "Yutani, bring up the local news station on your laptop, please."

While Yutani tapped away, I began to read the police report. Sure enough, Jasper had been a member of the Light Fae court. The photos were bleak, with blood and bone smeared all over the streets. One photo showed a woman kneeling over a young boy who didn't look more than six years old, her face in her hands.

"Got it," Yutani said, sliding the computer over to Herne.

Herne scanned the headlines, then clicked on a link, turning the computer around so we could all see. The video was a live feed from the mayor's office.

Whoever was responsible for damage control was speaking. The caption identified her as Deputy Mayor Maria Serenades, the mayor's right hand.

"We are calling in government experts, as well as *divine agency* to help us understand why this crime happened.

We have received no demands from the Tuathan Brotherhood, only a claim of responsibility for the act. The hate group has emerged from seemingly nowhere, and there's little evidence as to where they are located, or what is fueling the sudden spate of violent crimes."

In a world where gods often walked among the populace, "divine agency" referred to any divinity-appointed agency who had authority along with the government. The Wild Hunt was one of those agencies.

"What government experts? The FBI? The BIDB?" Viktor asked.

Herne snorted. "The FBI wouldn't be able to touch this. And the Bureau for Interdimensional Beings? They aren't to be trusted, and the mayor knows it. The United Coalition hasn't yet issued an official statement. They can't, really, until they gather more information. But I've talked with the mayor a number of times and she called me this morning, asking for us to intercede, since this involves the Fae. So she's on the same page as Morgana and Cernunnos."

"And Névé and Saílle? What did they have to say?" I tossed the police report back on the table, the image of the mother leaning over her son too fresh.

"They're begging us to find out who's doing this. Both claim they have no idea about this hate group, and that if there *is* any such hate group, the group is rogue. To be fair, neither Névé or Saílle have ever directed their anger at humans—not directly. Nor at shifters. They usually target each other and it's the spillover damage that we're directed to stop. The fact that they willingly contacted my parents does indicate that they're telling the truth."

"And what about other states?" Angel asked.

Herne nodded. "Four other states report similar attacks to the beatings last night. They may be copycat crimes, so Father's asked Kipa to go check it out. He's on the road, as of now."

"Where do we start with this?" I crossed to the counter and poured myself another cup of coffee, adding in sugar and milk. "I suppose we should head over to Jasper's home and check it out?"

"Right. Since the mayor asked us to lead the case, I was able to instruct the police to cordon off the apartment. They made sure there's nobody else inside, but haven't touched anything. Ember, you and Viktor come with me. Yutani, find out everything you can about Jasper and email us the information. Talia, stay on Amanda's case. We'll get back to that after we check out Elrich's apartment, but for the moment, this is top priority."

"More important than a little girl who's missing?" Angel said.

Herne turned to her. "Unfortunately, yes. We have three *dead* children and two *dead* adults thanks to this psycho. To top it off, I got a call from the hospital. One of the injured yesterday—a human—died during the night. Whoever these crazy fucks are behind the Tuathan Brotherhood, they're on a murder spree. I feel very badly for Eleanor's mother, but right now, this emergency has a much broader scope."

Angel hung her head, staring at the table. "I know. I just…"

Herne regarded her silently for a moment, then said, "I'm sorry. I didn't mean to yell, but we are in a code red situation and we have to do our jobs. We'll do everything we can to find Eleanor, but right now…" He stopped, letting out a long sigh. "It all sucks, Angel. *All of it*. But we only have so many resources, and time on both cases is running against us."

With that he stood and motioned to Viktor and me. "Come on, let's get a move on. Angel, stay by the phone in case we need you to email us info. Also, if anybody else comes in looking to sign us up for a case, tell them we won't be able to consult with them until at least next week. If they want to wait, great, take their number and tell them we'll call within the next week. If not, refer them to Isaak Durnholm. He's a good investigator and works with a lot of the SubCult."

"Isaak Durnholm. Got it," she said, standing up. "Is that all?"

"Yeah, that's it. Get to it, guys." Herne turned to me. "Grab what you need, you and Viktor, and meet me at my car in five minutes. Make it snappy."

As he headed back to his office, I turned to Angel, resting my hand on her arm. "He didn't mean to be abrupt—"

She shook her head. "No, I get it. I do. I just… I think Eleanor is out there, somewhere, and we can't do a thing."

"I'll see you later." I headed back to my office, grabbed my purse and tablet, and slid my dagger into my boot sheath before I hurried to the front where Herne and Viktor were waiting. Without a word, we stepped into the elevator and were on our way.

"Where does Elrich live—or rather, where *did* he live?"

I glanced out the window. We were headed toward North Seattle.

"He lived in Parkwood. On Meridian, in the Ella Marie Apartments." Herne turned onto an entrance ramp and picked up speed as we merged onto I-5. The freeway was fairly clear by now, rush hour was over, and it didn't take long for us to reach Exit 175. We then navigated the streets until we were headed west on 155th Street. From there, we turned left on Meridian, driving a couple blocks until we were in front of the Ella Marie Apartments. There were several police cruisers in the area, and we parked in back of the nearest one. As we exited the car and were walking toward the apartment building, one of the cops standing out front stepped out to stop us.

"I need to see your ID. What's your business here?"

Herne held out his badge, and Viktor and I followed suit. The cop blinked, then nodded us through.

"Radio upstairs that we're coming, would you?" Herne said over his shoulder and the cop gave him a wave.

The Ella Marie Apartments weren't kept up very well. The building was three stories, stretching toward the back of the lot like a motel. There weren't any elevators. At the end of each floor, an outdoor staircase led to the upper level. A long concrete walkway ran the length of both upper floors, passing in front of each door.

"What unit did he live in?" I asked as we clattered up the metal steps. I didn't touch the railing—it looked like cast iron and my feet tingled even inside my shoes.

"2-B. See the officer standing in front of the door?" Herne swung off the stairs, onto the second level. We stopped in front of the second door where, once again, we showed our badges. The officer opened the door for us, then stepped to the side and we entered the apartment.

The first thing I noticed was the incredible stench of the place, like stale beer and moldy food and unwashed clothes all run together. I coughed. The very air felt permeated by the smell.

"Haven't any of his neighbors complained?" I asked, trying not to gag.

"You were outside—we didn't smell anything there," Victor said, grimacing. "Geezus, this is bad. It smells like something curled up and died in here."

"Given the mess, maybe something did." Herne coughed. "This is pretty bad." He turned to the cop, who was watching us from the door. "Did you guys touch anything at all?"

The officer shook his head. His eyes were watering and I caught a whiff of his pheromones—he had to be a shifter. He was nervous, but not in that *I'm lying* sort of way. He was just jumpy, and I didn't blame him, given that Elrich had been aiming for both shifters and humans alike.

"No, we did our best to avoid walking on anything on the floor, though I can't guarantee we totally managed it, given there's hardly any bare spots. We just checked each room to make sure there was nobody else inside, then we shut it up, like you asked."

The apartment was silent, except for the ticking of a clock.

I glanced around, staring at the disarray. Either Elrich had been a hoarder, or he had been a total slob. There were stacks of magazines, tied in bundles, and scattered junk all over the floor—old takeout containers, crumpled napkins, half-eaten food. My stomach lurched when I saw half of a hamburger covered in maggots.

"What the ever-loving fuck?" I pointed to the computer. It had been trashed. Somebody had smashed it to bits. The monitor was shattered, and the computer was demolished.

"He was trying to cover his tracks, I'll bet. I wonder if the hard drive is still intact. We'll have Yutani check it out, see if he can pull any info off of it. If it's still all right, he can put it into a different case and see what's there." Herne stopped by the sofa, staring at a stack of pamphlets. "Bingo. Tuathan Brotherhood propaganda."

Viktor checked out the bedroom while I wandered into the kitchen. It was just as bad as the living room, but as I looked around, something caught my eye. I walked over to the fridge and stared at a picture taped to it. There was something off, but I couldn't quite tell what.

The picture was of our suspect—Jasper Elrich, with his arms wrapped around a beautiful young woman. She was probably around twenty. His lips were against her cheek, and they both looked radiant. And then, it hit me. She was *human*.

"Herne, come here!"

"What is it?" Herne maneuvered through the mess over to my side.

"Does this look like someone who hates humans?" I pointed to the picture. The timestamp on it read two months ago. "He looks pretty happy here, to me."

"People can hide all manner of prejudices," Herne said, but he took the picture off the fridge and turned it around. "Jasper and Penny, Whidbey Island." He looked around. "Any other pictures like this? By the way, I asked the cops and they said he didn't have his phone on him in the car, so look for a phone."

"That means moving the mess around." I grimaced.

"Here." Herne handed me a pair of vinyl gloves. "Wear these. We have no idea what kind of bacteria might be hiding in this mess."

I slipped on the gloves and walked over to the table. It was piled high with old food wrappers and paper. As I shifted through the garbage, I caught sight of a stack of unopened envelopes. They were all addressed to Jasper Elrich. I shook off the residue crap that was sticking to them, and looked around for a chair. There was one by the table that didn't have anything on it, so I sat down there and began opening the envelopes.

"What do you have?" Herne asked.

"Looks like bills—all late. None of them have been paid for...*two months*. Electricity, credit card, phone bill, cable bill. All of these are second requests for payment. So he was in arrears. I wonder if we can find his checkbook to see if he was out of money. And can you ask the cops to find the manager? If he was behind on his other bills, was he behind on his rent?"

I stacked the bills together and poked through the kitchen until I found some plastic zipper bags, then put the bills inside one. Herne handed me the picture, and I added that to another one while he went to speak with the police officer.

A moment later, Viktor emerged from the bedroom.

"I found his phone. He has a drawer full of women's clothes—mostly underwear, a pair of jeans, a couple tops. Definitely not his size, so he wasn't a cross dresser. There's a blow dryer in the bathroom, and there was an extra toothbrush there, along with some tampons in the cupboard, so I am pretty sure that a woman stayed here off and on."

I showed him the picture. "Ten to one, it was her. Can you unlock his phone?"

"Idiot didn't have a passcode on it, much to our good fortune." Viktor handed the phone to me.

I brought up the contacts screen and scrolled through, looking for…

"Bingo! Penny. And it's just her first name, so he probably knew her pretty well. Should I call?" I frowned. "Or maybe I should wait till we see if we can identify her and find out her background."

"I'd wait. But take a look at his text messages. See what you can find out from there."

"Good idea." I flipped over to his text messages and glanced through them. There were several recent ones, but the ones from Penny seemed to be older. I began to skim through them. "Penny texted him at least fifty times in August, asking where he was, what was wrong, what did she do wrong. There seems to be no response, until she threatened to call the cops to have them come check on him. Then he texted her a curt 'It's over. Leave me alone. I never want to hear from you again.' After that she texted a few times, begging him to call her, but after another text from him, 'You fucking slut, quit bothering me,' just…radio silence."

"What were his texts like before then?" Viktor asked.

I scrolled back. "Loving, thoughtful—oh," I paused. "They were engaged, Viktor. Right up until August, he was all over her, promising that when they got married, they'd go to France for a honeymoon, talking about having kids, all that."

Frowning, I stared at the messages. "What makes a person switch like that so quickly? By the date stamps, there seems to be about a week's break between the happy times and when Penny started to text him the first week in August. What happened in one week to make him go from being the loving fiancé to cutting her out of his life so harshly?"

Viktor pushed a pile of garbage off of another chair and, after making sure it was clear of any residue, sat down. He took the phone, staring at the texts. "I guess we ask her. Once we find out who she is and whatever background we can."

Herne returned at that moment. "The manager says that Elrich paid his rent in six-month increments. He's been living here for three years, and he's never missed a payment. Every six months like clockwork. Model tenant. Elrich always kept the place immaculate, so the manager was in shock over what I told him about the state of the apartment. And Elrich had been friendly with the manager, though standoffish from his neighbors, which isn't a surprise given that, apparently, the neighbor to the right is one of the Dark Fae, and the neighbor on his left works nights, so isn't around during the daytime."

"He say anything else?" Viktor asked.

Herne shook his head. "There haven't been any signs of trouble from Elrich. *Ever*. I talked with the cops—he doesn't have any sort of police record. I'm baffled."

We showed him the phone and I told him about the text messages.

"Then we have to figure out what happened to make

him do an about-face. We'll talk to his bank, see what we can find out about his spending habits. Talk to the utility companies to find out if he was ever late on his bills before. And once we get that computer back to the office, Yutani can see what he can find out. I'll have Talia check out Penny. Who are the other texts from?"

"I haven't checked them out yet," I said.

"Well, let's go. I asked the police to bring us any other evidence they find that might be important. They know we're in charge of the investigation and they seem relieved. This is the second attack on humans and shifters in just a couple days. People are going to be getting antsy, and we need to nip this in the bud."

"I just hope we can," Viktor said.

"Me too," I echoed as we filed back into the living room. Herne had the cops box up the computer parts and carry it down to his car, and we followed.

All the way back to the office, I kept thinking about Penny. What could make a person shift so drastically in such a short time?

BACK AT THE OFFICE, we met up again. Angel had ordered lunch in for everybody.

"I hope you don't mind subs for lunch. I also ordered chips, salad, and a box of cookies." She locked the elevator and followed us back to the break room, where lunch was set out across the counter. I washed my hands thoroughly, using more soap than I needed, just to scrub the feeling of grime off me. Elrich's apartment made me want to go home and clean. I noticed Viktor and Herne did the same.

After choosing a ham and cheddar sub, and piling my plate high with chips, I poured myself a cup of coffee and added cream and sugar. Finally, we gathered around the table, lunches in front of us.

"Thanks," Herne told Angel. "Good idea to order lunch in. We're working through today."

"I figured as much," she said. She seemed over her argument with Herne, and I glanced at Talia, suspecting that the harpy had managed to have a calming talk with my BFF.

Talia seemed to have a knack for bringing a sense of peace to the agency. Her silver hair was pulled back in a tidy braid today, and she was wearing a pair of blue trousers with a button-up shirt that had been embroidered with flowers across the top of the bodice. Talia looked like a fit, healthy woman in her mid-sixties, which was the glamour she had chosen when Morgana offered to give her a permanent illusion so she could fit in with society.

"Okay, let's start with what we found at the apartment," Herne said. He told them what the manager had said about Elrich, then added, "But here's the disconnect. The place was a cockroach's wet dream. It was a total wreck. We found stacks of propaganda about the Tuathan Brotherhood. The computer was trashed—somebody took a hammer to it, but we brought the remains back with us, in case the hard drive was still viable. Yutani, get on that after lunch. Ember, your turn."

I set the phone on the table along with the packets containing the unpaid bills and the picture of Jasper and Penny, while telling them about the texts between the two. "We need to do some digging and find out what her last name is, along with whatever else we can find out before contacting her."

Talia picked up the phone. "I'll tackle that this afternoon."

"The cops will let us know what else they come up with," Herne said, taking a bite of his sandwich. "So, what did you two find out?"

Yutani tapped away on his laptop. "I just sent you each a dossier on Elrich. He was a model citizen. I already can tell you who Penny is. She is—*was*, apparently—his fiancée. They met at work. Until the past two months, Jasper Elrich was an art teacher at one of the local schools. He taught a mixture of students—human, Fae, shifter—and there were zero problems. In fact, the kids loved him. But at the tail end of July, he abruptly quit with no notice. He'd been at that job for five years, and not once did he present a problem."

"There it is again. The end of July. What the hell happened?" I took a long sip of my coffee. "Gods, I needed this. I didn't get enough caffeine this morning."

Angel snorted. "That's because you forgot to buy coffee, and we didn't have time to swing by a Starbucks."

I snorted. "I know, I know. I forget these sort of things."

"You mean, you don't like to go grocery shopping. That's why I ran down to the local coffee shop and bought a couple pounds while you were out. I know you won't remember, since you and Herne have a date."

"Can we get back to the topic at hand?" Herne asked, sounding tense.

"Sorry," I murmured.

Angel grinned.

"Thank you. Go on, Yutani. What else did you find out?" Herne glanced at me, a slightly irritated look on his face.

"What happened at the end of July? That's the million-dollar question. Before you ask, I already ran his financials. He's got enough in savings to cover about six months of bills."

"Then why didn't he pay them in September? And obviously he didn't pay them this month either." It didn't add up. If he had the money, why not pay them? Then I thought of something. "Did he have a will? Who gets his savings?"

"That I can't tell you. But it looks like at the beginning of August, he dropped out of every organization he was part of. He was in good standing with Névé's Court—I already checked on that, though that's obviously over with. His family is going to have a buttload of fallout over this." Yutani shrugged. "As to what happened, I don't know. But I'll see what I can find out with the remains of his computer."

Talia picked up the phone. "I'll download all his text messages. I'll focus on those in July, August, September, and this month, to start. I can look through the older ones later." She paused. "Back to the missing girl. Do you want to hear what I found out about Amanda's relatives?"

Herne nodded. "Yeah. Anybody we should be watching?"

"Nope. Her family seems to be the poster family for functional. They're the most boring family I've ever seen. Not a whisper of scandal other than a few cousins ticketed for minor traffic violations. These are people who probably take cheesy pictures for the holidays and you know they must have an ugly sweater contest. Her late husband's family checked out too, though there are a couple drunks and one kleptomaniac on his side. But nothing to trigger alarm bells."

"Well, hell," I said. "Where does that leave us?"

"We still have the mall video footage, and we haven't yet looked into—"

"Excuse me, but Erica texted me this morning. In the furor over Elrich's attack, I forgot to mention it." Viktor pulled out his phone. "There have been three abductions and murders over the past few months, but the cops haven't been able to find out what's going on and given the manpower crunch, I doubt they've been as thorough as they might be otherwise. Let me download the document she sent me and see what it says." He fiddled with his tablet for a moment. "I sent it to the rest of you, as well."

I brought up my email, then opened up the document on my tablet so I could read it easier than on my phone screen. "Crap. Viktor's right. Three little girls, all between two to four years old. All blond. All found murdered about ten days to two weeks after they vanished. One a month since July, and all abducted on the 22nd of the month." I glanced up. "Eleanor was kidnapped on the 22nd. It *has* to be the same person."

"Then we have a couple days leeway, if the murderer hasn't escalated. Given Eleanor's been missing three days, we have, at best, eleven days left if it's the same perp," Herne said.

Talia scanned the document. "Well, this is odd. None of the bodies showed any marks—no bruises, no sign of sexual assault, thank the gods. They were all found in child-size white coffins, hidden out in the woods, and they were all wearing pretty dresses and bows in their hair."

"That's odd," Yutani said. "That shows remorse. What did they die of?"

Talia glanced back at the report. "They died of…" She stopped, looking puzzled. "An overdose? They were drugged to death with crackalaine."

Crackalaine was the hottest illegal drug in town. It hearkened back to old-school cocaine. It was as cheap as crack to make, and it provided the same euphoria as ecstasy. Incredibly addictive, it took as little as one dose before the user was physically addicted. Its effects included euphoria, carefree attitude, loss of inhibition, and in some cases—paranoia and hallucinations. The overdose threshold was low, and it was cheap and plentiful in the underground drug market. Usage had actually decreased once marijuana had been legalized, but there were always thrill seekers looking for the next, best high. And it made sex amazing, like ecstasy, so it had an extra appeal, especially to college age students.

"Let me get this straight," Herne said. "We have a serial killer out there who abducts two- to four-year-old blond girls, doesn't hurt them from what we can tell, then two weeks later, gives them an overdose and lays them out in child-size coffins, in pretty dresses?"

I thought about it for a moment. "My guess is that we're dealing with a female suspect. And it was a woman who abducted Eleanor in the video. Think about it for a moment. Women tend to utilize poison as a weapon far more than men do when they commit murder. And dressing up the girls and putting them in a coffin to protect them from the elements? It might be remorse, or it might be a maternal instinct to protect their bodies."

"Even after she killed them?" Yutani asked.

"We have no idea what's going on in her psyche. I don't know, maybe it's ritualistic. Or maybe it's remorse, or a dozen other things. But it's a pattern and, given the children aren't harmed…well, other than being killed," I added, realizing how incredibly bizarre that sounded, "at least we know she's not a pedophile or into torture."

"We shouldn't jump to conclusions," Herne cautioned. "The woman on the tape could be our serial killer, or it could be someone else entirely. But I grant you that Eleanor fits the profile of the other victims. I just don't want to assume anything. It might be a copycat, or someone trying to cover up another reason for kidnapping the child. We chance overlooking evidence if we only look in one direction." He skimmed over the document Erica had sent Viktor. "It says here, all the girls were abducted from outside the home." He glanced over at Viktor. "We should interview the parents of the murdered girls. I'll contact the mayor and ask if she can give us official access to any info the cops have on this. We don't want to step on toes."

"The cops didn't add Eleanor to the list of possible victims," I said, frowning.

Viktor shook his head. "No. Erica told me the department is stretched thin as it is, and Eleanor vanished right before the first Tuathan Brotherhood attack, which of course they're fixated on. Let me text her." He began tapping away at his phone.

"I wish we could have seen the woman's face on the security film." Angel frowned. "Did they check through all their other film that day—especially around that time—looking for any other footage that might match the woman in the video?"

Talia shook her head. "I doubt it. It's a blurry image, though Eleanor stands out pretty well, and they only got her from the back. The woman's petite, wearing a nondescript jacket and jeans, it looks like, and she's either a blonde or light red head or light brunette. There could be hundreds of similarly dressed women in that footage and I don't think mall security is going to spend the time combing through it. And before you suggest it, neither am I."

"I can write a program to scan through, looking for similarities," Yutani said.

"Before you spend time on that, let's see if we can even get hold any more of their tapes," Herne said. "Otherwise, it's a waste of time." He glanced at the clock. "All right. Input all your notes, and Yutani, you get busy on sorting out what's left of that computer. Talia, get cracking on the phone. As soon as I talk to Cernunnos, we'll hand out new assignments."

As we carried the rest of our lunches back to our desks, my mind was on the murdered girls, and I found myself murmuring, *"Mary, Mary, quite contrary, how does your garden grow? With silver bells, and cockle shells, and pretty maids all in a row."*

Yes, they were all pretty little maids, and all very dead. My thoughts somber, I began to type in my notes.

CHAPTER FIVE

By afternoon, Yutani had managed to salvage the hard drive of the computer and he was busy transferring data to his own computer. I was finishing some paperwork—entering notes from one of our recent cases into the system—when Herne called Viktor and me into his office.

"I got the go-ahead to interview the parents of the murdered girls. In fact, the cops are welcoming our help, given the situation. I'm sending the two of you out to interview the first set of parents now. Dana and Hadley Longtooth. They're puma shifters. They live in West Seattle, not too far from where Amanda lives. Be discreet, they're still in mourning."

"What was their daughter's name? And when did she die?" I asked, wanting to have as much information as possible before we went in.

"Her name was Cassie, and she was the first victim. She was abducted on July 22nd, and found on the 30th.

She was barely three." Herne handed us a photocopy of her picture. "The parents own Sappho's Bookstore."

I glanced up. "Sappho?"

Herne nodded. "Lesbian couple. Here's a rundown of what they told the cops. See if you can find out anything else." He handed me a sheet of paper. "Viktor, you drive. Try to get back before rush hour. It's one o'clock now, so…get back here by four if you can."

I nodded. "Sure thing."

Viktor and I informed Angel where we were taking off to, and then headed to the parking garage to Viktor's car. But instead, he stopped at a compact pickup.

"You get a new car?" I asked.

He nodded. "I bought it last week. Had to. My old clunker died the final death. I've had my eye on this model for a while, so I figured I might as well take the plunge. There's a surprising amount of head and leg room inside, which I need, given my size."

Viktor was six-foot-five, and well over two hundred pounds of solid muscle. He beeped the key fob and I swung into the passenger side, surprised to see that it had more than enough room for the half-ogre. As he fastened his seat belt, I played with some of the different buttons on the dashboard, which included controls for the passenger seat.

"Cool, you have heated seats!" I leaned forward, looking at what other goodies the truck had to offer.

"Keep your hands to yourself. I have everything pre-set the way I like it." Viktor gave me a stern glance, but then laughed and started the truck. "You want to stop for an espresso before we head over to the Longtooths?"

"Sure thing. I could use the buzz." I leaned back,

enjoying the feel of the leather against my back. "Nice truck."

"I know," Viktor said, as we headed down the street. He swung into the nearest Starbucks and we ordered our drinks. "This is on me. You're going to owe me a hundred bucks when Skyler beats Balentine."

We were back on the street in five minutes, and fifteen minutes later, we pulled into the Longtooths' driveway. They had a little house on a rundown street in the right neighborhood. Even though the house looked old, they had kept it up and it was painted sage green with brown trim. The yard was neatly trimmed, though small, and the fence was weathered but it was standing and looked like it would hold until the next big windstorm.

I stared at the door. "Are they home?"

"Herne said that Dana is. She gave him permission to send us over." He climbed out of the truck and, as I got out, beeped the fob to lock the doors. "You ready for this?"

"You mean, am I ready to face a parent who recently lost her little girl to a killer? No, but I don't think we have much choice." I took the lead, striding over the cracked sidewalk to the door. Tufts of grass poked through the broken concrete, though along the sides of the walk, rows of hearty primroses lined the path.

As we came to the porch, I darted up the steps. People responded quicker to me than to Viktor. It was purely a matter of threat—Viktor was huge and half-ogre, and even though he was handsome, he looked like some organized-crime thug. I, on the other hand, was five-six, sturdy but without bulging muscles, and I looked like the Fae girl next door. Kind of.

The woman who answered my knock was shorter

than I was, and plumper, and she was wearing a circle skirt and a form-fitting sweater. Her hair was pulled back into a ponytail, and though she looked perfectly made up, there was an aura of sadness about her that said to me it was a façade, probably to keep her going.

"Hi, are you Dana Longtooth?" I asked.

She nodded. "Yes, are you from the Wild Hunt?"

"Yes, we are." I pulled out my badge and Viktor did the same. She let us in, leading us into the living room.

The house was small, but tidy. The living room contained a sofa, a rocking chair, a television on an entertainment cabinet, and a bookshelf. It led into an equally small dining room, with a wooden table and four chairs, and what looked like an antique sideboard. From the dining room we could see the kitchen. Parallel to the kitchen, from where the dining room and living room merged, was a hallway leading back to three more doors. I guessed two bedrooms and a bath.

"Please, sit down." She led us to the table. "I see you have coffee. Let me get mine, and we can talk." Her voice was soft, as though sadness had put her on a permanent mute button.

Viktor and I took our seats and waited until she returned with her coffee. As she settled into a chair, opposite me, she let out a long sigh and shook her head.

"All right. Please, go ahead and ask me whatever you like." Everything about Dana seemed resigned to sadness. Her eyes were bleak, and it was hard to look at her without falling into her pain.

"I know you've already answered these questions for the police, but can you tell us where Cassie was abducted?" I was glancing through the report of what the police had asked her.

"From the Aurora Street Mall. We were shopping for a birthday present for my wife—for Cassie's birthmother. We used a donor to get pregnant, and Hadley was in better shape to conceive than me. So I took Cassie to the mall to buy a birthday gift."

"What time of day was it?"

Dana shrugged. "Right after lunch time. The mall was crowded. We visited several stores and then Cassie said she was hungry, so we stopped at a hot dog stand and bought hot dogs and some orange juice. We sat down to wait for them at one of the tables in the food court. When our order was up, I told Cassie to wait for me."

"So she was alone at the table?" I tried to put as little judgment in my voice as possible. We all made split-second decisions that turned out to have horrible consequences, but at the moment, seemed the right choice.

She started to cry. "The counter was only about ten feet away. I dashed over to pick up our dogs and juice. The cashier asked me a question—I think it was about the baseball game coming up, because I was wearing a Mariners T-shirt, but it only took a second to answer her. When I returned to the table, Cassie was gone."

Viktor glanced at me, but I gave him a quick shake of the head and let her sit for a moment. She looked on the verge of tears and I didn't want to push her over the edge if I could help it. After a moment, Dana pulled herself together.

"Dana, did anybody at the mall stand out to you? Did you notice anybody following you, or showing up in the same stores? Anybody at all?"

"I don't know," she said with a shrug. "*It's a mall.* When you go in, you're focused on getting your errands done, you know? And because Cassie was with me, I was paying attention to her." She paused, then bleakly said, "Hadley blames me. She doesn't say anything, but I can feel it. She blames me every day. Every time she has to go to a meeting, she blames me."

"Meeting?" I asked, looking up from my notes.

"AlkaNon. She's been a member for years, but she had been thinking she might be able to quit. I didn't think it was a wise idea—those meetings were her lifeline when she first started going. I guess they're her lifeline again, now. She's been hit really hard with the cravings since we lost our daughter." Dana leaned back in her chair, biting her lip. "If I could change the past, if I could give my life instead of Cassie's, I would do it in an instant. If only I hadn't left her at the table…"

Viktor cleared his throat. "Don't beat yourself up. I'll tell you one thing. If somebody was determined to take your daughter, they'd find a way. There are always opportunities, and if it wasn't at the mall, then it would be somewhere else."

I thought for a moment. AlkaNon had reared its head again, and I had a tingle in my spine that told me I was onto something.

"You said that Hadley thought she might be able to quit going to the meetings?"

She nodded. "Yes. Why?"

"Had she stopped? Or was she still going when Cassie vanished?"

"No, she was still going. She was just thinking about stopping. Why?"

I tried to search for a way to explain why I was interested. "Did she ever have any friends come over? Friends from the group?"

Dana shook her head. "No, that's one thing we agreed on. No potential drama in the house—and unfortunately, drama follows alcoholics. Hadley managed to wean herself away from her family drama that had pushed her into drinking in the first place. We wanted to keep that sort of stress out of our relationship."

"What kind of family drama?" I asked.

"Oh, you know, some shifter clans really don't appreciate the queer community, and her father and two of her aunts disapprove of the fact that she's gay. Needless to say, we don't spend the holidays with them." Dana's frown broke and tears filled her eyes. "Now, they're blaming our lifestyle for Cassie's death. I don't know what's going to happen to us."

"Before we leave, can you tell me which meetings Hadley goes to? Which branch?"

Dana gave me an address and after writing it down, I thanked her, and motioned to Viktor. We weren't going to get much else from her, and she was in a rough emotional patch.

"That was quick," Viktor said as we returned to the truck.

"I have an idea, but it's just starting to pull together. We'll need to talk to the other two families first. For now, let's get back to the office."

Back at the office, Yutani was waiting with news of his own.

"I found the list of passwords on Jasper's computer. I can access his email and we can find out just what's gone on since late July." He had brought his laptop into the break room and was furiously tapping away.

I told Herne what we had learned. "I want to ask the other parents if one of them attends AlkaNon meetings. If that's where the unsub is finding them, then we have a place to start looking."

"That's a good catch," Herne said. "If it checks out, then we can at least come up with some plan to shadow their meetings. The question is, though, what if all of the parents go to different meetings?"

"The meetings insist on privacy for the members, and they work on a first-name basis. It would be too noticeable if several members in one group suddenly had a child go missing and/or turn up dead. Suppose the kidnapper goes to different meetings? Maybe sets up a layer of trust with a parent? Then after kidnapping the child, the unsub quietly drops out of that particular group? The parents would be in mourning. Nobody else would really notice." I turned to Yutani. "Can you tell me how many AlkaNon meetings there are in the Seattle area?"

He paused what he was doing, brought up another screen, and went to town. A moment later, he said, "There are at least one hundred and fifty different groups. There are specialized groups for shifters, Fae, humans, multiracial groups, atheist groups, groups of just about every faith, groups for women only, men only, teenagers, couples-groups… You name your choice, the group probably exists."

"See? That's a *massive* hunting ground. And no last names, no personal information except what the member chooses to provide. No way to verify anything. No rolls, no logs. It's perfect for a predator." I stared at the list that Yutani showed us. "We have a serious problem on our hands, if what I suspect is true."

"I almost hope you're wrong," Herne said. "All right. Onto the Tuathan Brotherhood. You said you have Jasper's passwords?" He turned to Yutani.

"Roger that. I'm running his email through a program I wrote to scan for keywords. There are thousands of emails here—the dude was social, that much I'll say for him." He paused, then glanced up. "I've got Penny's info. Penny Sanders, human, lives over on the Eastside. I found their wedding registry. They were supposed to be married in December."

"So neither one bothered to cancel the registry. She was probably too heartbroken, and he probably didn't care by then." I jotted her name down. "Address and phone number?"

"The Juanita Bay Towers, Unit 5-E. Phone is 425-555-0110." He glanced at Herne. "Who should contact her?"

"Ember," Herne said. He glanced at me. "Please give her a call and ask her when she's available. Give her the option of coming into the office, or we can meet at her place if she wants."

"What if she doesn't know about what Elrich did? It seems unlikely but regardless of the internet, news doesn't always get around." I was dreading having to explain to the woman that her ex-fiancé had mowed down a group of people, including kids.

"I think you can figure out how to break it to her."

Herne shook his head. "It's not ideal, but breaking bad news is something that everyone in authority has to do at some time. You might as well get used to it."

"Gee, thanks." Rolling my eyes, I stepped out of the break room as they continued to discuss the cases. As I punched in Penny's number, I ran over what to say, praying she was already aware of the situation.

A moment later, she answered the phone. "Hello?" She sounded wary.

"Penny Sanders?"

"Yes, this is she."

"My name is Ember Kearney and I'm with the—"

"No, not another reporter! Please leave me alone. I don't want to talk to you."

"Wait, I'm not a reporter!" I tried to catch her before she hung up. At first, I thought I was too late, but then I heard her clear her throat.

"Who are you, then? And if you *are* a reporter, I swear I'll hang up on you so fast you won't be able to breathe."

I paused, then said, "My name is Ember and I'm with the Wild Hunt Agency. We're investigating Jasper Elrich's background by order of the mayor, and we need to ask you some questions about him."

She paused, then said, "Are you with the cops?"

"We're an enforcement agency, yes. We work with the police. We're what's known as a *divine agency*." I waited for her to process the information.

"Oh, yeah, the cops said someone would be in touch to interview me, and to not leave town until then." She hesitated, then said, "Where should I meet you?"

I wondered how the cops had found out about her.

"We can either come to your place, or you can come to our office. We're in downtown Seattle on First Street."

After yet another moment, she answered. "I'll come down. Is tomorrow afternoon at three all right?"

"That should be fine. Just let me give you our address." After she jotted it down, I added, "I want you to understand that we really *do* need to talk to you. If you skip the appointment, we'll have to come to you." Reluctant witnesses had skipped their appointments more than one time. I'd learned the hard way.

"I'll be there." She hung up abruptly.

I stared at my phone for a moment. I didn't blame her for being reluctant to talk to us. First, Elrich had broken her heart, and now she had to subject herself to being grilled. It couldn't feel good.

BY THE TIME the day was over, all I wanted to do was stretch out, relax, and have a glass of wine. I wasn't a big drinker, but now and then, it was the easiest way to get through an evening when we were in the middle of a rough case. And right now, both the Tuathan Brotherhood attacks and Eleanor's case were what I considered emotionally draining cases.

Angel headed home to meet Rafé for her date, while I followed Herne to his house. By the time I got there, I had managed to shake off most of my frustration by singing at the top of my lungs with the car radio.

Herne leaned against his SUV, waiting as I pulled into the driveway behind him. He was wearing black jeans with a dark gray top under his leather jacket. His hair was loose, hanging down around his shoulders, and the scruff he called a beard was just thick enough to give him that five-o'clock shadow look. His face lit up as I stepped out of my Subaru Outback. I walked up to him and he draped his arm around my shoulders as he led me into the house.

Herne lived in a gorgeous house bordering Carkeek Park. It was modern in every way, with a giant great room that looked out onto the park through floor to ceiling windows. The kitchen was a gourmet's delight, and more than once, Angel had tagged along to make dinner. She loved to cook, and what we had now at our house was a definite upgrade compared to what my condo had been, but it couldn't hold a candle to Herne's kitchen.

"Rough week, huh?"

"Yeah, and it's only Tuesday." I let out a long sigh. "I don't want to talk about work, if you don't mind. I just need to let it go. The picture of that little girl haunts me, and talking to Dana today was even worse. No parent should have to bury their child, Herne."

"I know," he murmured, kissing the top of my head. "Come on, let's make dinner and leave work back at the office, where it belongs." He unlocked the door and opened it, letting me in first. The alarm beeped and I tapped in the code. Herne had given me both a key and the code well over a month ago, and I was careful not to abuse the trust.

As I set my purse on the kitchen table, he opened the refrigerator and pulled out a bottle of wine. It was my favorite. Wild Moon mead was made by a group of Dark Fae who followed Mielikki, a goddess of woodland, the very same goddess to whom Herne's cousin Kipa had made himself persona non grata. The mead was only sold in specialty markets. The wine was rich and thick, and surprisingly tart. It was actually a meglethin, mixed with raspberry, lemon, and cinnamon. Herne handed me the goblet as I sat on one of the kitchen stools by the island, watching him.

"Oh, this is just what I needed," I said, my voice growing husky as I watched him. "I need something else, if you're up to it," I added.

Herne turned around, his eyes lighting up. "You know I never stop thinking about you. About your lips, your eyes, your body, the feel of your skin under my fingers." He set his goblet down and shrugged out of his jacket. "Bedroom. Now."

I drained the mead, swallowing it in one gulp. Then, wiping my lips on my sleeve, I set the goblet down, holding his gaze.

"Only if you can catch me."

I slipped off the stool and darted down the hall. Instantly, Herne was after me, dropping his jacket on the floor. He let out a hoarse laugh as I dashed into his bedroom. I spun around as he paused at the doorway, leaning against the doorjamb, his eyes glowing.

"Undress. Now." He pulled his shirt over his head and tossed it to the side. His chest glistened, from his pecs down to the V that led beneath his jeans. I caught my breath. He was gorgeous, and the wild light in his eyes was for me. He hooked his thumbs in the pockets of his jeans, a cunning smile on his face.

I held my ground, my own passion fueled by the mead. I was hungry for him. Riding a god was a high that nothing else could touch, and I had come to crave his touch, his lips, the heat of his body against mine.

"Oh, you beautiful minx, come here," Herne whispered, holding out his hands.

I shivered, my own passion fueled by the tone of his voice, the look in his eyes. I slid my top over my head and dropped it on the floor, then inched my jeans down my thighs, kicking them off. As I moved toward him, he caught me in his arms and pulled me to him.

"Do you trust me?" he whispered.

I stared into his eyes. "What do you mean?"

"I just want to know. Do you trust me? You've spent your whole life not trusting people, looking over your shoulder even if you didn't realize it. I want you to feel safe with me. I want you to trust me that I'm not going to hurt you." He leaned his forehead against mine. "You say you love me, and I believe you, but do you trust me?"

"I trust you as much as I can."

"Do you trust me as much as you trust Angel?" His question was simple, he wasn't demanding, he just wanted to know.

I thought about it, leaning against him, my breasts pressed against the warmth of his chest. Did I trust Herne as much as I trusted Angel? I knew the answer to that even before I spoke.

"No, I don't. I'm sorry, but I've known Angel all my life. I've known you six months. I love you, Herne, I do, but it takes me time." I gazed into his eyes, hoping I hadn't hurt him. I didn't want to hurt him.

But he smiled, a soft smile that told me he understood. "I get it. I intend to earn your trust. I'm sorry I didn't tell you right away about Danielle. It just took me time to process the news myself. Hell, *I* was in shock."

It had been a major revelation, not only to me but to

Herne, when he found out he had a daughter from an old dalliance. And it had been a rocky spot in our relationship, but we had come through it and I felt we were stronger because of it.

"I know. I understand why it took you awhile. You were processing the information. Herne, you've never lied to me, as far as I know, and that's of primary importance to me. I can handle a lot of problems, but lying? I won't stand for it. I know myself. I can't ever trust anybody unconditionally. It's just not in my nature. *But...*I trust you more than anybody except Angel, and it takes a lot of work to earn that spot in my heart." I kissed his neck. "What brought up this conversation?"

He hugged me close, rocking me gently from side to side.

"I love you so much. I never want to hurt you. I never want to do anything to compromise *us*. The past six months has been amazing. When Reilly lied to me, I shut down. I pushed aside the idea of another relationship, at least for a long, long time. And then you showed up. It was like a light went on and my heart woke up. If I ever do or say anything that frightens you, scares you, makes you not trust me, tell me. I don't want to mess this up."

He kissed me then, long and deep, and picked me up in his arms, carrying me to the bed. I wrapped my arms around his neck and drew him toward me, my breath coming in hard pants as he entered me, driving into me first softly, then fast and hard, riding me like the King Stag rides his mate. He rolled over, then, pulling me down on top of him, and I rocked against him, gasping as he slid his hand down between my legs.

We made love for over an hour until I rolled to the

side, as limp as a washrag. Herne leaned over me, smiling, his gaze fastened on mine.

"Had enough for one night, my love?" He stroked my cheek, tracing his finger down to my lips where I kissed it gently.

"Yeah. Are you good? I feel guilty that I can't go all night. You're a god. Do you ever get hungry for someone who has more stamina than I have?" I hadn't voiced the insecurity before, but it was there, and had been since the beginning.

Herne snickered. "Oh, love, if I wanted someone to bang for as long as I could keep it up, I would have just hired a concubine. There are plenty of minor goddesses out there looking to make it big as the consort of a major deity. And since my father is a major deity, I've had my fair share of offers."

"Have you ever taken any of them up on it?" I asked.

"Once or twice," he said, leaning down to kiss my nose. "But the thrill wears off when you realize you're being used for your pedigree as opposed to who *you* are. I left off playing those games a long time ago. As far you're concerned? I'd rather have an hour with you in bed, than all night with a succubus."

And by the tone of his voice, I believed him.

"Come on, let's go run through the woods to clear our heads, then we'll eat a late dinner and get some sleep." He pulled me up. "We can take a shower before bed. I need to stretch my legs."

We dressed and headed out to the sliding glass doors that led onto the patio overlooking the park. Herne locked the door and handed me his keys, which I slipped into my jacket pocket and zipped it shut. Then, as I stood back, the air filled with a fine mist around him and everything near him began to blur. I squinted, looking away from the brilliant flare of light. A moment later, a magnificent silver stag stepped out of the fading glow. Herne, in his massive King Stag form, nudged me with his muzzle, his breath hot on my face.

I laughed. "You goon. Kneel so I can climb on your back."

As I swung over his back, I let out a groan. Herne glanced back at me, and I leaned forward, patting his head.

"You wear a girl out, dude. My thighs are sore." I laughed as I adjusted myself on his back. "Okay, I'm ready. Let's go."

He began to lope softly into the woods. There wasn't a trail from his lot into the park, but he had carved one out with his paws over the months. Within moments, we were racing through the park as he loped along, his great hooves thudding against the ground.

Herne went off track, up a ravine, as I leaned forward, wrapping my arms along the sides of his neck, hanging on for dear life.

Riding him was different than riding a horse. Horses had thinner bodies, generally, and usually riding a horse involved a saddle. But this was more primal, and I had to admit, the constant shifting of him between my legs usually only served to stoke my hunger. But tonight, I was still sore enough that sex was the farthest thing from my mind.

We rode until we were deep into the woods. Granted, we were in a park, but Herne could traverse the terrain to where most people never went. The leaves were thick on the ground from the scattered maple trees that emblazoned their way through the tall fir. The air was pungent, smelling of mold and mildew and mushrooms, of dark earth churned over to expose the roots of plants gone fallow for the winter.

I could see my breath in front of me as the darkness closed in around us. And then, I felt it. A deep longing to be on my feet, creeping through the forest, bow in hand, hunting down my prey. The bloodlust rose within me, and I shuddered as the images flooded into my mind.

Time to hunt, to kill, to eat the bloody heart of my quarry, to merge and become one with the forest. Time to stalk my prey, to follow silently as it wound through the woodland unaware.

As the hunger swelled up, I felt oddly homesick, though I didn't know where or what I was missing. Tears started to trickle down my cheeks as the feeling flared from a memory that I couldn't pinpoint. I let them fall, not understanding where the emotions were coming from, but accepting them.

We journeyed through the park until close to midnight, and then home. By the time we were in the shower, Herne was quiet and so was I, each of us lost in our thoughts. I curled up in his bed, with him spooning me from behind, but for a long time sleep eluded me as I sought through my memories, trying to figure out what had been calling me, and why it had inexplicably filled me with sorrow.

CHAPTER SIX

"You ready?" Viktor held up his keys. We were headed to interview the second victim's mother. Samantha Trifor was waiting for us at her job.

I nodded. "Yeah, let's head out. At least we've got some questions to lead with," I said as we headed toward his truck. "I just hate sitting there, putting the parents through this."

"The more we learn, the more we can spare more parents the same pain. And we might be able to find Eleanor. If she's with the same unsub, then there's a good chance she's got at least a few more days to live." He fit the key into the ignition and eased out of the parking garage.

"Why do you think the woman takes them?" I asked, staring out the window.

I was still feeling the effects of the ride into the park. The longing had stayed with me, the feeling of being displaced. I hadn't told Herne, mostly because I didn't want him to worry, but all I could think of was that my Autumn's Bane side was bleeding through.

"I don't know," Viktor said. "Why does anybody do anything? It fills a need they have, however twisted that desire is. For some reason, this woman—if it's the same woman we saw nab Eleanor on the film—can only fill that vacuum inside by stealing children."

"And then she kills them," I added softly. "Don't forget the other side of the equation."

"I never do," Victor said, turning on to the main drag. Traffic was light. It was nine-thirty and the business sector was in full swing with everybody at work.

We reached the school where Samantha Trifor taught third grade. She was a single mother, and her daughter had been second to vanish. Samantha was waiting for us in a conference room, looking nervous.

"Have you found her killer yet? Have you found the person who killed my little girl?" The hope in her eyes was palpable.

"I'm sorry, no, not yet. We need to ask you a few questions, because a fourth girl has been abducted and we're in a race against time." I paused as her crestfallen expression revealed more than any words ever could.

"I'll do what I can. No other parent should have to go through this." She hung her head for a moment, then finally looked up at us. "How can I help?"

"I'm going to ask you a couple of questions that might be personal in nature. Please understand we're just trying to gather as much information as possible."

She nodded.

"All right," I continued. "First, it says in the report you were at the mall when Nexie vanished?" I glanced at my notes, making sure to get the right ones. Nothing made a victim feel like you didn't value them more than getting their name wrong. Or the name of their child.

"Right. It was August 22. I took Nexie to the mall to see the petting zoo." Samantha met my eyes. "You know that already, though."

"Yes, but we want to make sure we have our facts straight. Can you tell us what happened when she vanished? What was she doing? What were you doing?"

"I was standing there, watching her interact with the ducks inside the zoo—it was ringed off with a metal fence. I thought I heard someone calling my name and I swear that I recognized the voice. I glanced over to where I thought it was coming from. There was nobody there, so I took a quick look around. Nexie was safe inside the fence. When I couldn't find anybody, I decided whoever it was had been calling someone else. I turned back to the petting zoo, but Nexie was gone."

"How long were you looking for the person who called you?"

Samantha thought for a moment. "Maybe two minutes? Maybe three? It wasn't more than that, though."

"What did you do when you realized Nexie was gone?"

"I thought maybe she had wandered over to see the sheep, so I moved over to that side of the zoo, but she wasn't there. At that point, I started to get worried. I began calling for her, but she wasn't there, so I ran inside the pen. I was hoping she had just wandered out of sight —there were a lot of people there with their kids. But I couldn't find her. The mall went on lockdown, but it was too late. Whoever kidnapped Nexie was gone."

"You said you recognized the voice who called you?"

"I thought I did, though I couldn't pinpoint who I thought it was. I don't know, everything just became a blur at that point." She shook her head, a bewildered look on her face. "They took her on the 22nd of August. On the 28th, a man was walking his dog along one of the shoreline parks and found…"

"He found her?"

Nodding, she choked up. "In a coffin. Why would they do that to my baby? Why would anybody kill her? She was so little. She never hurt anybody."

"I don't know," I murmured, reaching out to place my hand on hers. "We're trying to find out." And right then, I realized it was true—we weren't just on the hunt for Eleanor's abductor. We were hunting for justice for the other victims.

"I have a difficult question to ask you, but I need you to trust me that it's important." I waited for her to look at me. "Are you an alcoholic? Do you ever go to AlkaNon meetings?"

One beat. Two beats. Then, finally, Samantha nodded.

"Yes," she whispered. "I've been sober for a year. AlkaNon is my saving grace. Without them, I'd have lost my baby years ago."

"Please, tell us about it. I promise you, we need this information."

She paused for a moment. "I was divorced right after Nexie was born. My ex couldn't handle being a parent and he didn't want anything to do with Nexie or me. He cut and ran. I served papers, but they couldn't find him. I started to drink and realized I couldn't stop. My mother intervened and dragged me to the AlkaNon meetings—she's also an alcoholic. She reminded me that Nexie was all I had and that if I kept up the drinking, I'd lose her. That scared me, so I started going out of fear. Now, I go out of love."

I asked for her regular meeting place and then asked, "Has anybody at your meetings ever showed an overt interest in your life—I mean, during the month before Nexie vanished? Did anybody seem *too* interested in your home life and daughter?"

Samantha stared at me for a moment. "You mean that someone there could have taken her?"

"We don't know. We're just gathering information." I hoped to hell she wouldn't go off on the group. We needed her to be discreet. "Listen to me. You can't talk about this to anybody. The more information we gather, the better we can assess who's doing this. But we need it to stay quiet because we don't want to scare away whoever's killing these little girls. Do you understand?"

After a pause that felt entirely too long, Samantha nodded. "Yeah. Actually, I do understand. I used to work for the Department of Children's Services, and we investigated abuse claims. We had to be cautious so that if we found abuse, we didn't muddy our case. And we had to make sure we had the right suspect. After a while, I couldn't take the parade of abuse—it ate at my heart, so I went back to school and got my teaching certificate. I wanted to make a difference in the children's lives in a more positive manner that didn't leave me drained."

"Then you get it—why neither you nor our agency can go off half-cocked."

She nodded. "Yes. And there *was* a woman at the meetings for a while who seemed odd to me. She was constantly asking how Nexie was, even though she had never met her. I was uncomfortable around her and did my best to avoid her. Do you think she…"

"We can't answer that. But the more you tell us, the better. Can you tell us what she looked like? If we send a sketch artist to you, can you work with them?" The Wild Hunt had a sketch artist they occasionally employed.

"I can. She was blond, short—about five-two. Very thin. I remember thinking she looked like she'd had a hard life. Weathered, if you know what I mean. She was there because she had been an addict—addicted to crackalaine. Oh, and she was a shifter."

Bingo. I jotted down what she said. "Do you remember her name?"

"Only her first name—we never give last names in the group. She told me her name was Naomi. She never told me much about her own life, though, even though she was prying into mine. But she stopped coming to the group…sometime…shortly before they found my daughter's body." Samantha squeezed her eyes shut. "Oh good gods help me. Was I talking to Nexie's killer?" She leaned her head on her arms on the table and began to cry.

I glanced over at Viktor, who looked both uncomfortable and incredibly sad. I leaned over and rubbed Samantha's shoulder.

"Just breathe. We don't know for sure, so please, just breathe and rest. We'll be in touch as soon as we know more, and I'll arrange for a sketch artist to come over today, if you have time."

After a moment, Samantha raised her head and wiped her eyes on a tissue. "I'm going home, so send him there. I took this afternoon off because I needed to wait for the cable guy anyway." She paused, then softly added, "Find her. Find the woman who killed my Nexie, and those other babies. Find her before she kills the little girl she has now. Please."

"We're doing our best," I said, slowly standing. "Do you want me to call someone to be with you?"

Samantha shook her head. "No. I promised myself I wouldn't drink today, and I keep my promises. Every day, I wake up and promise myself that I won't drink for just one day. That's how I make it through."

As Viktor and I headed out, I glanced at him. "We need to find that bitch and fast."

"I agree," he said. "And I hope she puts up a fight so we have an excuse to take her out."

ON THE WAY back to the office, I asked Viktor if we could stop by my bank so I could make a deposit and take out some cash. "I won't have time after work, given I have to go home and get ready for my session with Marilee tonight."

"No problem. Where to?"

"We're near the main branch—the ASCU." The Associated Shifters Credit Union wasn't just for shifters, and they offered the best rates on car and house loans. I had been going to them for years because I didn't like dealing with the Fae, and I wasn't inclined to bank with the vampires, either.

Viktor parked across the street in the parking garage. "Change a twenty for me? I need fives." He handed me a twenty-dollar bill.

"Sure thing. I'll be back in a few." I slipped out of my

car and headed across the street, waiting till there was a lull in traffic so I could dash across. I crossed between a black sedan that was parked in front of the credit union with its motor running and an SUV. The credit union took up the bottom two stories of an office building that also housed a gym and several apartments.

As I jogged up the front steps, stopping at the double glass doors, a crow suddenly swept down to circle around me. I paused, turning around to watch as it flew away, my back to the entrance. The crow shrieked at me, and the next second, there was a sudden change in pressure as a great roar blasted past me. My ears felt like someone had jabbed ice picks in them and I couldn't hear.

A split second later, I felt an eerie calm descend, and everything seemed to move in slow motion. A shower of glass blew past me and I felt some of the shards lodge in my back. And then, the blast picked me up to carry me with it.

I'm flying, I thought, feeling oddly calm as I sailed over the stairs, toward the road past the sidewalk. I was gliding on the wind, sailing with my arms spread out like wings. As the pavement rose to meet me, I suddenly realized that I was going to land hard on the asphalt. I caught a quick glimpse of Viktor racing across the street toward me, and then, time speeded up again and I hit the road, hard, skidding along it till I came to a stop as the black sedan pulled out and rolled down the street.

I still couldn't hear, and I could barely breathe—the landing had knocked my breath away. As I lay there, the pain in my back increased and I saw blood begin to trickle down my arms, pooling on the ground below me.

I tried to move, but Viktor was kneeling by me. He

was trying to talk to me, but I couldn't hear him. I stared up at him, unable to comprehend what had just happened. He had pulled out his phone and was talking frantically on it, while he held me down with one hand so I couldn't move. I began to feel queasy, and my head was spinning. I tried to tell him how I felt, but I couldn't hear what I was saying, and panicked, I began to hyperventilate.

Viktor leaned down, staring into my face. He formed his words carefully as I watched his lips. "Breathe slowly. Take a slow breath and let it out gently. The medics are coming."

I nodded, trying to control my breathing. The pain in my back was increasing at a rapid rate. I grimaced, trying to shift so that I was more comfortable. Viktor was on the phone again and I couldn't tell who he was calling. My ears were ringing now, which was somewhat comforting. At least I could hear *something*.

A moment later, flashing lights filled the street as a parade of police cruisers, medics, and ambulances crowded into the area. As people raced by, a team of paramedics stopped beside me, kneeling. Viktor was talking to them, and they felt for my pulse. I was wondering why they didn't roll me onto my back, but then they gently rolled me up on one side to slide a back board beneath me, then laid me back down on my stomach. The next thing I knew, they were lifting me up and carrying me to an ambulance. Viktor leaned down to where I could see his face again.

"I'll be driving right behind you. I'll be at the hospital," he mouthed.

I nodded that I understood, and then closed my eyes, not wanting to think about what might be wrong with me. All the way to the hospital, all I could think about was the crow, and how it had probably saved my life.

AT THE HOSPITAL, they took me right into the emergency room. The doctor was cutting my jacket, my shirt, and my jeans off me. I was beginning to feel faint. A nurse hooked up an IV and I saw blood trickling into my arm. Another moment and she had plugged yet another IV into my other arm.

The doctor leaned down and, like Viktor, began to speak to me. "Can you understand me?"

He was speaking clearly, and I could see the words form on his lips. I nodded.

"Your back is riddled with shards of glass. We're going to remove them now. I've given you pain medication in the IV. Then we'll have to check you for broken bones. Stay as still as you can," he said, then vanished around the table.

I could feel the tug as he removed each piece of glass, and started counting, trying to keep my mind off what was happening. By the time I got to fifty-eight, I decided to stop. More time passed and then I felt the sting of antiseptic as they began to doctor the wounds. As the minutes ticked by, I suddenly realized I could hear faint sounds, then they became louder.

Another five minutes and I could faintly hear the doctor speaking.

"She's damned lucky. If she had been facing the door, the glass could have punctured her heart and other organs. As it is, she's going to feel like a pincushion."

"Yes, Doctor," the nurse said.

"I can hear you," I spoke up, my voice raspy and harsh.

The doctor peeked around at me. "Good, that means you probably didn't sustain permanent damage to your ears. We're going to turn you over and check you for broken bones now. It's going to hurt, even with the pain meds, but we need to make sure you didn't bust anything up with that swan dive."

"Trust me, it wasn't intentional." I blinked as they carefully shifted me over to my back. He was right—it hurt, but I bit my lip and didn't say a word.

"First, since you can hear me now, does anything feel like it's hurt?"

I shook my head. "No, I don't think there's anything broken, though my stomach hurts."

They peeled what remained of my clothes off me and began a thorough examination. My stomach hurt, and even my boobs hurt, because while I had managed the landing without busting a single bone, apparently I had a lot of scraped skin from body surfing the pavement. As the doctor helped me sit up, I grimaced.

"Yeowch, those cuts hurt."

"They're bound to. Somehow, you managed to survive fairly intact. A few of the cuts required a stitch or two, but they're self-dissolving and you should be healed up in a week or so. You're going to have some scars on your back," he warned.

"Hey, at least I have my life and my limbs." I paused, shaking my head. "How are my ears?"

He peered into them, then checked my eyes. "No concussion, but I'm going to bet you have a nasty headache for the next few days. You probably need a good chiropractic adjustment, and at the first sign of anything else seeming wrong, get yourself back here. There's always the chance we're going to miss something."

"Can I go home?" I really didn't want to be stuck in the hospital for long.

"I'm afraid we need to let you go. While I'd like to keep you overnight, the fact is that we've got multiple victims coming in from the explosion and we're going to need every room we have." He paused, then gazed in my eyes. "You're lucky, Ember. You're *very* lucky. If you had arrived at the bank five minutes earlier, we wouldn't be sitting here talking."

I read between the lines. "How many?"

"We don't know, but the credit union was busy this morning, and then there were all the employees there. And the explosion brought down part of the building so the apartments and gym above it were impacted, too. I'm going to discharge you now, because I've got a long day ahead, and multiple victims are waiting. Unfortunately, most of them aren't as lucky as you are."

"Go on, help them. I'm all right." I waited till he signed off on my chart and headed out the door.

The nurse turned to me. "I'm afraid your clothes are ruined. You'll have to wear the hospital gown. Your boyfriend is waiting for you, along with your friend who followed you in."

"Do you have a robe I can put over this?" I asked.

She brought out a thin robe and at least between it and the hospital gown, my butt and boobs were covered.

"It's not pretty, but it will keep you covered. Here are your prescriptions for pain meds, and an antibiotic to prevent infection. They're geared toward Fae physiology so they won't conflict with your makeup." She paused, then touched my arm. "The doctor's right, you're a lucky young woman. We've seen ten dead come through already, and the injured are piling up. A lot of traumatic burn cases. Whoever did this, they were out to kill."

I stared at her for a moment, my heart sinking. I knew precisely who had done this. As she wheeled me out to the waiting room, I saw Herne pacing the floor. The room was overflowing, and there were several security guards milling through the crowd.

Herne rushed over when he saw me, Viktor on his heels.

"Ember, oh my love." Herne started to hug me but I held up my hand.

"No touching me right now. My back is a minefield of cuts from the glass in the door."

Viktor nodded. "I saw just how many shards were poking out of you. If you'd been human, you would have died from that blast."

The nurse signed off with the receptionist, who handed me my discharge papers. She had a peculiar look on her face, but I didn't want to ask what was wrong. As we headed out the door, though, one of the men in the waiting room turned a cold eye on me.

"You—*your kind* did this. You're the reason my wife is fighting for her life!" He started toward me, but one of the guards intervened, taking him by the shoulders and moving him back, talking softly to him.

Tears welled in my eyes. I had managed not to cry over the pain, but I was feeling on edge and in pain and right now, that was the last thing I wanted to hear.

"Come on," Herne said. "Let's get the hell out of here."

Once we were at his SUV, Herne insisted on lifting me in instead of letting me climb in myself. I locked my door and tried not to lean back against my cuts while still fastening my seat belt. Herne slammed the door and then dashed around to the driver's side. We were on the way before he'd even fully closed his door.

As we threaded our way out of the parking lot, I watched the ambulances that were still arriving, sirens screaming. They were lining up, five deep at one point, and I watched the medics wheeling gurney after gurney into the hospital.

"The Tuathan Brotherhood?" I turned to Herne.

He gave me a terse nod. "I'm afraid so. We're on the precipice of a really bad scene, Ember. I'm in close communication with the cops right now. So far, there are at least twenty dead, and more than forty injured so far, a number of them critically."

"All shifters and humans?"

"Mostly. A few Fae, but mostly shifters and humans, yes. And the TB hacked into one of the local news channels to claim responsibility on the air. They wore masks, so we couldn't see their faces," he said bleakly. "We have to get a handle on this before people start to retaliate."

"I think that horse already left the barn. Did you see the look on that man's face in the waiting room? If the security guard hadn't been there, he would have attacked me. What the fuck is this brotherhood? We need to talk to Saílle and Névé. No more pussyfooting around."

"You are going straight home and going to bed," Herne said.

"Oh hell no, *I'm not*. I'm in pain, yes, but lying down isn't going to do anything for me. I'm coming into the office. Besides, Viktor and I may have caught a break in Eleanor's case." I told him about the woman Samantha had told us about. "I'm pretty sure that she's getting to the families via AlkaNon meetings. And if she *is* a crackalaine addict, and she's killing the girls with crackalaine, there has to be something about that angle."

"I hate to admit it, but you're right. And we can use all hands on deck. But if you need to rest, you take a nap on the daybed in my office, you hear me?" He flashed me a stern look, and I nodded.

"Deal. Come on, let's get back to the agency. We've got a lot of damage control to do." I stared out the window all the way back to the Wild Hunt, wondering where the Tuathan Brotherhood would strike next.

By the time we arrived, Angel was in tears. When she saw me, she rushed over and threw her arms around me, which of course, brought an instant reaction from me.

"Mother of pearl! That hurts!" I pulled away, groaning.

"I'm sorry," she said, pulling back. "I'm sorry!"

Feeling instantly contrite, I shook my head. "No, it's just that my back feels like some sadist took a knife to me. Trust me, I'm glad to see you too." I gave her a kiss on the cheek. "I'm just sore as hell and the pain meds are wearing off. Can you get my prescriptions filled for me?" I started to hand her the scrips, but Herne grabbed them.

"I'll run down to Urgent Care on the first floor and take care of these. They have an in-house pharmacy. Angel, help Ember into the break room. We'll meet when I get back. Order in food. I'm pretty sure we all need something to eat by now. No pizza, though—we've had entirely too much the past few days, thanks to you girls. Something else. Fish and chips or tacos or whatever." He headed back toward the elevator.

Angel helped me into the break room and I chose the cushiest chair there. She handed me a loose gauzy sundress and a pair of underwear and a soft sports bra, then brought me a cup of coffee and a package of cookies. "I ran home when Herne called me and I brought you some clothes. Now, get something in your stomach now. I'll go order lunch."

I changed clothes with Talia's help while Yutani turned around. After I was out of the hospital gown and dressed, he regarded me with somber eyes.

"Can I get you anything?" he asked.

"My laptop, please. And can you ask Viktor if he has my purse? The last time I saw it was when I was sailing through the air toward the pavement." I realized that my throat was hurting. I took a slow sip of coffee, and the warmth soothed the rough patches. "I must have been screaming and not realized it."

"That wouldn't surprise me." Yutani leaned forward. "Are you sure you're up to being here?"

"I have to be. If I went home, I'd just fret myself into a state. I'm exhausted and feel like I got hit by a sledgehammer, but other than that, I'm okay. I'm lucky, the doctor said, and from what I could see, he's right." I held his gaze. "A crow saved my life. It distracted me, and I turned around to look at it. Otherwise the blast would have hit me face on and this would have had an entirely different ending. Maybe I would have survived, but I would have been injured far more seriously than I was."

Crows and I were intimately tied together. I wasn't sure how, though I had the suspicion it was via Morgana, given the crow necklace she had given me. But I knew that the crow hadn't just randomly appeared to help me.

Yutani nodded. "Your spirit animal. The crow, that is."

Viktor appeared in the doorway, and he tossed my purse on the table.

"Thanks. I don't know what happened to your twenty, by the way. It was in my hand when the explosion happened."

"Don't sweat it. Not an issue," Viktor said.

I thanked him and dug out my tablet and phones, checking them to see if they were still working. My phones were, both the home and work cell phones, but the tablet's glass was cracked. I showed it to Yutani.

"Here, let me check it out." He played around with it for a moment. "Okay, I think this is fried. I'll set you up with a new one. Luckily, we back up everything on an encrypted cloud base." He disappeared out the door.

I ate three of the cookies, then sipped more of the coffee, but I was feeling shaky as hell, and I wasn't sure whether it was the injuries themselves, or just the shock of the morning. Talia noticed and brought me a throw from one of the armchairs over by the window. I draped it over the back of the chair and around my shoulders, so it wouldn't lay against the cuts.

"You need more than coffee right now. I know that Angel is ordering lunch, but here." She poked around in the fridge and came up with a blueberry yogurt. "Here, eat this. It has some protein in it."

At that moment, Angel came in. "Lunch will be here in about ten minutes. I ordered from Anton's Fish Shack.

Clam chowder, fish and chips, slaw, and biscuits. I ordered enough for an army, so eat as much as you need." She slid into the chair next to me, looking at me with worried eyes. "How are you feeling?"

"Like death warmed over. But I'm lucky, I really am. So many dead and injured." I motioned to the TV. "Can somebody turn it on so we can see what they know?"

"You know they won't be broadcasting everything, but all right." She turned on the TV and then headed back to her desk to wait for the food.

While we waited for Yutani and Herne to return, Talia, Viktor, and I watched the news. The damage was devastating, and had destroyed the entire bottom level of the building. It had damaged the upper floors as well, and everybody had been evacuated while the fire department fought the flames that were still burning.

"THE TUATHAN BROTHERHOOD has claimed responsibility for this explosion. While little is known yet about the method of delivery, or the explosives involved, we do know that at least twenty are dead, and over forty people have been injured, most of them seriously."

THE NEWSCASTER SOUNDED FAR TOO chipper for my tastes, and I glared at her as she rattled off the standard shtick that the broadcasters were expected to parrot. The scenes of the explosion were hard for me to look at. As I stared at the outside of the bank, where the doors had once been and where I had been standing, I suddenly remembered the black sedan.

"I remember something—Viktor, do you remember the black sedan that was parked in front of the bank? I remember thinking it was odd because the motor was still running. It pulled out as I was flying through the air, toward the road."

He straightened. "You're right. Do you remember anything about the car?"

I closed my eyes. Everything was jumbled up, but I did my best to visualize the sedan. I could see it, engine idling as I passed between it and the SUV.

"Nobody came out."

"What do you mean?"

"I mean, nobody came out of the bank as I was heading up the stairs. Unless somebody got into the car who was already down on the sidewalk, it was just parked there until the explosion and then drove off. Which could mean that whoever was inside was waiting for the blast to happen."

Talia handed me a pen and a pad of paper. "Can you see the license plate?"

I closed my eyes, letting my mind drift, which wasn't difficult. I brought my attention to the car, trying to visualize the sedan. It was black, sleek—a foreign build—and then the emblem jumped out at me. It was a crouching lion. Not a Jaguar, but…

"It was a Panther XL—I remember thinking that must be one hell of an expensive car."

"Good, that helps. Anything else stand out, any part of the license plate?" Viktor asked, keeping his voice low.

I let myself drift deeper, tumbling down the rabbit hole that felt like it was growing so large and deep that I might not be able to pull out should I let myself freefall.

And then, there it was, floating in front of me, a license plate. Only the first four digits were visible, but those were clear as day.

"Yeah, I remember four of them. GFR5…the other three are cloudy, but those were the first four." As I opened my eyes, Talia was already tapping away at her keys. Finally, we might have a break in the case.

CHAPTER SEVEN

By the time Angel brought in the food, Herne was on her heels. He handed me the medication, gently kissing the top of my head.

"I can't believe I came so close to losing you," he whispered.

I stared up into his eyes. "I know. I'm going to have to process all of this." I paused, then told him about the license plate and sedan. "I think whoever was in that sedan was also responsible, at least in part, for the bombing. It's not a certainty, but I just have a feeling."

Herne nodded. "I'll check it out."

Yutani returned as Angel was setting out the food. "Here's a new tablet. I transferred all of your data. It's good to go."

"Thanks," I said as Angel handed me a bowl of chowder and a plate of fish and chips. She knew I wasn't all that fond of coleslaw. She added a couple biscuits to my plate before setting it down in front of me.

As I dug into the food, I was all too aware of the

strained tension in the office. When everybody was settled in around the table, I decided to tackle it head on.

"I know we're all on edge, but as for me, please—quit worrying. I'll be all right. The doctor checked me out and I'm bruised up, cut up, and banged up, but I'll live. I'll need help for a day or two, but I heal fast so don't treat me with kid gloves, all right?"

"If you're sure?" Herne asked.

"Yeah. We have too much to focus on, and we're in over our heads on this one, I'm afraid. As you said, we need all hands on deck, and I don't want anybody distracted by my welfare. I'm all right. I was in the wrong place at the wrong time, but I lucked out and so let's just move on." Truth was, I was highly uncomfortable when people fussed over me.

"I'm checking on that license plate right now," Talia said. "I'm in the DMV's database and…bingo. The only Panther XL with the beginning four digits you saw belongs to… Well, this is interesting. It belongs to one Grimspound Mica." She froze, then looked up from the screen. "He's a Fomorian."

I stared at him. "What?"

"I know what you're thinking, Ember," Herne warned. "But there's no evidence to link them. Not yet, at least."

I wanted to jump to conclusions. It made sense to me that the Fomorians might be involved, but Herne was right. If we approached this from the wrong angle, the collateral damage would be far greater than it already was. As I had warned Samantha, we had to move cautiously to make sure we had the right culprit.

"I hear you," I said. "What else do we have?"

"Let me check. Okay, yes, Grimspound is actually a

customer at the bank. Oh boy," Yutani said. "A number of Fomorians have signed up with the credit union." He shook his head. "That would just give the Tuathan Brotherhood *more* reason to bomb them, if it really is a group of renegade Fae behind the mask."

"Fuck!" I didn't want to accept that the Fae were actually behind this, but I couldn't deny the possibility. The Fomorians were a group of giants who had been out to exterminate the Fae since the beginning of time and recently had made an attempt on the Fae race. And *that* would give any fanatics plenty of reason to target places that did business with them.

"You see, we have to walk softly. This could play out any number of ways." Herne's phone rang. "It's Cernunnos. I'll be back in a minute. Go on."

"What else have we got?" I asked.

Yutani shrugged. "I'm looking over Jasper's email that my program flagged. It looks like all this began when he contacted the Tuathan Brotherhood, offering to volunteer. But…" He sounded puzzled. "The documents they sent him aren't about a hate group. What I see here portrays the Tuathan Brotherhood as an organization out to help Fae who are on the skids. They read like some homeless shelter–recovery center. There's not a single word about supremacy or anything of that nature."

"When is the email dated?" I asked.

"July 7. And it seems that Jasper volunteered to go stay with them for a week, in order to go through the necessary training. Actually…this isn't a volunteer position. He was applying for a job with them." Yutani scrolled through the email. "They told him they'd take him on for a trial period, including paid training. Then, if all worked well, he'd be hired on permanently."

"So they were misrepresenting themselves?" Talia asked, looking perplexed.

"Very much so. And they say right here that they've 'had multiple responses' to their ad." Yutani scanned through a few more emails. "Jasper accepted and made plans to go into training in mid-July. Isn't his fiancée supposed to come talk to us today?"

I glanced at the clock. "Around three o'clock, she said, so she'll be here in about fifteen minutes."

"Then we need to ask her whether Jasper ever mentioned anything about the potential job." Yutani paused, looking at me. "How are you feeling?"

I frowned, assessing my condition. "I feel like somebody took a sledgehammer to me and then decided to play tic-tac-toe on my back with a knife. Other than that, I'm just dandy. My ears are still ringing, but it's dying down. At least I can hear." I shifted in my chair and my body protested. "I think I'm going to be a mass of sore muscles for a few days though. And I can't even get a massage because of all the cuts on my back—they're all the way down my body, back of the legs included."

Herne let out a sigh. "I don't care how important these cases are. I'm taking you home after Penny's visit. You can afford one evening off. I'd tell you not to come in tomorrow, but I know how well that would go over."

"You said it, not me." I grinned at him, then sobered. "I'm just grateful to be alive. The crow saved my ass. If I had been facing the door when it blew out…I don't even want to think about it." I shook my head, trying to clear my thoughts. The glass alone would have killed me—or blinded me, or ruptured vital organs, or so many potential things. My jacket had taken the brunt of it, and still, the glass had been lodged in my skin, slicing right through the leather. "Hell, now I need a new leather jacket."

"That's the least of your worries, given what could have happened," Talia said.

"I'd better get back to my desk and unlock the elevator, given Penny is supposed to show up soon." Angel excused herself and headed back to her desk.

I finished my lunch while the others discussed both cases. I felt utterly exhausted. My thoughts kept slipping back to the moment when I found myself sailing over the steps, toward the pavement. That moment when you think, *"What's happening?"* and then the fraction of a second when it turns into disbelief—*"No, this can't be happening!"*

And then the aftermath sets in.

"Can we turn on the TV again? Find out what's going on with the bomb scene now?"

Talia flipped on the remote. The all too perky announcer had been replaced by a more somber reporter who was announcing that there were now twenty confirmed dead, and sixty-three injured, eighteen of them critically. There were fourteen people missing that authorities knew of. The fire had been extinguished, but the inspection was going to take awhile.

My heart dropped. "So many. Who knew enough about the credit union's traffic to know that this was a heavy-use time?"

"Remember, people in the apartments and gym above the credit union were also injured. There were a lot of people in that building. And the bomber planned for maximum injury. The credit union's prime time is during mid-morning, and that wouldn't be hard information to get," Viktor said. "While I don't like the thought, we should consider the entire city a potential target. Any place run by humans or shifters could be a potential target."

"We can't mention that," Herne said. "It would induce a city-wide panic, which would lead to a backlash. Like the guy in the hospital this morning who yelled at Ember."

"What's that?" Talia asked.

I glanced at her. "There was a guy in the waiting room who blamed my 'kind' for his wife fighting for her life. Not the Tuathan Brotherhood, but the Fae in general. And you know the animosity toward the Fae is only going to grow."

Angel popped her head through the door. "Penny Sanders is here. Should I bring her in here or into your office, Herne?"

He glanced around. "Give us a minute to clear off the table, then bring her in here. We all need to hear what she has to say, given the nature of the case."

Talia immediately began clearing the plates and tossing the remains in the garbage. She washed the table, then nodded to Angel. "We're good."

Angel vanished, then reappeared a moment later with Penny in tow. The woman looked exactly like she had in the photograph, only the wide smile was nowhere to be seen. Instead, she looked haunted.

"Please, have a seat," Herne said. "Thank you for coming down."

"It's been nonstop reporters at my door. Somehow, they picked up on the fact that I was engaged to Jasper, and they won't leave me alone." Her bottom lip quivered as she looked at me. "Were you one of the people that Jasper hit with his car?"

I realized that the various bruises and cuts that showed up all over my arms and chest were all too visible with the sundress on. I glanced over at Herne.

"Actually, Ember was caught in the bombing this morning."

She stared at me for a moment, then hung her head. "I'm so sorry. And I'm so sorry for those people that Jasper killed and hurt. I don't understand what happened. He was the most soft-hearted man I ever met."

"Can you tell us if he ever mentioned a potential job with a group called the Tuathan Brotherhood?" Herne asked. "This would have been in early to mid-July."

"That was shortly before he changed. Let me think." She glanced at the coffeepot. "Do you mind if I have a cup of coffee? I'm exhausted."

Talia crossed to the counter. "Cream, sugar?"

"Just cream, please." After Talia handed her the mug, Penny took a long sip, then visibly relaxed. "I needed this. Thank you. Now that you mention it, I do remember Jasper mentioning something about getting a new job. I know it seems strange that I wouldn't recall that, given we were engaged, but June was a crazy month for both of us. My mother was in the hospital, undergoing a hysterectomy for cancer, and my sister brought her kids to my place to stay for a couple weeks—her marriage was falling apart. Jasper was getting really tired of his job and he wanted to find more meaningful work. So we didn't see much of each other for a couple weeks. But when I think back, yes, he *did* say he was taking some time off to go into training on what could be a fantastic new opportunity."

"Did he tell you what it entailed?" Yutani asked.

"Only that it was a new organization that was focused on helping those members of the Fae community who had been ostracized to find a new path. Or something like that. He told me he'd call me when he got there, and he did, but after that, he never called again. I tried phoning him several times during that week, but then my mother needed me, and I figured that Jasper was just neck-deep in training. That he'd call me when he got back." She twisted a ring on her right hand that looked like an engagement ring.

"You're still wearing your ring?" I asked.

She gave me a sad shrug. "I couldn't take it off, so I just put it on my other hand, hoping that whatever was wrong, would just…fix itself. I needed closure. I needed to know why he had turned against me. I suppose I'll never get that."

"We'll try to figure out why." I glanced over at Herne.

He cleared his throat and leaned forward, resting his elbows on the table. "Did Jasper have any good friends? Anybody who he might have told about the job? We'd like to find out where the organization is located."

Penny finished her coffee and gently wiped her lips on a napkin. "He had a lot of friends, but if he were to tell anybody else, I think it would have been Warren. Warren Mossly—a shifter who owns a deli in Shoreline. The two were football buddies. If you'll wait a moment, I'll give you his number." She glanced through her contacts list. "Here it is," she said, turning her phone around for us to see.

Yutani immediately copied the number down and began searching on his laptop. "Warren Mossly, married to Larinda Mossly for thirteen years. Owner of the Veggie-First Deli in Shoreline. Deer shifter. Member of several local organizations—Audubon, Nature's Helpers, Community Gardens. He's a master gardener as well."

"Warren's won several awards for his participation in Keep Seattle Green." A smile broke through Penny's gloom. "He's a good sort, and so is his wife."

Talia stood. "I'll go give him a call." She left the room.

"When Jasper returned, what happened?" I asked.

Penny winced.

"I know the memories are painful, but we really are trying to find out what happened, and what could have led him to run down those people," Herne said softly.

"I know," Penny said. "All right. My mother was feeling better, and I realized that I hadn't heard from Jasper in a while. I dropped by his place and saw his car parked near his apartment. I knocked, but nobody answered. I have a key so I tried to let myself in, but the inner chain lock was on and I couldn't get the door open. I called out, and he yelled to leave him alone. I tried a couple more times, but he wouldn't come to the door."

"What did you do?"

"I left. After that, I kept calling, but he wouldn't return either my calls or texts until he sent me a curt note basically calling me a slut and telling me to leave him alone. He said we were done and that he didn't want anything to do with me. Finally, I quit trying. I didn't know what was wrong, but obviously, he had changed his mind about marrying me. I left him alone, though I couldn't bring myself to take off my ring. I really don't know what happened."

"Is that everything? Is there anything else that you can remember?"

Penny shook her head. "No, everything seemed like it was in limbo until I woke up to reporters calling me and pounding on my door on Monday because they found out we used to be engaged. That's how I found out what he did." She gave me a bleak look. "Why did he do that? Before he left, he went out of his way to help people. He wouldn't even hurt a spider—always scooped them up and put them outside. For him to turn into a killer? It makes no sense."

There wasn't much more she could remember, so Viktor escorted her out. Talia followed him back into the break room.

"Did you find out anything from Mossly?" Herne glanced up as she entered the room.

"Only what Penny told us. Warren heard from Jasper as he was headed out of town. He was all excited about the new job, and he was worried how Penny would hold up if her mom didn't make it. Sounded every inch the doting fiancé. He wouldn't tell Warren where he was training—said he had signed an NDA about it."

"That's odd. Who signs a non-disclosure agreement about where they're headed?" I asked.

"Somebody who's desperate for a change. According to Warren, Jasper hated his job. He was on the verge of quitting, but according to Warren, he decided to hold on until he knew if this new position was going to work out. He took vacation to go to the training—he taught summer courses—and didn't tell his boss where he was going. He just said he needed to get out of town. He was apparently worried that if it turned out to be a bust and his boss knew he was looking for work, he'd be fired." Talia carried Penny's mug over to the sink and washed it out.

"So he truly believed it was going to be a new opportunity to help other Fae members." Herne glanced at me. "I think we need to pay a visit to Saílle and Névé. Are you up to it? And what about Marilee tonight?"

I groaned. "I forgot all about the session. Let me call her." I eased my way over to the sofa, where I lowered myself into the soft cushions, groaning in both relief and pain. "Remind me to download my mobile banking app. I'm never going into a bank again," I said as I pulled out my phone.

Marilee was home, and when I told her what happened, she sputtered.

"You're not going to be working any magic or trance work tonight, my dear. Not in that condition. Let's make it for Saturday morning. You have to have one more session before next week, and that way, you can still go to your dinner Saturday night."

"I should be good to go by then," I said. As I hung up, I glanced out the window. The break room overlooked the same street as my office. As I watched, the sun broke through the clouds for a brief second, illuminating the entire block. I shaded my eyes, welcoming the light, but it faded and once again, gloom descended on the city.

"Do you think you're up to the drive?" Herne said.

"You really need me there?"

"I don't know why, but I think—even if they don't like you—the Fae Queens respond better when you're there. Maybe it's a desire to prove they aren't the bigots they are, or something like that. If you aren't up to it, no worries. I'll take Viktor."

"I'll go. But you get to help me out to the car." I handed him my purse. "I'm not putting anything over my shoulder right now. Are you sure they'll see us on such short notice?"

"Oh, they'll see us. They've been on my back to meet ever since Jasper mowed down those kids." He shouldered my purse, then gently steered me out to the waiting room.

"I take it we're working late tonight?" Angel asked.

"Yep. We'll be back within a couple of hours, if traffic is kind." Herne held the elevator for me. As we settled into his SUV, I gingerly fastened my seatbelt.

"You know I'm just doing this because I love you," I said, only half-joking.

"Seriously, if you need to go home instead, I'll drop you off there." Herne paused, his hand on the gearshift. "Ember, when Viktor called us, my heart almost stopped. He saw you blown into the street, and he called us as he was running over to you. All I could think of was that I might lose you." His voice was strained. "I couldn't bear that."

I leaned my head back against the seat. "It takes more than a little bomb to get rid of me," I joked, though it came out strained. Licking my lips, I said, "Herne? I want a piece of these jokers. I want whoever set off that bomb. I'll heal, but a lot of people died today."

"You don't think the Fae are behind this, do you?" He eased out onto the street and turned right, heading toward the entrance to I-5.

I thought over my answer. "My gut says no. But I can't deny that Jasper was Fae, or the guys who beat up those partiers. But there's more to it than my instincts. The Fae don't pay much attention to humans or shifters. Why would they suddenly divert thousands of years of hatred toward each other toward someone else? If anything, you'd think a Fae hate group would go after the Fomorians."

"Maybe when the United Coalition gave the Fomorians a seat on the council, that pushed a group of activists over the edge? After all, the vote was two to two at first—the vampires and the Fae dissented, while the shifters and the humans agreed to let them in. The deciding factor was that the courts would have overruled a veto on the Cryptozoid Association if the measure hadn't passed. That's when the vampires swung over to approve the measure." He paused, switching lanes and speeding up. We were about twenty minutes away from rush hour, and hopefully we'd stay ahead of the rush.

"I don't know. I don't know the answer. All I know is this mess is going to get uglier before it gets better. And I admit it, I'm scared. I've been in danger before, I've fought the *enemy*, but random violence frightens me. *Collateral damage* is an ugly term. I can handle a battle with someone I know is coming after me, but when you're not sure where safety lies—when some random stranger holds your fate in your hands—then you lose any control over the situation. We lose any ability to predict what's going to happen next." I paused, then finally added, "Today I almost died, not because I was someone's particular target, but because I was simply in the wrong place at the wrong time. And the randomness terrifies me."

"You're going to suffer some PTSD, I think. I'd like to set up some counseling sessions for you with Marina—

she's one of Ferosyn's healers. She's a good person to talk to."

Ferosyn was Cernunnos's main healer, and he had treated me before. While I thought that it was probably going overboard talking to a counselor, I also trusted that Herne had seen a lot more in battle than I had and he might have a point.

"All right. Go ahead. But not till after the Cruharach. I have to focus on that, because it's coming and there's no stopping it."

"You're facing a lot right now," Herne said. "You've been fast-tracking your training for the ritual, and then we've been slammed. Now this."

I could hear the worry in his voice. "Herne, I've been through a lot of stress in my life. Look at what happened with my parents."

"Yeah, I know, but it changed you. And this is bound to change you. I just want to make certain it doesn't hinder you." He shook his head. "It's not that I don't think you're perfectly capable of carrying on. I know you. But that doesn't mean that the scars aren't there."

I pressed my lips together, feeling like we were on the verge of an argument. But I didn't want to argue, and I had already agreed to see Marina, so I just looked out the window as we drove over the 520 bridge to the Eastside.

"Tired?" he asked after a few minutes.

"Yeah. If you don't mind, I'd just like to rest while we're on the road."

It wasn't a lie—I was exhausted, and the last thing I wanted was to be fussed over or needled. Herne could be overprotective in some ways, but he never recognized it. I had the feeling it was because he was so aware of the fact that he was immortal, while I wasn't. Oh, I would be long lived as long as I didn't get myself killed, but the fact remained: I was mortal. My life had a definite beginning, and it would have a definite end.

We drove in silence, through the increasing traffic, until we arrived at Ginty's bar. This was where we always met the Fae Queens. Not once had I ever entered the great cities of TirNaNog or Navane. And I doubted that I'd ever be invited into the ranks.

As Herne opened the door and helped me down, I looked over at the bar. Seemingly one-storied from the outside, Ginty's Bar and Grill was a Waystation, providing sanctuary to members of the SubCult who asked for it, until they could either get the hell out of Dodge, or undergo a fair trial. The bar was interdimensional, much bigger on the inside than out, and it was run by Ginty McClintlock, a dwarf who kept order with an iron fist. Even the Fae Queens couldn't overrule him, or the gods.

"So once again, into the mouth of hell," I muttered.

"It's not that bad. They're a pain in the ass, but at least they're not out to get you," Herne said, chuckling. "And they're scared spitless over this Tuathan Brotherhood mess, so they shouldn't be too hard to corral."

This would be the first time I had seen Saílle since I killed my grandfather and she paid me off for what he tried to do to me. While I knew that they couldn't do anything to me on sanctuary grounds, I still dreaded looking her in the face. I wasn't sure what I was afraid of. Perhaps her judgment, though that had never stopped me before. Or perhaps that she would mirror my feelings of guilt back to me, amplified. Because, regardless of how much I had been in the right—it had been self-defense, all the way—I still felt oddly responsible for the whole mess. It made no sense, since the man had tried to force me into a ritual where he was going to strip my mother's bloodline out of me. But I had let him in instead of turning him away.

Angel had tried to shake the guilt out of me. "You're just caving to that archaic belief that women are responsible for men's actions," she had said.

I knew she was right, and I knew part of my squeamishness came from the way I had killed him. On one hand, it had been fitting, but on the other hand? I had deliberately made it painful.

"What are you thinking about?" Herne asked.

I shook my head. "Nothing. Everything. Come on, let's get this over with." I pushed ahead as Waylin, the extremely large and muscled bouncer, opened the door.

Herne stopped to peace-bind his dagger, wrapping the leather thong around the hilt so that it couldn't be drawn without a lot of trouble. I had left mine back at the office. I handed Waylin my purse and he peeked through it.

He stared at me for a moment, arching his eyebrows. "You're... You look different today." He handed my purse back to me.

"Yeah, yeah. Gunnysack sundress, no belt, sports bra. I get it. I'm not exactly a fashion plate." I winked at him, though, to let him know I was joking.

He shook his head, rolling his eyes. "That's not what I'm talking about. I mean, your arms and legs. You look like you ended up on the wrong side of a wildcat."

"I got on the wrong side of a glass door, actually." I shook my head at his puzzled look and stood back so he could check Herne's dagger.

"You are now entering Ginty's, a Waystation bar and grill. One show of magic or drawing a weapon will get you booted and banned. Do you agree to abide by the Rules of Parley, by blood and bone?" He rattled off the words and by now, I realized that while binding, they were also rote. Everybody who entered the bar had to agree.

"We do, by blood and bone," Herne said, pushing through the inner doors into the main bar.

A roped-off staircase behind the bar led to an interdimensional space where seekers of sanctuary could stay, as well as offering meeting rooms for formal parley. The bar itself was beautiful, polished to a warm sheen. Behind the bar, Wendy, Ginty's second in command, was serving drinks. Six-two, with a platinum Mohawk and skin the color of rich earth, she looked like an Amazon. In fact, I wondered if she *was* an actual Amazon. We took our places at the bar, sitting on two empty stools to wait for Ginty.

"What'll you have?" Wendy asked, giving us an infectious smile.

"I want a pint of Bitter Ale. What about you?" Herne turned to me. "You want an actual drink or you want something gentler?"

"I think I'll just have a Lemon Beam."

Lemon Beam was a gentle drink—half white wine, half lemon-lime soda, with a grating of lemon zest and a touch of honey in it.

Wendy stared at me. "Herne, those marks better not be from you, or I'll kick your ass."

Herne coughed. "Trust me, they're not. I wouldn't want to get on your bad side any day of the week."

I blushed, feeling all too conspicuous. First, I was dressed in a pretty, but vulnerable dress. I had a sports bra on that barely contained my boobs. I wasn't wearing a jacket. And to top it all off, my bruises and wounds were out in the open for all to see.

"I got caught in the wrong place at the wrong time," I muttered.

She stared at me for another long minute, then her eyes widened. "You get caught in that bombing?"

I nodded. "Yeah. And I'd rather not talk about it. I was lucky to walk away."

At that moment, Ginty came down the stairs, appearing out of a fog that covered the upper part of the staircase. He motioned to us.

"They're waiting."

Herne carried our drinks and my purse, as it was all I could do to drag myself up the steps. We followed Ginty into the fog, turning the corner to ascend yet another flight. Finally, we entered a hallway that seemed like any normal hotel or office hall. Doors on either side were closed, but we stopped in front of the first one.

"Ready?" the dwarf asked. He seemed subdued today and I wondered what was wrong. Ginty was usually in good spirits.

"As we'll ever be," I said.

He opened the door and we followed him in.

CHAPTER EIGHT

I knew right off, by the looks on their faces, that both Saílle and Névé were worried sick. For the first time since I had been in contact with them, they weren't covered in finery. Oh, they were regal, there was no getting away from that. Both women were raised from birth to be queens, but today they were both dressed in stark colors—Saílle in black, Névé in white. Their hair was done up in neat chignons, and they were wearing their crowns—Saílle's, sapphire and diamond, while Névé's was emerald. They were sitting on opposite sides, as usual, and neither looked happy to be here.

"Is Callan here?" Herne asked.

Ginty cleared his throat. "You're always ready to jump before it's time. I haven't called the Parley to order yet."

Herne let out a grunt. "Fine. Get on with it. We need to get this meeting under way."

"A fine *good evening* to you, too, Lord of the Hunt," the dwarf said, scowling. But he shrugged and pulled out a scroll, unrolling it. "I hereby declare the Samhain Parley of the Courts of Light and Darkness, in the year of 10,258 CFE, open."

He glanced up. Usually at this time, somebody ended up interrupting him. But today we all sat silent, waiting. Clearing his throat, he continued.

"Under this mantle, all members are bound to forswear bearing arms against any other member of this parley until the meeting is officially closed and all members are safely home." He looked up. "This is becoming all too frequent of a routine for me, you know."

"Go on, Ginty, get this over with," Herne said.

"I also remind the Courts of Light and Darkness that they are forsworn by the Covenant of the Wild Hunt from inflicting injury on any and all members of the Wild Hunt team, under the sigil of Cernunnos, Lord of the Forest, and Morgana, Goddess of the Sea and the Fae. Let no one break honor, let discussions progress civilly, and remember that I—Ginty McClintlock, of the McClintlock Clan of the Cascade Dwarves—am your moderator and mediator, and my rule as such supersedes all other authority while we are in this Waystation."

With a big sigh, Ginty rolled up the scroll. "If you stay, you agree to the rules. If you disagree, leave now, or you will be bound to the parley. I have spoken, and so it is done." He glanced around. "Anybody out?"

"We're in, little man," Névé said. "We're in."

"You're in, and don't you ever call me that again, *Oh Fairest of the Light*," Ginty said, his voice dripping with sarcasm.

"Very well," Névé said, leaning forward. "If the parley is open, then what the hell are we going to do about this mess?" She looked over at Herne. "What are you doing about it? We know very well that your father and mother have set you to the case. What's happening? Who is this Tuathan Brotherhood and when are you going to stop them?"

As she paused, Saílle frowned, staring at me. "You were injured in the bombing today, weren't you?"

"Word travels fast," I said. "Yes, I was." I was so weary I forgot to add her title but then I decided it didn't matter. I'd play the injured card if necessary.

"Did you bring Callan?" Herne asked.

"You know the Triamvinate awarded us the right to keep him here," Névé said, a dangerous glint in her eye.

"*I know that*. I just wondered if he's going to be helping you out on this. *Is he here*? That's all I asked." Herne sounded ticked. Positioning him and the two Fae Queens in the same room was just asking for sparks to fly.

"No, he's not here," Ginty said. "Kindly keep to the subject at hand."

Herne took a long swig of his ale. "We've just discovered that the Tuathan Brotherhood, at least on one occasion, set themselves up to be a philanthropic organization in order to lure people in to work with them. Jasper Elrich visited them to be trained for a job he thought would involve helping ostracized members of the Fae community. He came back hating humans and shifters, at the very least. And then on Monday, he went off the skids and mowed down innocent people. We don't know what he was doing between his return and the incident."

I decided to cut to the chase. "Does the Tuathan Brotherhood reside under the dominion of either the Light or the Dark Court?"

Both Fae Queens turned to stare at me. Herne rubbed

his forehead. I knew he had wanted to approach it more diplomatically, but *I* had been the one on the receiving end of a bomb.

Saílle looked me up and down. "You're lucky you came through the explosion alive."

"How *does* the rumor mill work so quickly? But yes, I am. And yes, I want the head of whoever planned it served up to me on a silver platter." I leaned forward, wincing as the wounds on my back pulled. They were starting to scab over, and the skin was pulling as I moved.

For once, neither Fae queen looked at me like I was an alien with two heads.

Saílle nodded. "I understand. Given the circumstances, I think we can set diplomacy to the side. On my word, I have no knowledge of who this Tuathan Brotherhood is, and I want them stopped as much as you do. This is already producing serious ramifications throughout the Fae community. There's a rising fear toward us, and it's likely to cause a major rift in society."

"I concur," said Névé. "And I add, on my honor, that I know nothing of this group, either. They must be stopped before permanent damage is done." She let out a slow breath, then said something I never expected to hear. "I'm sorry you were caught in the attack, Ember. We will honor and mourn the dead in our courts."

"Has there been any unrest in your cities toward humans or shifters?" Herne asked. "Perhaps because of the UC's decision to allow the Fomorians to join?"

"Of course there's been unrest over that, but it hasn't been directed toward any one group in particular, except the UC as a whole. However, I've heard no talk of humans or shifters being to blame. If this group spawned in our cities, they've been keeping underground. And I would think they would directly blame the source—the Fomorians themselves. The giants secured their position simply to have a better access from which to target us, and you know it, son of Cernunnos." Saílle frowned. "They attacked us outright, and yet they gain a voice over the governance of the country?"

"We couldn't prove it was them who engineered the Iron Plague. You *know* that. If we *had* enough proof, we would have taken it to the UC." Herne rapped his knuckles on the table. "And don't even mention the group of Bocanach who attacked us when we were searching for the antidote. While they are usually found with the Fomorians, we have no way of linking that band to Elatha."

Ginty cleared his throat. "I usually do not intervene or even comment on the parleys that I oversee, but I have to add a voice in here. I cannot speak for all of my people, but I will put out feelers to see if we can find out anything about the Tuathan Brotherhood. They're a deadly snake, creeping through the grass. And they have already harmed the reputation of the Fae."

"The problem with figuring out who's behind them is that we have two very likely possibilities: one, that it's actually a front for someone trying to discredit and smear the name of the Fae—and we all know who I'm thinking of. But on the other hand, when you think of zealots and fanatics, they *don't care* if they harm those who don't band behind them. You could have a band of Fae who think that this is the only way to regain some power they feel has been lost. Either option is entirely feasible." I looked at Herne. "Saílle and Névé should set up a press conference and formally disavow any knowledge or approval of the group. The sooner the better."

"That's a good idea," Herne said. He leaned back and folded his arms. "Are you willing to do that?"

Saílle nodded. "I am. Névé, you and I should both go on at the same time. We need to present a united front."

I blinked. I had honestly expected their truce to last about two or three days. Instead, it had held for several weeks. Even though it meant less for us to do given their constant attacks at one another were at a lull, it gave rise to more worries. I had no doubt they were working in private with the Fae warrior Callan whom they had freed from the past, and that they were working on a plan to destroy the Fomorians. And that would be diving down the rabbit hole.

"Can you send your spies through your cities, looking for anybody talking about the group? And before you deny it, we know you have agents that spy on your populace. Every government does." Herne shook his head. "We're really running on empty with this one so far. Maybe the investigators will have leads for us when they have sorted through the remains of the bombing."

"I can tell you this," Névé said, motioning to one of her servants. He handed her a tablet and she glanced at it before saying, "Jasper Elrich was in good standing with the Court. He never presented a problem, he was well liked, and even though he was engaged to a human, he was loyal to the crown. We were going to intervene in the proposed wedding, but we were sure we could do so without any problems. Now, of course, that's moot. But if what you say is correct, if he changed personality so abruptly, then I wonder if he was drugged or brainwashed? There are spells to control behavior that experienced witches can use."

I frowned. I hadn't even thought of that. "That didn't even occur to me, but you're right. A personality switch that drastic doesn't just happen out of the blue. Either he had to be a closet bigot already, or the shift was precipitated by something. I suppose we could ask at his workplace, but he wasn't happy there and I don't know if that would give us any insight."

"I'll text Viktor to check into it," Herne said, then turned back to the Fae Queens. "Set up the press conference for tonight or tomorrow morning. You want to come out against this as soon as possible." He paused, then said, "Do you think there are Fae who are capable of creating a group like this?"

Saílle closed her eyes, looking strained. "Yes, I'm sorry to say it, but there are those who resent our interaction with the world at large. And they would be more than capable of this. But I have always thought they were few and far between, and more talk than action. I admit, I cannot rule out that the Tuathan Brotherhood is actually a group of renegade Fae."

"What she said," Névé added. "Keep in close touch with us on what you find out. And we will contact you if we find out anything. This can't be allowed to go any further."

"I'm afraid things may get a lot uglier before they get better," I murmured, and no one contradicted me.

By six-thirty, we were on our way back across the

bridge, and I was done in for the day. I felt nauseated from the pain, and kicked myself for leaving my prescriptions back at the office. I hated admitting that I needed the pain medication, but the fact was, I was hurting pretty bad.

Herne glanced at me, worried. "Are you all right?"

"The pain meds have worn off and I hurt like a son of a bitch." I grimaced. "As soon as we get back to the office, I'm taking one of those pills." I leaned my head back, staring out into the growing darkness. The sun was setting earlier every day, and the night had set in. The clouds were socking in and we were due for rain and wind. I welcomed the storm, feeling it brewing in the distance. Its energy matched my mood.

"When both Saílle and Névé are scared into cooperating with us, you know things are bad," I said. "I have no clue what to think now. My gut says somebody other than the Fae are behind this, but that they both agree that the Tuathan Brotherhood could be exactly what it says it is, well…that makes me nervous." I pressed my head against the window. "What do you think?"

"I have no idea. I see both possibilities and either way, it's a mess. I'm almost hoping it's a frame-up because if it's not, then the Fae will have so much more damage control to do. But if it's not the Fae, how the hell will this play out?"

I fell into silence, listening to the sound of the traffic as we inched our way across the bridge. Rush hour was easing up, but we were still going half-speed of normal. By the time we got back to the office, Angel was waiting with my pills.

"You look like hell," she said. "Let's get you home."

"I drove in this morning, but I don't think I'm capable of driving home," I said, popping one of the pain pills.

"Then leave your car and ride with me," Angel said. "Herne, can you walk us to the car? It's late, Ember's out of it, and I'm feeling on edge."

Herne lifted me in his arms and carried me into the elevator, ignoring my protests that I could walk by myself. But I didn't object too hard. I was in pain and tired and frazzled. He carried me to Angel's car and slid me into the passenger seat.

"I'll wait till until you're on the road," he said to Angel, then kissed me gently on the lips. "Love, go home. Rest. If you need anything, call me. Angel, that goes for you, too. I'll keep my phone with me."

Thanking him, Angel pulled out of the parking garage as I leaned back against the seat. The pain pill was kicking in. When we got home, she helped me into the house.

"Can you make it upstairs?"

I stared at the staircase, groaning. "I can, but it's not going to be fun."

"I'll walk behind you, to make sure you don't fall."

"Trust me, if I fall, I'll just bowl you over. Why don't you take the lead. I'll just crawl up."

I motioned for her to go in front of me, and then, on my hands and knees, I crawled up the steps. I probably could have walked, but every muscle in my body ached, and my back felt like every movement pushed it toward a spasm. I made it, though, and Angel helped me to my feet. She guided me into my bedroom, and helped me undress.

"Your back looks like somebody took a knife to you." She glanced toward my bathroom. "Do you want a shower, or a bath?"

"Yeah, but I don't feel up to standing."

"Wait here." She motioned for me to stay on the bed and dashed into the bathroom. When she returned, she said, "I put the plastic stepstool in the shower. It's high enough for you to sit on. Come on, let's get you washed up and then I'll doctor your cuts."

As the hot water streamed over me, I closed my eyes, enjoying the heat as it worked its way into my muscles. Angel lightly washed my back, being careful so that she didn't re-open any of the cuts. When I finished, she wrapped a beach-sized towel around me and led me over to the vanity bench, where I dropped the towel so she could dab the antibiotic ointment onto my back. It was a blend specially for the Fae, and it numbed the sting of the cuts.

She brought me my robe, and then got out the blow dryer and began drying my hair for me.

"You don't have to do all this," I said, feeling a little teary.

"Yes I do. You would do the same for me." She gently brushed the strands back. "When Viktor called, I swear my heart stopped. All I could think about was the thought that you were hurt, that we didn't know how severe your injuries were, and that we might lose you. I couldn't take that, girl." Her face was soft, her eyes welling with tears.

"Well, I'm alive. But a lot of other people aren't. Angel, I'm scared. Not for myself, but this is one of the most dangerous cases we've worked on. If we don't find the headquarters of the Tuathan Brotherhood and put a stop to them, things are going to get a lot worse. I'm just afraid we won't find them in time." I rubbed my forehead. "I'm so tired, and I'm hungry."

She finished drying my hair and then lightly braided it back. "There. Tomorrow, your natural waves will be all sorts of dreamy." As she walked with me back into my bedroom, pulling my covers down, she said, "I'll bring your dinner up. Would you like it if I eat with you and we can watch a movie or something?"

"Please." I nodded as I climbed into bed and she adjusted my pillows to cushion my back as I leaned against the headboard. I didn't feel like being alone with my thoughts.

As Angel headed downstairs, Mr. Rumblebutt jumped on the bed and curled up on my lap. I cuddled him, cooing softly, trying to focus on all the good things in my life, but the images from the morning kept replaying themselves over and over in my mind and I was relieved when she appeared with a tray full of grilled cheese sandwiches, potato chips, and mugs of tomato soup.

As we ate, we talked about Herne and Rafé—Angel and he were getting along nicely—and what we wanted to plant in the gardens come spring, and anything and everything that didn't involve violence and pain and loss. Finally, I began to doze, and she carried the tray away as I curled under the covers. Mr. Rumblebutt burrowed in beside me as I fell asleep. But I kept a dim lamp on all night, and only woke up once, gasping as I thought I heard another explosion. But it was only in the back of my mind, and I calmed myself before once again, closing my eyes.

By morning, I was still stiff and sore, but feeling a lot

better. I desperately needed coffee, but that wasn't out of the ordinary, and while I decided to forgo any scratchy tops and to wear a skirt instead of jeans because of the cuts on the backs of my legs, I wasn't feeling too shabby.

Angel looked up as I made my way downstairs. "You up to work today?"

"Yeah, I'm just not going to race around getting into any fights." I adjusted the skirt and then cinched it with a patent leather belt. The shirt was a low-cut peasant top that I usually wore in summer, but it was gauzy and light against my skin. I was wearing a sports bra again because the material of my regular bras was just too scratchy, and I needed to avoid compressing against the cuts. "I need a new leather jacket."

"We'll go shopping this weekend." Angel handed me a plate of waffles and bacon. "Here, I made your favorite breakfast."

I gave her a wide smile. "Did I mention that you're the best roomie ever?"

"Only a dozen times, but what's one more?" She paused as a text came in. After glancing at it, she groaned. "Dear gods, what now?"

I was about to ask what was wrong, but she was already talking to somebody on the phone. She moved back into the kitchen, and I dug into my waffles. They were so fluffy and yet crisp that they felt like an oxymoron. I was famished and had half-finished my breakfast by the time she came back.

"You really are hungry. Another one?"

I nodded, wiping syrup off my chin. "Please. Everything okay?"

"Not exactly. That was Cooper. DJ's got himself in trouble."

"Oh good gods, what did he do?"

DJ was Angel's younger half-brother, and he lived with a foster family of shifters to help guide him through the changes that would beset him at puberty and to keep him safe from our uncertain lifestyle.

"He hacked into the school computer system to change the grade of a classmate from a D to a B. He admitted it. When they asked him why, he said he didn't want Timothy to get in trouble for his grades. I can believe that, but my guess is that he's just trying to prove he's one of the guys. DJ is small for his age and he always feels left out." She paused, then shrugged. "Cooper has grounded him through Thanksgiving, and he's been suspended, so he's on home study until after the holidays. He can return to school in January."

"Ugh. That's a long time."

"It's a private shifter school. They'll send out a tutor once a week for him. But it's going to cost Cooper money—the parents have to pay when that happens—and DJ has to keep his record clean till the end of the school year to get off probation."

I thought about the punishment. It seemed a little harsh, but then, it wasn't corporal, and the tutor would probably put him through his paces at a harder rate than if he were actually going to class. The school seemed to care about the kids getting their education.

"Are you still going down for Thanksgiving?"

Angel nodded. "Cooper said I'm welcome there. He had already promised DJ I could come, and he's not going to renege on that. But you can be sure that boy and I will have words once I arrive." She brought her plate to the table and joined me, handing me another waffle.

As we ate, I ran through the day's schedule. We hadn't fully set it by the end of work the day before, but I wanted to talk to Amanda to find out if she remembered anybody who might have been too interested in Eleanor at Alka-Non, perhaps someone named Naomi. Other than that, I'd be doing whatever Herne asked me to.

We reached the parking garage and, as Angel pulled in next to my car and I got out, I noticed that, across the side of my Subaru, somebody had keyed the words "BITCH SLUT."

"Fucking hell!" I stared at the gouges. They were deep enough to mar the metal as well as the paint. Whoever had done this was either hyped up on something, or they were angry. It wasn't just some kid passing by.

"Ray?" Angel asked, glancing at me.

I stared at it for a moment, then nodded. "Probably. I guess I could call the cops, though right now this isn't going to be a major blip on the radar. But I'll damned well take pictures." I snapped a few photos on my phone and then, grumbling, checked my tires and anything else I could think of that might have been tinkered with. Luckily, everything else looked intact.

"Let's get inside. You can stop by an insurance adjuster after work," Angel said.

We skimmed through the morning meeting quickly. Luckily, there hadn't been any other attacks that we knew of, though the death count to the bombing was up as five more of the missing were found. Or rather, parts of them. The injured were still managing to hold on, some of them very close to death but maintaining.

Herne gave me a long kiss when he entered the room, stroking my chin. "How are you?"

"Better—at least my body is. Some asshole keyed my car while it was in the parking garage." I waved him off when he asked more about it, not wanting to deflect from the matters at hand. "I want to ask Amanda something—based on what Samantha told Viktor and me yesterday. I was going to give her a call after the meeting."

"That's fine," Herne said. "Yutani, I'd like you to poke around on the Dark Web. I know you've been peeking, but arm yourself and go in. We need to find this group and we need to find them now."

"Do you want me to dive into the cesspool too, Herne?" Talia asked.

Yutani abruptly put a stop to that. "Nope. I'm telling you now, I know my way around the Dark Web, but if you don't, you're just asking for trouble. I'll feed you info to look up as per usual, and we'll divide the work that way."

Angel frowned. She had been scanning her tablet. "We've got trouble brewing. There are four businesses cited as closing their doors to the Fae. And a vigilante group beat the hell out of a Fae couple last night—they were shifters. They claimed 'payback' for the beatings on Sunday night. The couple has no known connections to the Tuathan Brotherhood."

"Victims of opportunity. I was afraid this was going to start happening," Herne said. "Do we have a fix on the perps?"

"The cops picked up two of them and they're in jail.

The other three got away, but their buddies will probably turn tail on them." Angel shook her head. "Bad juju."

"Well, Cernunnos received an irate call from the United Coalition this morning, asking what the hell we're doing. They seem to expect miracles. My father managed to put them off, but we can't go on this way much longer without wide-scale backlash." Herne tossed his pen on the table. "We need a break on this."

The office phone rang, and Angel dashed out to her desk to get it. When she returned, she was waving a piece of paper.

"We may just have got our break," she said, her eyes sparkling. "That was the cops. They have the name of the bomber. They found the security footage, which survived, and they saw a man come in with the bomb. It matches what a few witnesses remember—they're just now managing to interview them. The suspect pulled off his coat and held a gun on people to keep them from leaving. Ember," she said, turning to me. "If you had gone in the bank five minutes earlier, you would have seen him."

I froze. "I could have stopped him."

"No! Don't you even go there," Herne said. "You would have just been caught with the rest of them. There's no way you could have disarmed a suicide bomber, and even if you carried a gun, you probably would have triggered the explosion if you shot him. He wouldn't have surrendered, given he willingly put his life on the chopping block. Do you understand me, Ember? Don't go there." He leaned forward, shaking his head, a fierce look on his face.

I tried to process what he said along with the fact that the bomb hadn't just been planted, but it had been on a living, breathing fanatic who willingly stood there, holding those people hostage, knowing he was going to kill them at any minute, dying with them.

I suddenly gulped, realizing I had been holding my breath. "Yeah," I said slowly as logic took over. On this one, Herne was right. If I had gone inside a few minutes earlier, I'd probably be dead now.

"Right," I said. "You're right. I couldn't have done anything." After another pause, I turned to Angel. "Do they have an ID on him?"

"Yeah. Footage places him as one of the bank's clients, actually. His name is Menhir Ryma, and he was a loyal customer for ten years. Then…boom." She handed Herne the paper. "Here's his address, phone number—landline—and next of kin's information. He leaves a wife and two kids." She shook her head. "Can you imagine what they're going through?"

"How do we go about interviewing her? I mean, I know we have to, but how do you walk up to somebody and ask them if they knew their spouse was going to blow himself up along with as many people as he could take with him?" I shook my head.

"We'll tackle that later today," Herne said. "This morning, you go ahead and talk to Amanda. I'm sending Viktor out to interview Grimspound Mica—the Fomorian who owns the Panther XL you saw at the scene."

I frowned, starting to protest because I remembered the car and it felt like my fight, but then when I thought about it, I agreed. "Yeah, come to think of it, you're right. It wouldn't be wise to send me along with him—given how much the Fomorians hate the Fae. I don't want to be on his radar."

"No, you do not." Herne sat back, frowning. "I feel like

we're running five steps behind this group. They came out of nowhere, and now their name's on everybody's lips only a few days after they appeared. I hate to even think it, but what happens if we can't shut them down? What do we do if they just keep evading us?"

"Then the Fae are going to become mighty unpopular, regardless of whether they have anything to do with the group or not." Yutani gave a little shrug and finished off his coffee. "I suggest we dive in for the day. We can only do so much with what we know. I'll check on the Dark Web and see if I can find any sort of manifesto or target list or anything like that."

Herne nodded and adjourned the meeting. As I returned to my office, I passed him and he caught my wrist, pulling me to him.

"Ember, how are you feeling?"

"I'm sore and aching, but I'm all right." I paused, thinking back to the blast. "But a lot of people are mourning today, including Amanda's mother. At least we have a couple leads in Eleanor's case. If we can bring that little girl home safely, then maybe the world will make some sort of sense again."

He pressed his lips against my forehead, kissing me gently. "Oh, my love. The world has never made much sense, and I doubt it ever will. That's one thing you'll need to get used to as time goes along." With a soft smile, he let me go. "Come on, we've got work to do."

I nodded, thinking that he was right. As long as the world held humans and Fae and shifters, and all other manner of people, it probably never would make much sense.

CHAPTER NINE

I waited until nine-thirty to call Amanda, wanting to avoid waking her if she were sleeping in. "Hey, it's Ember from the Wild Hunt."

"Have you found Eleanor?" The hope in her voice made me cringe.

"No, I'm sorry, but I do have some questions I need to ask you. We can either do this on the phone, or I can drive over if you like."

I could hear the catch in her voice and realized I had dashed her hopes. "No, the phone is fine. What do you need to know?"

"We've talked to a couple of the parents of the…" I didn't want to say *dead girls*, but I wasn't sure how else to phrase it. "I need to know, at your AlkaNon meetings, was there ever a woman there who was of a slim build, possibly a blonde, and she would have shown more interest in your home life than you'd expect a stranger to. Her name might have been something like Naomi. She's a shifter."

There was a pause, then Amanda gasped. "Yes, actually. I usually hang out with Tawny, but I do remember that a new member started coming at the beginning of the month. She's a shifter. Her name…it's not Naomi but rather, Natalie. She's a blonde, and very thin. Why, do you think she may know where my Lani is?"

I wasn't about to tell Amanda that I suspected the woman might be the kidnapper—shifters went off half-cocked all too often, and if she thought that Naomi—or Natalie—had swiped her daughter, there was no telling what Amanda might do.

"She's a person of interest. We're trying to reach her to find out what information she might have. Do you happen to have her last name?" I knew, given AlkaNon's policy, it was likely she wouldn't have it, but on the chance, I asked anyway.

"No, I'm sorry. We don't give out last names in the group. The only reason I know Tawny's last name is because we've become good friends. But Natalie—something about her bothered me, so I shied away from her when she began to ask too many questions."

"When was the last time you saw her at the meetings, and do you remember what she said she was there for?"

Amanda hesitated, then said, "I think…a week ago? Meetings are on Tuesday nights. Eleanor disappeared on Saturday, so yeah, last Tuesday. As to what Natalie's problem is, she said she's a recovering crackalaine addict."

Bingo.

"Thank you. If I send a sketch artist out to your house, can you work with them to create a picture of Natalie?" I still had to send one out to Samantha, as well.

"Of course." Amanda paused, then asked, "Do you think we'll be able to find my baby?"

"We're going to do everything we can, Amanda. That much I can promise you." I hung up, then called the sketch artist the Wild Hunt kept on retainer. I made appointments for him to visit both Samantha and Amanda, then called them both to pin down the times. By the time I was done, it was ten o'clock. I thought about calling Dana Longtooth back, to ask if we could talk to her wife Hadley about the meetings, but given how tense their relationship seemed, I decided to wait until we had no other choice.

I picked up my tablet and headed for Herne's office, tapping on the door first before entering. "Herne? I wanted to interview the last couple that we have left in the missing-girls case."

He held up one hand. He was on the phone.

"Yes, Father. Yes, I know. No, I didn't think about that. Of course." He motioned for me to wait outside and so I shut the door behind me, wandering over to Angel's desk.

"What's up?" she asked, glancing at me. Her desk was a swamp of paperwork. "I swear, next time Charlie comes in to use my computer, I'm leaving him a strongly worded note to put my files back in order, or I'll stake the little geek myself." She pointed to the scattered files.

"I'm just waiting for Herne to get off the phone. Cernunnos called him." I stretched and yawned, wincing as the scabs on my back pulled. "Good gods, those cuts hurt."

"Most of them looked fairly light and should heal without too much of a scar. A few are going to be there for a while, though. The ones with stitches were jagged." Angel frowned. "You want to see a plastic surgeon?"

I stared at her. "What for? It's not like the bomb got my face, though I do have some nice little skid marks on my nose. But they should heal up without a problem."

"You're okay with the scars then?" Angel glanced at me as she shifted around a stack of file folders.

"Yeah, I'm okay with them. I can't see them and if anybody who does see them gets offended, that's their problem. Battle scars, Ange. War wounds." I winked at her as Herne peeked his head out of his door, motioning for me to join him.

Angel laughed as I waved at her and followed Herne into his office.

"What did you need?" He seemed preoccupied, frowning as he stared at something on his tablet.

"I just wanted to let you know that I've arranged to send a sketch artist over to both Amanda's house and to Samantha's place. Amanda said that a new member had joined her meetings this month who seemed overtly interested in her home life. She said a woman—a slim blonde—by the name of Natalie kept asking prying questions, and that she got a bad feeling from her. She was a shifter. And *that* matches the description of the woman Samantha mentioned, only *her* name was Naomi."

"Hmm…Natalie, Naomi. Both begin with the letters N-A." Herne slid into his chair, leaning back and propping his feet on the desk. "What's your gut reaction?"

"That it's the same woman. And the fact that she was addicted to crackalaine has to play into it. I can't believe the cops didn't piece it together." I frowned.

"Sometimes, people are ashamed of their failings and do what they can to hide them. My guess is that they didn't even think of telling the cops about the meetings.

We're not the police—we may have a similar authority, but in a lot of people's eyes we're less threatening. The cops lock up crackalaine heads right and left. We don't."

He had a good point. "True that. I want to interview the last set of parents. When do you want to head out to talk to Ryma's wife?"

"I called her and she said we could drop by around one-thirty today. So you have time, if you like." He set his tablet down on his desk. "Who keyed your car?"

I shrugged. "I don't know. I found it like that when I arrived at work."

"It was Ray, wasn't it?" Herne's eyes had a dark look to them, and I could feel his mood. It wasn't the best.

"I don't really know, Herne. I suspect him, yes, but I can't prove it and I don't want to accuse him without any evidence." I was half-afraid that Herne would hunt Ray down and beat the crap out of him. "At least Marilee's counterspell has worked on him and he's no longer obsessed with winning me back."

"No, now he's just obsessed with revenge for what he sees as a deliberate action. One day, that boy is going to overstep himself when I'm around and I won't hold back. Your glamour may have lured him in, but there's still such a thing as taking responsibility for your actions, and Ray isn't willing to do that."

I held up my hand, trying to stave off this train of conversation. The last thing I wanted to do was talk about Ray right now. "Can we change the subject?"

With a grunt, Herne acquiesced. "Fine, but this isn't over. Go ahead and interview the last couple. Be back by twelve-thirty."

I blew him a kiss and ducked out the door, stopping in

my office to pick up the names and addresses of the third couple. Tim and Verka Wochosky were also wolf shifters. I called them. Tim Wochosky said I could come over. Jotting down their address, which was less than a mile from where we were and, sliding a rain poncho over my head, I headed for the elevator.

THE WOCHOSKYS LIVED in the Cornish Apartments on Third and Blanchard. It took me five minutes to reach their place. The building was nine stories tall, and took up half the block. The bottom-story windows all had bars on them but the higher ones didn't, and the building looked relatively old but updated. I pulled into the parking garage, finding the visitor parking, and took the elevator up to the sixth floor. The Wochoskys lived in apartment 605.

The halls were carpeted in a quiet beige, and the walls were muted taupe. Neutrals that I detested, but they made sense in a building like this. I passed a potted palm tree and stopped in front of the door to apartment 605, ringing the bell. A moment later, the door opened and a tall, thin man greeted me.

"I'm Ember Kearney, from the Wild Hunt Agency?" I held out my badge.

He glanced at it for a moment, then nodded and let me in. "I'm Tim Wochosky. Please come in."

The apartment was small but tidy, and it felt cozy. The living room was neater than any place I'd ever seen. Everything looked ready for a magazine ad, but it felt natural here, and calm. Some places were neat out of desperation. This one felt like everything had its place and was comfortably snuggled away.

Tim Wochosky was a thin man, and his face looked gaunt. His eyes were too bright—the brightness that only happened with speed or too much caffeine. His movements seemed jumpy.

"Please, sit down." He pulled out a chair at the table for me and I sat down. I was feeling more shaky than I thought I was, and when he offered me tea, I gratefully accepted.

"I'm sorry my wife's not here, but she works. I take care of the house and of..." He paused, grimacing. "I took care of Mallory."

Taking a deep breath, I dove in. "Mallory was your daughter?"

He nodded. "I still... We can't..." He paused, choking up. "I'll get your tea." He disappeared into the kitchen.

The apartment was small enough and open enough that I could see him standing at the stove, pouring water from the kettle into two mugs. His head was down, and his shoulders were slumped. He was defeated, even if he didn't realize it.

When he returned, he had wiped his eyes and he placed my mug in front of me. "Here you go. I hope you don't mind peppermint. I'm out of black tea."

"That's not a problem," I said, pulling the mug toward me. "Are you up to answering some questions?"

"I'll try, if it can help." He played with the string attached to his teabag. "You said on the phone another little girl is missing?"

I nodded. "Yes, and we think we may have time to find her. But we need every bit of information we can gather."

"I already told the cops what I knew, but they don't seem to be doing anything." He glanced over at the TV. "I suppose they're busy now with the bomber…"

"Yeah, they are. My agency is trying to help them on that case, too. The fourth girl went missing on Saturday and her mother came right to us, as well as the police. So we're involved. Tell me, where was your little girl abducted?"

He shrugged. "The mall. I took her there to pick up something my wife had ordered. We were waiting in the customer service line. There were five people ahead of me. My phone rang and I let go of Mallory's hand to answer. I was looking the other way and when I turned around, she was gone. That's the last time I saw her."

He rocked gently back and forth, his face strained as he tried to avoid crying. I knew the signs by now. The rocking helped to focus and keep control.

"Her name was Mallory?"

He nodded. "Mallory Jean. She was three years old. I let go of her hand…"

"I have a delicate question. Please know, it's important or I wouldn't ask you."

Tim frowned, looking wary, but he waited for me to speak.

"Are either you or your wife members of AlkaNon?"

There was a pause. "I am."

"Have you been going to regular meetings?"

After a moment, he nodded, his expression guarded. Finally, he seemed to find his tongue. "My wife forced me to go. I admit, my drinking was out of hand, but I was going to quit on my own. She told me that if I didn't start going, she would take Mallory and leave me."

"Where do you go for your meetings?"

"The Pike Place branch. Why?"

I jotted down the name. Four abducted girls. Four different meeting places. Whoever the killer was, she got around, all right. "I have another question, and I'm afraid I can't explain to you right now why I'm asking, but we need the information."

"All right, what is it?" Tim wiped his mouth in a gesture I had seen several alcoholics use.

I was wary about asking him. Once it came out that this woman had been preying on AlkaNon members, I could see him blaming his wife for forcing him to go.

"At the meetings, was there a woman—she would probably be a blonde. Slim. She might be named Natalie or Naomi or something similar, and she would have asked a lot of personal questions about your home life."

The words were barely out of my mouth when he whispered, "Nadine."

"Nadine?" I frowned. She also had a variety of names.

"She was a member of the group. She dropped out sometime last month. I didn't notice because Verka and I were so wound up in trying to find Mallory." He straightened up, staring at me. *"Did she kill my daughter?"*

"I can't answer that. We're just gathering information right now. There's no way to know for sure what's going on yet, but we're doing our best to find out."

He was holding something else back, I could tell. "What is it? Anything you could tell us can help."

"My daughter's already dead. What good would it do?" The words were bitter, but there was something hiding behind the anger.

"You might be able to help keep this from happening to other little girls, Tim. Talk to me."

"You won't tell my wife?" He paused, his mouth twisting.

"Not if I can possibly avoid it," I said, sidestepping a promise.

Finally, he dropped his head and muttered, "I hit on her. On Nadine. We had sex in one of the unused rooms in the community center the last night I was there. I was so angry at my wife for making me go, and I was so cocky. That weekend, Mallory vanished."

I leaned back in my chair. Talk about conflicting emotions. And now, they'd be even more convoluted. "Is there anything you can tell me about her? Any birthmarks or other identifying marks?"

He shook his head, the look on his face painful. Then he froze. "A scar. She had a scar across her belly. Under her belly button. I asked her where she got it and she just brushed it away. Oh gods, did I have sex with the woman who killed my baby?" He burst into tears, burying his face in his hands.

I sat there, unsure of what to do or say. Finally, I leaned forward.

"We don't know for sure how she's involved, or even whether she's involved. Breathe. Just breathe. We'll be in touch with you when we know more. For now, though, I suggest you find a good therapist to talk to, perhaps together with your wife? This isn't something that's easy to navigate by yourself."

He continued to cry, nodding as the tears raced down his cheeks. "She blames me. I blame her. We blame each other. We always had problems but now, it's like my wife has locked herself behind a massive wall and she won't let me in. She never says to my face that she holds me responsible, but I know she does." He paused, then asked, "Have you ever lost someone who was your entire world? Mallory kept my wife and me together. She was the reason I went to the meetings. She was the sunshine in our clouded marriage. And now...it's all storm clouds."

I thanked him for talking to me, then let myself out. There was nothing I could do for him. He needed a qualified therapist, and probably a good divorce lawyer. Statistics said that couples either bonded tightly or were pushed apart after the death of a child, based on how close they were before the death. I couldn't see much hope for him and his wife.

On the drive back to the office, I found myself thinking about the people whose lives we touched. We brought some justice, to others we brought closure, and to others, we made painful situations worse. But at least we worked to uncover the truth, and that was most important.

By the time I returned to the office, Angel had ordered lunch.

"I ordered Italian. Hope you guys are up for spaghetti," she said. "It's in the break room." She was eating at her desk, and the smells were good enough to make my stomach rumble.

I dished up a plate and joined her, telling her what had happened.

She frowned. "You said she had a scar across her stomach?"

I nodded. "That's what he said. Underneath her belly button."

"Did he describe it?"

"Not really, just said it was a horizontal scar beneath her belly button. Does that mean anything to you?"

Angel nodded. "Mama J. had one, from when she had DJ. She had to have a C-section to deliver him. Whoever she is, your suspect has had a child."

I blinked. "She has kids? Then why…" I paused, thinking hard. "She comes to the groups. She's told every group so far she's a former crackalaine user. So…maybe her child got taken away from her and she's angry? Maybe she's on a self-righteous trip and believes other addicts should lose their children? But why would she kill them?"

"I don't know, but you should probably tell Herne." Angel motioned to the break room. "I think he just went in there."

I picked up my plate. "Thanks, *chica*. This could help us figure out her motive, and if we have a motive, it makes it easier to find the person."

Herne was in the break room, along with Viktor. He glanced up when I entered.

"Ember, can you call everyone in? Viktor's back from interviewing Grimspound."

I set my plate down, heading back out to the front desk. "Meeting. Lock the elevator and come on in." On the way to the break room, I peeked into the office Yutani and Talia shared. "Meeting in the break room."

We gathered around the table, everybody carrying their lunch, and settled in.

"We've got to stop meeting this way," Talia intoned, vamping for us.

I snorted. "Yeah, trust me. Angel and I never get to go out to lunch anymore."

"Deal with it," Herne said, snickering. "Okay, so Viktor, go ahead."

Viktor had just served himself up a big plate of spaghetti and garlic bread, and he carried his plate to the table and sat down. He took a big bite of the pasta, moaning softly as the savory sauce hit his tongue, and then, after swallowing, he cleared his throat.

"That is delicious. I want the name of the restaurant."

"Roma's—down the street and around the corner. They deliver," Angel said, breaking off another piece of bread.

"Thanks. All right, I interviewed the Fomorian. Trust me, Ember, you would not want to have been there. He's an asshole in every way possible, and then some. But I can tell you this, he's not part of this Tuathan Brotherhood organization, not unless I'm reading him way off. Neither is he part of Elatha's brood, from what I can tell."

"How do you know?" I asked.

"He's been living in Seattle for twenty-three years, and Elatha didn't arrive till this year. He's also a pacifist and a follower of Savisanism." Viktor rolled his eyes.

I groaned.

"What's Savisanism?" Angel asked.

"Savisanism's an esoteric cult that was started by a monk named Savisa, about sixty years ago. Savisa's one of the Fae and he turned his back on the Fae conflict, preaching tolerance and a live-and-let-live attitude," I said.

"What's wrong with that?"

"Nothing, until you start charging your followers a thousand dollars a year just to belong to the movement. Those who want to become his guardians, as he calls them, are those who can afford the ten-thousand-dollar initiation fee, and their yearly bill skyrockets to five thousand." I shook my head. "It's a scam. Well, not in that they profess to be one thing and turn out to be another. To maintain your place in the Savisanism movement, you have to keep your nose clean and avoid bringing disharmony into the group. But that's a lot of money just to be told to keep your nose clean and be open to differences."

"How do you know so much about it?" Herne asked, a curious look on his face.

"One of my mother's friends, a shifter woman we used to know, was into it. She was always bringing pamphlets over, trying to convert my folks. I just ignored her, though I swiped a couple of the pamphlets once and read them. They were filled with a bunch of buzzwords and generic affirmations." I laughed. "And for every person you bring into the fold, you get a small percentage of the initiation fee. In other words, a finder's fee."

A lightbulb seemed to go on over Viktor's head. "That's why he kept pushing me to come check out the meetings with him to make certain he was for real. He was hoping I'd join and he'd make himself a little payday."

"No doubt. So our Fomorian is a Savisarian? Then it isn't likely he would have anything to do with the bombing." I frowned. I had wanted to be right on this, desperately so. I was disappointed. I had to admit it. It would have been so tidy for Mica to be involved. I was still angry at the Fomorians for what they had done, and I would happily turn them over for whatever we could pin on them. But if he wasn't involved in anything underhanded, I couldn't pretend he was. At least I was reasonable about it.

"Yeah, I don't think so either. Grimspound is arrogant and pushy, but he's no killer. The movement may be shady, but he firmly believes what they teach. And he insists that nonviolence is at the root of the organization." Viktor tossed his notes on the table. "I asked him what he was doing there. Turns out he lives in the apartments above the bank and was on his way to work. He heard the explosion as he drove down the street and says that he didn't want to get in the way of emergency vehicles. He called the cops when he got to work, and that checks out with their reports."

"Well, another dead end." I frowned. "On Eleanor's case, I have another lead." I told them what I had found out, along with Angel's mention of the C-section scar. "Is there a way to check for children—little girls, probably—who either were kidnapped and killed over the past, what…ten years? Might as well include those who had an accident or went missing?"

"I can run some files," Yutani said. "It will take me a few minutes, but I might be able to come up with something for you." He began tapping away while the rest of us dug into our lunches.

Angel raised her head. "Somebody's asking permission to come in. The elevator is locked. I'll be right back." She slid out from her chair and dashed back to her desk.

I broke off another piece of bread to mop up the leftover sauce, and then frowned as Talia, who was sitting opposite me, stiffened. She was staring at the door behind me.

"I didn't know you were already in town," she said, slowly standing.

From behind me, a voice—a melodic woman's voice—answered. "That's because I knew if I gave you much warning, you'd find a way to put me off."

Angel sidled back to her chair. Swinging around the other side of the table, another woman appeared. She was gorgeous, but there was something to her looks that told me that she was wearing some sort of illusion. Tall, statuesque, almost regal, the woman had hair the color of platinum, and her eyes were an arresting gray. She wasn't young, nor was she old, but she had a sense of timelessness. She was wearing a pink pantsuit, and looked far too *Barbie* for comfort.

She approached Talia and stood beside her chair, staring down. "Aren't you going to welcome me into your place of business, *sister*?"

As we watched, Talia slid her chair back and stood, staring at the woman. After a moment, she turned toward the rest of us. "Excuse my manners. I'd like you to all meet my sister, Varia. Varia, don't be shy. Introduce yourself."

And with that, Varia let her illusion drop and there, in the flesh, stood a living, breathing, harpy.

THE NEXT MOMENT, Varia reclaimed her illusion, but not before we had seen her true nature. She had been massive, a good seven feet tall with flame red hair and brilliant blue eyes. Her head, breasts, torso, and arms had been those of a woman, but her lower body had reminded me of a massive vulture, and her wings had been folded in back of her.

Herne was the first to react. "Varia, welcome to the Wild Hunt Agency. I'm Herne, son of Cernunnos. I run this place."

She accepted his hand graciously, nodding as she took it. "Lord Herne, well met."

Talia quickly recovered her tongue. "Varia, allow me to introduce the others. This is Ember, she's one of our investigators. And Angel, our receptionist. Yutani, our IT wizard, and Viktor, another one of our investigators."

Varia nodded at each of us in turn. "I knew you wouldn't see me if I asked in advance, even though I told you I was planning on coming out. So I thought I'd just drop in and surprise you."

"Won't you sit down? Viktor, grab another chair," Herne said, offering his own chair to Varia.

She gracefully sank into the seat, putting her designer bag on the table. She looked around, then cleared her throat. "I assume they all know your background?"

Talia nodded, looking wary. She still hadn't held out her hand or made any move to welcome her sister. "Yes. What you have to say can be said in front of them."

"Well, then, I have what I imagine will be welcome news. I've been tracking Lazerous for years now, and I know where he is. He actually lives about forty miles from here—and if you like, I'll go with you and we'll force him to return your powers."

With that, Talia let out a cry and ran out of the room.

CHAPTER TEN

Varia looked at the rest of us, clearly surprised. "I thought she'd be happy for the information. We can force him to return her powers. I'm certain she had no idea that he was camped out so near to her. I'm not sure why she's upset."

I glanced at Herne and he motioned for Angel and me to follow Talia. We slipped out of the break room, shutting the door behind us.

"Well, that certainly was a showstopper to lunch," I muttered as we headed to Talia's office. She had slammed the door behind her, and now I tapped on the door, peeking inside.

Talia was sitting in a recliner, staring out the window, her expression bewildered. "Is she still here?" she asked, leaning forward as we sat down on the sofa under the window.

"I'm afraid so, and she seems thoroughly perplexed as to why you didn't jump for joy at her offer." I paused. "Can you really get your powers back from a liche?"

She shrugged, looking like she'd rather be anywhere than here. "I don't know. I had no clue that Varia had been tracking Lazerous, or that he was over here now. I tried to forget about him. Sometimes, it's better to leave the past in the past."

"But if you can, don't you want to try?" I could understand her not wanting to face him, but surely she had to try if the chance was there?

Talia let out a grumpy sigh. "I don't know. All I know is that my mother drove me out of our home when my powers were drained, and neither of my sisters did anything to find me or help me for, what…a thousand years or more? Finally I left the country and had no clue of what happened to any of them. I learned to relegate them to my past and leave any thoughts of them there. I've been who I am now for…I don't know…hundreds of years. I don't know if I want to go back to being a harpy."

Just then, Yutani stuck his head in the door. "Get back in the break room, all of you. Now." It wasn't a request.

We hurried behind him to find that Herne had the local news site running. A live feed was coming through. Varia was nowhere to be seen.

"What's wrong?" I asked, but Herne motioned for me to be quiet.

"In a case that has apparently gone unremarked on by police, the Q-14 News Team has uncovered threats of a serial killer preying on children in Seattle. According to our source, the Angel of Mercy has abducted and killed three young girls so far, and a fourth is missing. The children—all girls around two to three years old—have gone missing on the twenty-second of each month since July and their bodies have been found about ten days to two weeks later. In talking to Timothy Wochosky, the father of one of the missing girls, we learned that the Wild Hunt Agency is on the case, since the police have been unable to locate the killer—"

"Crap! What the hell did you tell him this morning?" Herne turned to me. "*We do not need this*. If the killer thinks that we're on to her, then she may dispose of Eleanor in order to skip town."

I crossed my arms, glaring back at him. "I told him nothing more than we were looking into the case. I was afraid of this, though, given his demeanor. He and his wife are at each other's throats. He's riddled with guilt because he fucked the killer."

Talia did a spit-take with her tea. As she wiped her mouth and the table with a napkin, she said, "What did you say?"

"I said, Tim Wochosky is nursing one hell of a bruised ego. He's a reluctant member of AlkaNon, and he blames his wife for making him go. He thinks he can handle the booze, but he can't. He fucked little Miss Angel of Mercy, as the newscaster dubbed her, and while I didn't outright tell him that she's the killer, he's smart enough to put two and two together. I'm pretty sure this gives him the ammunition to blame his wife for his daughter's death, because his wife pushed him to join the group, and that's where he met Nadine. Or whatever her name of the month is."

"And he slept with her?" Herne asked.

I nodded. "Yeah, he did. I don't know if his wife knows about that part." I shook my head. "He was a powder keg set to go off, and I guess my visit just lit the fuse."

"Okay, let's go on the assumption that the killer has

seen the newscast. I don't think we can safely assume anything else. What's she going to do?"

"Did they mention anything about the connection to the AlkaNon groups?" I scrolled down on the news site, looking for a written transcript of the story. As I skimmed through it, I was relieved to see that they hadn't mentioned the connections to AlkaNon. That would be the last thing we needed.

"Talia, contact the station and ask them to please coordinate with us before releasing any further information on the case." Herne turned to me. "I'm sorry I yelled. I wasn't expecting that surprise and it threw me for a loop. We need to go visit Menhir Ryma's wife now. But we can talk about ways to mitigate the damage that report may have done on the way."

"What do you want us to do?" Viktor asked.

"I want you to talk to Erica. See if you can find out who leaked the report to the news. It was likely Wochosky, but there may be someone on the force with a grudge. Yutani, start a search for this Nadine person. Look through old cases of missing children, especially if they vanished on the twenty-second of the month. If any of them were little girls, especially blondes, we need to know. And if any of them had a mother whose first name begins with an 'N-A,' we want to know."

He glanced at Talia. "I'm sorry, but I asked your sister to contact you later. We don't have time to deal with her right now."

"That's fine with me," Talia said. "I'm not prepared to answer her, anyway." Her phone rang and she glanced at it, then let it go to voice mail. "And *right* on cue. One thing about my sisters, they're stubborn as hell and they have no tact."

"Well, tact or not, tell her to talk to you on your own time." Herne motioned to me. "Let's get moving."

I grabbed the lightweight jean jacket I had worn, since my leather jacket had yet to be replaced. "I'm ready. I'll get my purse."

"Meet me by the elevator." He bundled together a couple case files and headed toward the front.

I turned to Talia. "You going to be okay?"

"Yeah, I'm just a little shaken. But at least this buys me some time to process everything." She let out a long breath and headed back to her office, Yutani right behind her.

I waved at Angel and Viktor, then headed toward the elevator where Herne was waiting. He took my purse from me, slung it over his shoulder, and then we were off, down the elevator, through the lobby, and into the parking garage.

"How do you want to handle this?" I asked in the car. "I've talked to victims' families before, but never to someone this close to grief and so hard hit by it."

"First, never assume. His wife may be a rock. Hopefully, she'll be able to do more than just cry." Herne sounded more brusque than usual. I knew that Varia's visit had shaken him as well, given how close he was to Talia.

"Aren't you being a little harsh?" I asked. "The woman just found out her husband blew up a credit union, a gym, and an apartment building, killing a couple dozen people and injuring far more. I'm thinking we'll be lucky if she's even up to crying."

He sighed, his hands on the steering wheel, then turned to me. "I know I sound like an ass. I'm sorry. The news report rattled me, as did Varia's appearance. She's up to no good. None of Talia's family has given a damn about her since she lost her powers. I don't trust Varia. And Cernunnos is pressuring me about the Tuathan Brotherhood. Apparently Saílle and Névé are pressuring my mother as well. On top of this, we've got a little girl who's missing and I feel we can't give adequate attention to her case, but the cops aren't going to be prioritizing it right now, either. We need extra legs, you know?"

"Why not call in help? Is there anybody you can ask to come in? I'd say Kipa, but Cernunnos has him on the road already."

Herne shrugged. "Kipa would be a help. I'll talk to Mother. Anybody else you can think of?"

"What about asking Raven if she can contact the little girls' spirits? She's a bone witch. She might be able to get some information." I wasn't sure if Raven could conjure up anything, but it was worth a try.

"It's an idea, though I'm rather hesitant to disturb the spirits of dead children. I suppose we could put you undercover in a few AlkaNon groups—attend a couple different meetings a day until you catch sight of our kidnapper and then follow her home from there." Herne started the ignition and eased out of the parking garage.

"That's not a bad idea, but my guess is that once she has a child, she lies low until she needs to go hunting again. I pray I'm wrong, but I doubt if she'll surface again until she kills. Plus, I'm not a shifter and she only targets shifters."

I stared out the window. The clouds were banking up and it looked like we were due for a nasty storm. I could feel it building inside me as well, and I knew that I was responding not only to the weather, but to the approaching ritual.

"I wonder…" I paused.

"What?"

I shook my head. "Nothing. I was just thinking about my Autumn Stalker—the Autumn Bane side blood. That part of me understands the hunt—and hunters. And Nadine or whatever her name is, well, she's a hunter. She stalks her prey. She knows how to catch them."

"How would you start?" Herne asked, casting a glance my way.

"I think in order to train the powers, maybe I need to talk to someone who understands my nature. My grandfather and father are dead, and my grandmother is dead as well. So I suppose, I need to find someone in the Dark Court. Maybe a relative. Possibly I can ask Marilee to guide me on a personal journey again."

Or maybe, I thought, I could do it myself. Marilee was focused on getting me ready for the Cruharach. She might not be willing to take me on the journey I was thinking of.

"I'm not sure you should do this before the Cruharach." Herne paused, then added, "It could be dangerous, you know."

"Life's dangerous." I jumped as a bolt of lightning split the sky and thunder rumbled shortly after. Another flash, and the clouds burst, sending a hail of tiny ice pebbles down to skitter across the road. Herne slowed down—hail like this made the pavement all too slick.

"We're almost there," Herne said, nodding toward an apartment building ahead of us. "He and his family live in the Mulden Apartment Towers. I wonder what they'll do now. They're going to be facing a nasty backlash from all of the victims' families."

"What court was he from?"

"They're Dark Fae."

"Then, perhaps Saílle can help his family relocate. Get them out of the area so they aren't targeted by vigilantes. Two little kids. Geez, what the hell is their mother going to tell them about their father when they grow up?" I was grateful to see a parking space only a few steps away from the front door of the building.

"I don't know," Herne said softly. "Maybe I can get Mother to suggest it—Saílle might take the advice better from a goddess." He shook his head. "I'm not ready for this, but let's go."

As we stepped into the maelstrom of the storm, I gazed up at the lightning playing across the sky. It matched my mood, and I could feel my blood quicken and pulse in response to it.

Alina—Menhir Ryma's wife—was petite. As she opened the door, she gave us a look like she had fallen down a deep hole and was unable to climb out. She let us in without a word. Two children were eating a snack at a low table, while a puppy laid his head on his paws, staring at them, hoping to win a bite of the sandwiches that smelled so good.

"Sit down, please." Alina was quiet, but the resilience in her stance surprised me. Though her face was ravaged with sorrow, she was managing to hold herself together. "I'll just take the children into the bedroom, and then be right back. There's tea in the kitchen, if you'd like some."

She gathered the children and their snacks, and led them through one of the doors that led out of the living room. The puppy followed. I watched as the door closed behind her.

"Either she's in shock, or she's holding herself together because of the kids," I whispered.

"Or she's got a stronger constitution than we expected," Herne whispered back.

Alina reappeared, settling herself in a rocking chair that was kitty-corner to my chair. "Whatever I can help you with, I will." She shook her head. "I just…"

"Thank you," I said. "We'll try to be out of your hair as soon as we can."

"Alina, did you notice anything odd about your husband lately?" Herne asked.

"Yes, actually. Once he joined the Tuathan Brotherhood, he changed. He grew sullen and withdrawn. I thought it was strange for him to act like that, given the Brotherhood was supposed to be such a philanthropic organization." She was holding her purse, and now she rummaged through it, bringing out a note. "He left this for me. I assume he wrote it yesterday before he… I thought he was going to work."

She handed the note to Herne. He opened it, and I looked over his shoulder.

> *Alina, do what you need to for the children. Never let them forget me, or the great deed I have done today to free them from the tyranny of mediocrity. I want you to contact the name on this note and he'll help you with everything you need. Be proud of me. I fought for our freedom, and to preserve our heritage. —Menhir*
>
> Contact Sebastian at 206-555-8883

I glanced up at her. "Did you show the police this?"

She shook her head. "I just found it."

"Have you called the number yet?" Herne asked.

Again Alina shook her head. She seemed to be going through the motions, but I couldn't feel any spark coming from her.

"No. I don't know who it is, and if he belongs to this Tuathan Brotherhood, he can fucking die. My husband... How can Menhir have truly thought he was doing something wonderful? He murdered two dozen people in cold blood." She paused, glancing at me. I was all too aware of the bruises covering my body. "Were you..."

I nodded. "Yes, I was caught in the blast. I was outside at the time, so I managed to escape with a back full of broken glass and some bruises." I spoke softly, not wanting to add to the guilt that I could see churning in her eyes.

She let out a soft cry. "So many dead. So many hurt. And my husband was responsible."

"Do you know when he joined the Tuathan Brotherhood?" Herne asked.

She heaved a sigh, then nodded. "About two months

ago, he went on a retreat that he saw advertised. It was for men who wanted to make a difference in their community. He convinced me that it was a personal journey he needed to make. He liked his job but it didn't offer a lot of variety or personal enrichment. And Menhir wanted to help. He saw so much pain day after day, and he wanted to do something to give back."

"What did he do, if I may ask?" I caught her gaze, holding it gently.

"He managed a local grocery store—a specialty market. He saw people come through daily who needed special foods but couldn't afford them. Sometimes his paycheck was barely enough for us to pay our rent, because he gave out free food at work and absorbed the cost through his own account. I tried to convince him that his children should come first, but he would just say that we were among the lucky ones and to quit complaining."

Herne rubbed his chin. "Do you know how he felt about humans and shifters?"

That struck a chord. Alina ducked her head. "Well, the majority of the time we've been together he certainly didn't count them as a problem. We have several good friends from both heritages, but they haven't come over lately because he broke contact with them. I haven't been able to invite them over for the past couple months. He grew increasingly obnoxious about anyone other than of Fae blood. I kept asking him where the hell he copped the attitude from, but he wouldn't answer. He just told me to mind my place and raise the kids to be true Fae."

"*True Fae?*" I asked.

She shrugged. "I have no clue what he meant by that,

and I didn't ask because anytime I asked for clarification, all I got was a dressing down or an argument."

Herne glanced over at the desk in the corner. "Is that his computer?"

"Well, it's the family computer, yes."

"Did your husband have an email account?"

Alina nodded. "Yes, he did. Why? Do you need to see it? I found his password one day, but I never used it." She paused. "I thought he might be having an affair, but then decided to trust him." She motioned for us to follow her and led us over to the desk, where she sat down and brought up their email program. Within a few seconds, she had tapped in the password and then sat back. "There, that should take you into his email."

Herne motioned to me. "Can you skim through?"

I took Alina's place, and while she was giving Herne information on Menhir's friends, I started poking around in his email. Finally, I found something in the deleted mail program. Like most people, he didn't empty it often enough.

"Herne, I found something." I glanced through the letter. It was a welcome letter to the Tuathan Brotherhood, and it requested Menhir's presence at the next weeklong gathering to meet the others. I glanced at the date it had been sent, and it tallied up with the week that Jasper had gone in for training. The letter promised that they would text him the address, after he signed the enclosed NDA.

"Did he go on the retreat?" I asked.

Alina nodded. "He convinced me that it was something he really wanted, so I agreed. He wouldn't tell me where it was, just said he'd be available via his phone. I noticed something odd, though. I checked the Friend Finder app—we have it enabled on our phones—while he was gone and it wouldn't go through. He had to have disabled it."

"Or someone disabled it for him," I muttered. "When he returned, did you notice a change in his behavior?"

"Definitely. Before he left, he was a good-hearted, if misguided, man. He came back snippy and terse. We started arguing a lot. But I was busy with the children and he began staying later and later at work. I thought maybe he was having an affair at that point, but frankly, I was too pissed to check on him. So I ignored it. Then yesterday, he left early, before either I or the children woke up. And he left that note, apparently." Her face crumbled and she stared at the ground.

"It's not your fault, you know," Herne said.

She glanced up at him. "I know that. But nobody will believe me. Do you know what my children's lives are going to be like? They'll always be the children of *that fanatical bomber*."

Her despair permeated the room. I was seriously worried for her. "Do you have family who can take you in for a while?"

"His family will expel his memory, and me and the children along with it. My family won't want to be associated with the act. I don't know what to do." She reached out, her hand landing on Herne's arm. "Can you help us?"

Herne stared at her for a moment, then glanced at me. "Stay here. I need to make a phone call." To Alina, he said, "I'll be right back."

He ducked out the front door, and I could hear him arguing with someone outside. Reporters, no doubt. I turned to Alina.

"Is there anything I can do for you? Make some tea or something?"

She shook her head, tears streaking down her cheeks. It was as if the realization of how much trouble she was in had finally hit.

"I don't know. Taking care of the children is hard enough. I don't know what to do now."

I took her hand, moving over to sit beside her, and we sat there in silence until Herne returned, a faint smile on his face.

"My mother will escort you to Annwn, if you would like to move there. She can help you find a new home over there, and a position, where you and your children won't be known. If you're interested, then pack your bags and she'll send an escort tonight."

Alina looked frightened. Uprooting her entire life wouldn't be easy, but she didn't have much choice. She was right—people would always judge her by her husband's actions, and her children would grow up under a shadow. They were still young enough that they could make a change easily enough. But she would have to give up everything that was normal to her.

She thought for a moment, then let go of my hand and straightened her shoulders, wiping away the tears. "I have to be strong for my children. Yes, thank you. Who will be coming?"

"Her name is Ylanda, and she'll be here at eight o'clock tonight. Take only what you need. You won't need money, or furniture. My mother will get you started. Take family mementos, clothes, jewelry, your children's favorite toys." Herne stood. "I'll let Morgana know you've agreed. Be ready."

As we left, Alina whispered a "Thank you" that I barely heard as the door shut behind us.

"She's got a hard road ahead," I said as we headed back to the car. A handful of reporters swarmed us, but with one look from Herne, they backed off. Apparently, god-glamour worked wonders.

"It would be harder here," Herne said. "Can you imagine growing up under those conditions? I know people do, but she seemed so lost that I thought I'd intervene. I was afraid she might do something reckless, and the children deserve better than that."

"I had the same thought. Thank you for caring," I said, leaning my head against his arm for a moment. As we drove back to the office, it occurred to me that sometimes the gods were more humane than the rest of humanity. Not always…but sometimes.

When we reached the office, Angel had some news for us.

"The tox screen came back on Jasper. He was carrying a buttload of Ropynalahol in his system. Enough to drug an elephant. Apparently, it had been building up for some time, so he must have been taking it every day. If he had taken one dose to bring his levels to what they were, it would have killed him." She handed Herne the printout.

He glanced over it. "Ropy, all right."

Ropynalahol was a behavioral drug that was highly illegal to possess other than for medical uses, and it was used to alter behavior and mood. In high-enough doses, it could effectively make someone prone to follow suggested actions, and it also tended to stoke aggressiveness.

"Isn't that commonly known as 'brain-drain' on the streets?" Viktor asked, joining us at Angel's desk.

"Yep. Brain-drain, the 'zombie-pill,' and several other nicknames." I had learned all about it by watching *Criminal Case Files* on TV. "It's hard to get hold of, has an especially powerful hold on the Fae, and can totally reprogram your personality. If someone were medicated with the drug, and was then subjected to reprogramming, they could effectively become a different person. Or at least, a different personality."

"How long do the effects hold?" Herne asked, scanning the page.

"Until the drug is withdrawn. Which means, if Jasper was taking it every day, it had to have either been voluntarily, or he was being doped. Was there any sign of medications at his apartment?" I asked.

"Already on it," Yutani said. He had wandered up as we had been talking. He disappeared again into his office.

"So any news we should know about?" Herne asked as we waited, turning pointedly to Talia.

She blinked, then shrugged. "Don't worry, I'm not about to run off and try to kill Lazerous to get my powers back. At least not right now. I called my sister and told her she has to back off for now. That I can't even think about this until our cases have died down a little. She was impatient and irritable and gave me Lazerous's address, then took off. She said when I came to my senses, to contact her again and she'd come help."

"Impatient much?" I asked.

"That's the harpy's nature. I've learned to curb it, but

she hasn't and so far, she hasn't found a good reason to be patient. As I said, I have to think long and hard before I even consider attempting what she suggested. There's a lot to lose, as well as a lot to gain."

A moment later Yutani returned. "I got in touch with Jasper's doctor. He was never prescribed Ropynalahol. His fiancée has no memory of him taking any sort of prescription medication. But a bottle of the pills was found among his personal possessions, according to the police. I found the picture—everything is documented with pictures now, it seems." He turned his tablet around so we could see.

"Can you enlarge the photo to see who prescribed them? It should be on the bottle," Angel said, leaning in to look closer.

Yutani fiddled with it for a moment, then broke into a wide smile. "Got it. Take a look."

We leaned in again. There on the bottle was the name "Dr. Nalcops" and part of a phone number. The bottle was turned so that we couldn't see it all, so we had the area code and the first four digits, which were 555-8.

"Angel—" I started to say, but she held up one hand.

"On it." She was searching through one of the many databases that the Wild Hunt had accumulated over the years. "Dr. Nalcops. 360-555-8553. He's over on the peninsula."

"Bainbridge Island?" I asked.

"No, somewhere near Bremerton. In Port Gamble."

"Crap," Yutani said. "I hate that place. It's haunted as hell."

I stared at him. "Haunted?"

"The entire peninsula is. It's creepy as hell over there."

He shrugged. "You think it will do any good to call this dude?"

Herne thought for a moment, then shook his head. "I think we'll overplay our hand if we do. We don't want them to know we're onto this. Not yet, not until we know more of what we're dealing with. Meanwhile, I'll call Alina and ask her if she can check on Menhir's medications. If he had those in his possession too, we can assume we're dealing with unasked-for conversions." He vanished inside his office.

I turned to Yutani. "Did you ever run the files on little girls who were taken from their parents or who went missing?"

He nodded. "Let's take this in the break room so that I don't have to drag all my toys out here to the reception desk." He headed back to his office.

Angel glanced at me. "Should I lock the elevator and join you?"

"Sure. We aren't expecting anybody else tonight. If Herne wants it unlocked, he'll tell you." I picked up my purse and followed Yutani.

Herne appeared a couple moments later. "Bingo and confirmation. Alina found a bottle of Ropynalahol in Menhir's dresser. It was a third full, and the label stated that it contained ninety tablets, and to take one a day."

"Let me guess. Dr. Nalcops?" I was jotting down everything he said.

"On point. And here's the phone number." He texted it to me, and I added it to my notes.

"We found out Nalcops practices on the peninsula in Port Gamble," I said.

"Lovely. Just what we need." Herne's smile vanished. "I

don't go over there if I can help it. The land is beautiful, but it's haunted by dark secrets and even darker creatures. A number of the Ante-Fae live over there, too."

"Maybe Raven can help us there, if we need." I caught his gaze, hoping that he wouldn't squelch the idea. But he seemed all for it.

"That's a good idea," he said. "We need as much information as we can get."

Yutani came in at that point. "Okay, I have a little girl who went missing that fit the profile. Rhiannon Shields. But this was ten years ago. Rhiannon showed up dead a week later. She died from a crackalaine overdose. Her mother, Natasha Shields, was accused but the prosecutor couldn't prove that she did anything to harm the little girl other than neglect. She was imprisoned for neglect and spent the next ten years locked away, where she went into rehab and joined the AlkaNon program behind bars. She was released six months ago, and returned to her mother's house in early July."

"That's right before Cassie Longtooth vanished." I frowned. "This *has* to be her—what's her description?"

"I can do you one better. Here's her mug shot." He brought up another window. The woman in the photograph had that lean shifter look, and she was barely five-four. She was also petite, and a bleach-bottle blonde.

"Can you save that image and email it to Dana Longtooth, Samantha Trifor, and Amanda Skellig? Ask them if that's who they talked to in the meetings. Don't bother with Tim. He's caused enough trouble already."

I turned to the others. "If she's staying with her mother, then we have an address. Even if she's not, we have somewhere to start. And a name, which helps a lot."

"Her mother, Jenna Shields, lives in the Briarcliff District, on Perkins Lane West." Yutani texted us the name and address. "Finally, a break in at least one of our cases."

Herne glanced at the clock. "It's almost five-thirty. Should we shelve this till tomorrow?" He didn't sound like he wanted a "Yes" from any of us.

"The sooner we talk to her, the sooner we can hunt down her daughter," I said. "I vote for heading over there now. Should we call in advance?"

"If we do and Natasha's there, then we'll chance losing her. I say we just drop in on them." Herne grabbed his jacket. "Who's with me?"

I raised my hand, and Viktor. Yutani volunteered to stay at the office in case we needed him to look up anything. Talia and Angel decided to go home. Talia was trying to sort out the crap with her sister, and Angel was looking worn.

Herne, Viktor, and I headed out to our cars. We'd meet up there, in case we needed more than one vehicle. I glanced up at the darkening sky as the rain pounded down around me. For once, it felt like we'd been given a gift. I just hoped we were in time to rescue Eleanor before Natasha heard the news reports.

CHAPTER ELEVEN

The drive up to the Briarcliff District through rush-hour traffic was *ever so delightful*, I thought. Right up there with getting teeth drilled and having somebody pound on you with a sledgehammer. Though maybe not so much the latter, given the way my bruises still ached from the bomber. I followed Herne, and Viktor was right behind me. As the rain drove down, flooding the gutters, I turned my windshield wipers up to high.

But the thought that we might be able to find Eleanor raised my spirits. If we could find her and return her to Amanda, it would make the whole miserable week worth it.

Finally, we were on Magnolia Boulevard, and then came to the turnoff onto West Raye Street. From there, we swung a circular path down to Perkins Lane and eased into the driveway of the waterfront property belonging to Jenna Shields. It was a small house, but expensive-looking, built onto the side of the hill. One of the problems with waterfront property in the Seattle area was the frequency with which houses tumbled down the hills, thanks to the frequent mudslides. An older BMW sat in the driveway, and the lights were on in the house, so somebody was home.

"Did Yutani say if there was a father in the picture?" I asked after we parked on the side of the street and gathered by the driveway.

"I don't think he mentioned it," Herne said. "Call him before we go in."

When Yutani picked up, I asked, "Hey, before we go in, is there a father in the picture? Natasha's father? And what about the father of her baby? Of Rhiannon?"

"Give me ten seconds and... Let's see here." Yutani paused, then said, "Jenna Shields is a widow. Her husband died while Natasha was in jail. They're wolf shifters, and he ran a shipping business. It looks like he ended up in a major argument with one of his workers."

"He was killed?"

"No, that night after he went home, he had a heart attack. He had high blood pressure, and had already had two bypass surgeries. He refused to retire or take care of his health and the stress of the argument got to him, it seems. He died in the ambulance on the way to the hospital."

"And Jenna hasn't remarried?" Wolf shifters usually did at some point, when they were widowed.

"Nope. She's taken over the company and apparently she's making a success of it."

"What about the father of Natasha's child?" It seemed he would have had something to say about the death of his little girl.

"Never hit the radar. Natasha got pregnant after she left home and ended up on the streets. She didn't list the father on the birth certificate, and no one ever seems to have come forward." Yutani cleared his throat. "Natasha scored extremely high on her college board exams, but it looks like she began to slide around then. Before she graduated from high school, she was already on the road to junkie-ville."

"Okay, thanks. That gives us some idea. You can't tell if Mom has a boyfriend, do you?"

"Does not look like it."

I thanked him and pocketed my phone. "This is most likely Jenna's car. No husband—he died. No boyfriend that Yutani can find mention of. Natasha never listed the father of her child on the birth certificate, so it's unlikely he's in the picture."

"Let's go." Herne took the lead. We wound down the driveway toward the house, bracing ourselves against the steady rain. Beyond the tidy cottage, we could see the waves of the sound crashing against the beach below, the wind tossing foam high into the air. There was probably a trail down, but it couldn't be seen from where we were standing, and by the very nature of these houses, it was mostly steep. While the views were gorgeous here, the access to the water wasn't necessarily guaranteed or—if it existed—easy to navigate.

Herne rang the bell and a moment later, a young woman wearing a black dress and a white apron answered the door.

"May I help you?"

"Is Ms. Shields at home? We need to talk to her." Herne showed the girl his badge.

"Please wait here. I'll be right back." She closed the door again and we heard a soft click as she locked it.

I huddled under the eaves. "I hope she makes up her mind soon. What do we do if she won't talk to us?"

"We'll cross that bridge when we get to it. We can always bring a cop back with us."

But the girl returned and ushered us in. The foyer was filled with potted plants, and the floor was a gray-veined marble. The walls were a muted gray, and all in all, it looked like an expensive place.

"Ms. Shields is in the living room. Please allow me to take your coats." She stood firm and I understood. We'd be dripping water on her floors if we wore our jackets into the living room.

I shrugged out of mine and handed it to her, and Herne and Viktor did the same. The maid hung them in a coat closet, then led us through the foyer into the living room, where a massive bay window overlooked the sound. A door led out to a railed balcony, and from here, the storm was putting on quite a show.

Jenna Shields didn't look middle-aged—shifters wore their ages well—but she had that timeless quality that truly elegant women possess. She looked neither old nor young, dressed in a linen dress caught at the waist by a leather belt, and an infinity scarf was looped around her neck. It was, I wagered, a form of cashmere. Her hair was caught back in a chignon, and was blond streaked with a few strands of gray.

She held out her hand, a gracious smile on her face. "How do you do? I'm Jenna Shields. Won't you sit down? Amy, bring us some coffee, please." In one smooth motion, she greeted us and then returned to her seat.

"Ms. Shields, I'm Herne, and I'm with the Wild Hunt Agency. We're investigating the disappearance of a little girl." Herne motioned to me. "These are my associates, Ember Kearney and Viktor Krason."

"A missing child? And you think I can help?" Jenna looked puzzled.

"Ms. Shields, where is your daughter?" Herne asked.

"My daughter?" The blood seemed to drain out of her cheeks. "I don't know."

"Were you aware that she was released from prison a few months ago?" I asked. There was almost no chance that Jenna couldn't be aware, but I wanted to listen to her answer, to get an idea of her feelings about Natasha.

Jenna sighed. "Yes, I know. She came back here after she was released, but then she insisted on moving on. I told her she didn't have to. She could stay with me for as long as it took to get on her feet. The last thing I wanted was for her to feel like she had no place to go." She paused, then said, "If you know my daughter was in jail, then you know why she was there. She's clean now, she's off the drugs and the booze. At least prison seemed to give her that much of a leg up on coping with her life."

"When did she leave?" Herne asked.

She frowned, thinking. After a moment, she said, "Natasha came home on the second of July. She left on the ninth. I begged her to give herself more time. I was going to give her a job in the company—I own a shipping business. But she refused. I promised her that she could start fresh, but she wouldn't listen." Jenna's lips scrunched up in that way lips do when you're trying not to cry. She folded her hands across her stomach, staring at the coffee table.

"We need you to tell us about Rhiannon," I said. "We need to know what happened."

Jenna shivered as another bolt of lightning flashed outside the window. "You think she has something to do with that missing girl, don't you? I heard the news reports."

Herne glanced at me, then nodded. "I'm sorry, but yes. And it's not just this little girl who's missing. There have been three murders over the past few months—three little girls, all blond and blue-eyed, all between two to three years old."

"No!" Jenna covered her hand with her mouth, letting out a soft cry. "Why would you think Natasha is involved?"

"Ma'am, did your daughter attend AlkaNon meetings while she stayed here?" Viktor asked.

Jenna nodded. "Yes, she did. Every night she could manage."

"Her little girl was blond and blue-eyed, wasn't she?"

Again, the nod. "Yes. Rhiannon died on May 22, eleven years ago." She suddenly folded, slumping like a deflated balloon. "My daughter wasn't arrested for murder. They couldn't prove that she gave my grandbaby the crack-alaine. But…I don't know who else could have. Maybe one of her junkie friends. Maybe she did it. We'll never know. And now you think she's hurting other children? Why would she do that?"

"Sometimes, something can act as a trigger. Can we see the room Natasha stayed in while she was here in July? Did she leave anything around—a diary or anything that might tell us anything?" I knew I was grasping at straws, but it seemed worth a shot.

Jenna led us toward the back of the cottage, stopping in front of a door. "I kept her room the same, so when she was released she'd have something familiar to come home to." She opened the door and stepped aside.

As we entered the room, I was hit by the overwhelming color of pink and purple. The room looked like it had been decked out for a teenager, and it probably had been. Jenna probably hadn't changed a thing since Natasha went to prison. The bed had a purple comforter on it, and there was a white desk in the corner. On the desk were several dolls and stuffed animals.

"Were those hers?" Viktor asked.

"No," Jenna said. "Those were Rhiannon's. I thought she might want them, so I kept them, along with a couple of the dresses that I bought my granddaughter. I'm surprised she didn't take them with her."

I walked over to the stuffed animals and picked one up. "These were Rhiannon's, you say?"

"Yes." There was something she wasn't telling us. I could feel it hanging between us.

"That may have been the trigger—seeing her daughter's toys. Did Natasha ever talk about her?" I glanced over at Jenna, holding her gaze.

After a moment, Jenna sank down on the bed, clutching a white unicorn plushy to her. "Yes, she did. But she seemed to think that Rhiannon was still alive. She kept talking about the 'kidnapper' who took her away and how she was going to find Rhiannon once she had a home of her own."

"And this didn't strike you as odd?" Herne asked, scowling.

"I... I was just happy to have her home. I didn't want to

stress her out, so I just ignored it. I never thought...is that what she's doing?" Jenna asked, jumping to her feet. "Is she trying to find Rhiannon?"

"How much do you think she remembers from around the time of Rhiannon's death?" I asked. Jenna's guess was probably on the mark, but anything we could find out to back up the guess might help us.

"Probably not much. She was so strung out. I tried to drop by every day because I knew how dangerous it was for my granddaughter. She was a type 1 diabetic from birth and needed insulin on a daily basis. I had tried to win custody of her but the courts insisted she needed her mother. They didn't do a home visit, didn't check on Natasha's drug use. They waved away our worries like we were just interfering grandparents."

"What about when Rhiannon vanished?" I asked.

"We were all frantic, but Natasha couldn't even remember where Rhiannon was. She said she had given Rhiannon her medicine. We searched and searched, and then a couple days later, my husband went down to the lake by our lake house, and he found Rhiannon by the shore, dead. She hadn't been given her insulin, but an overdose of crackalaine."

"But your daughter wasn't charged with murder?"

Jenna shook her head, wiping her eyes. "My husband and I were sure that Jenna did it, but there was no actual proof. Natasha blamed her boyfriend, but he had disappeared a week before. The case went cold. The only way to get my daughter into rehab would be to get her locked up. So my husband and I pressed the courts and they finally charged my daughter with child neglect. She spent ten years in prison. I thought when she came out that things would be different. She's been clean for years, and I thought she could make a new start."

"Except she wasn't all right. And you had to know it. Even in the short time she stayed here, you had to know." Herne opened the drawers of the desk, glancing through them. "Was this Rhiannon?" He held up a worn picture of a little girl in a straw hat.

"Yes," she said and nodded. "That was my granddaughter."

"Natasha must be trying to find her daughter. She must truly believe that somebody out there has Rhiannon, and she's stealing her back. But then, the little girl doesn't act like her daughter or call her 'Mommy,' and so she kills them, like she did Rhiannon, and goes after another." I shuddered, the thought churning my stomach.

Herne turned back to Jenna, his voice imperious. "Where could your daughter be now? We need your help. Three little girls are dead and another is in danger because of her. Natasha doesn't have a handle on reality right now. We have to find her before she kills Eleanor, the little girl she most recently abducted."

Jenna frowned. "I don't know."

"Where is this lake you were talking about? Do you still have a house there?" Viktor asked.

"Lake Ballinger. And yes, I do have the house. I haven't been there since May, though. I've been too busy." She raised her head. "Do you think that my daughter's there?"

"We'll find out. Can you give us a key? And what kind of car does Natasha have?" Herne stood.

"Yes. Wait just a moment." She crossed to a side table where her purse was. Taking a key off of a key chain, she handed it over to him. "The address is 23750 74th Avenue

West." She paused. "I gave her my late husband's Lexus. If she *is* hurting those children…"

"Three girls are dead. We're trying to prevent the death of a fourth child now. If your daughter is responsible, we'll do whatever we can to stop her," Herne said.

"Whatever you have to do," Jenna said. "I don't know why I thought that I could get my daughter back." She hung her head. "I lost her when Rhiannon died. I just didn't want to believe…"

"That it was too late," I said softly. "Hope can be a wonderful thing, but it can also blind us to the facts right before our eyes."

"You'll let me know?" she asked.

"We'll let you know," Herne said, heading toward the door. We followed.

ONCE WE WERE BACK at our cars, Herne said, "Let's go. The moment it dawns on Natasha that Eleanor isn't her little girl, she's going to get rid of her and try again."

We headed out toward Highway 99, joining the flow of traffic to the north. Lake Ballinger was thirteen miles north of Seattle. While the heart of rush hour was over, the drive was still slow, and it took us forty minutes given traffic.

By the time we turned onto NE 205th Street, traffic had eased up, and we made good time to 74th Avenue, which was a two-lane street that ran along the lakeside properties. The road ran along the west side of the lake, and I watched Herne's signals. He suddenly turned onto the side of the road, and I followed.

He was out of the car and coming around the end when I parked behind him. Viktor joined us. "All right, the house is right down that drive. But we can't let her see us coming, if she's there." He glanced around. The houses were at the front of the lots, their backyards extending out toward the lake. We were parked two houses down from our goal.

"How do we approach, then? If she's at the house with Eleanor, there's no real chance to sneak up on her from the road."

"We can't go around behind the house," Viktor said. "Not without cutting through the neighbors' yards."

I frowned, trying to think. When I had been a freelance investigator, I had cut through plenty of yards and went over the top of a number of houses. But it had just been me, and I could manage it without being noticed. I was certain Herne could too, but somebody Viktor's size would have a hard time blending in.

"So we wait till it's fully dark. We don't have that long to go," I said.

"There's a good chance that a neighbor will notice us and call the cops. Even now, we kind of stand out," Herne said.

"Then let's just go. Rush the place before she has time to think or take action." I paused, then said, "Let me go in. I can always play the part of a neighbor who needs to borrow a couple of eggs." It was an old ruse, but it might work.

"Fine. Go, then. We'll be close outside. Find out what you can." Herne didn't look happy, but he knew I was right. If we tried to pull a raid, there were so many ways it could go wrong.

I jogged up to the driveway, then steeled myself and headed toward the house. It was a pretty house, two stories, with white siding and blue trim. The place had a nautical feel to it, and almost looked Cape Cod in style.

As I passed the Lexus in the driveway, I stopped to take a quick picture of the license plate. It couldn't hurt to have extra insurance in case she got away. The rain was still pouring, and I was drenched by the time I reached the door and rang the bell.

A moment later, and the curtain on the door inched back as the porch light came on. Another moment, and the door opened.

"May I help you?" Natasha asked. She looked just like the picture in her mug shot and I wondered if she had planned on dyeing her hair. Apparently, she hadn't thought about it.

"I'm your neighbor from a few houses down. I wonder if you have a couple eggs I could borrow. I'm making a cake and didn't realize I was out." I put on my best smile, and shivered. "Can you believe how much it's raining?"

Natasha stared at me a moment longer, then opened the door and invited me in. "Come on in. I'll get your eggs." She left me in the foyer and vanished. I took advantage of the moment to look around.

The house was decorated in a minimalist, breezy fashion. I craned my neck, trying to see into the nearest room. Natasha had vanished through a different door, so I edged over toward the archway and managed to peek in. I was looking into the living room.

Nothing. The TV was on, replaying some old game show, but I didn't see Eleanor anywhere. I listened, my hearing focused to pick up any faint sound I could hear.

There were several sounds of movement, but I thought they were probably from the kitchen.

Another moment, and Natasha returned, startling me. She gave me a long look.

"Here. Your eggs." She handed me a container with three eggs in it. "Is that all?" Her voice had gone from wary to frigid, and I recognized the shift in mood. If I set her off in any way, there was no telling what she might do.

"Thanks." I glanced back outside. "It's really coming down out there."

She nodded. "Yes, it is."

"I'm Ember, what's your name?" I decided to try to forge some kind of bond.

"Do you really need to know? I'm sorry, but I'm not that interested in joining the welcome wagon or whatever little group you might have going. In fact, I'm not much of a neighborly person. And I'm busy, so I'd appreciate it if you'd leave."

There was a sound from up the stairs and she glanced nervously over her shoulder. "I have to check on something. You need to leave."

I had the feeling that if she went up those steps, we'd never see Eleanor alive again.

"I don't think so. You need to come with me." I tossed the container of eggs on the floor and lunged for her, grabbing her wrist.

She was surprising strong—I had forgotten how strong shifters were—and she twisted away from me, breaking free. As she raced toward the back of the house, I punched the speed dial for Herne.

"Get down here. She knows and she's bolting. I'm

going after her. Check upstairs for Eleanor." Stuffing my phone in my jacket pocket, I dashed through the house. The door onto the back porch was open and I followed, glancing out into the night. There was no one in the yard that I could see. "Crap," I said, swinging back inside. She was still in the house. I charged for the stairs, thinking maybe she went after Eleanor, but I froze when I heard a soft click behind me.

I turned in time to see the door to the patio close. Natasha had darted out the door, which meant she probably didn't have a gun, or she would have used it on me. I was headed toward the door when Herne and Viktor raced in.

"She's gone out back. Viktor, check upstairs for Eleanor. Herne, come on." I yanked open the door in time to see a woman running toward the lake. But even from here, in the floodlights that illuminated the backyard, I could see that she wasn't alone. She was carrying something in her arms. "She has the child!"

Herne and I went sprinting across the yard, trying to gain ground on her. Herne could run faster than I could, but I wasn't far behind, though every muscle was protesting. Natasha headed for the lake. She looked over her shoulder and tossed her bundle to the side, putting on speed.

Herne sped up. "Check that!" He gestured to the bundle that she had let go of. I wanted to keep after her, but Herne was faster, and so I peeled off to the side, kneeling by the mound of blankets. There was crying from within, and I frantically untangled the layers to reveal a little girl. She was blond, about two years old, and she held her arms up to me, wailing at the top of her lungs. I caught her up in my arms just as Viktor came charging out of the house.

"Nothing but a dog up there—" he started to say, but stopped when he saw that I was holding the toddler.

"Herne's after Natasha. Here, take her inside and see if she's okay. I'll catch up to him." I thrust the girl into Viktor's arms and took off at a dead run, putting on the speed. My muscles complained but, thanks to the regular gym workouts, responded.

Natasha had run out on a pier, and Herne slowed, walking toward her with careful deliberation. I slowed too, joining him.

"Natasha, give yourself up. We can help you." Herne had his hands up, and was slowing his pace.

"No, I can't. I have to find Rhiannon. She's out there, and somebody has her. I have to find her!" She was crying, standing at the end of the pier, eyeing the water.

"Rhiannon is dead, Natasha. Don't you remember? You killed her, just like you killed those other little girls. Let us take you to someone who can help you." Herne was speaking slowly, his voice persuasive and soothing. He motioned for me to stop and I froze.

"You can't help me. No one can help me. I'm lost. I'm so lost," Natasha said, taking another step toward the water. "I didn't kill my little girl. I didn't... Somebody took her. If I don't find her, she'll never let me rest." She was babbling now, tears streaking her cheeks. "I told her I'd find her again once I was free. I can't break my promise—*I have to keep my promise*."

Herne glanced at me. "If we get any closer, she'll throw herself in the water."

"I can swim and so can you. We can't just leave her

here." I gauged the distance between Natasha and where we were standing. "I can make that in one good leap."

"But can you stop her? Can you—" He stopped as Natasha withdrew something from her pocket. It looked like a syringe.

"You have to let me go back to the house. I need to give her medicine. She's sick. She needs her medicine." She waved the syringe toward us, looking more and more frantic with each passing minute.

"Oh my gods. Maybe she *hasn't* been realizing they're not her daughter and then killing them. Maybe she thinks she's giving them insulin like Rhiannon needed, but she's really giving them crackalaine, just like she did her daughter. She's reliving her daughter's death over and over, trying to change the outcome." I stared at Natasha, simultaneously feeling sorry for her and wondering if it would be such a bad thing if she just vanished off the face of the planet.

"Please," Natasha begged, sinking to her knees. "You have to let me help her."

"Come on, then. We'll go back to the house. But you have to put the needle down." Herne stretched out his hand, waiting.

Natasha stared at it, and then a look dawned in her eyes and she shook her head. "No. No, you're going to lock me up again for trying to help my daughter." She glanced toward the lake, but instead of jumping in, she brought the needle up and stabbed it into her leg, injecting the crackalaine.

Herne and I raced toward her, but she had already slumped on the ground before we could reach her side. I felt for a pulse. There was one, thready and weak, but there.

"She's alive," I said.

Herne nodded. He caught my gaze and held up his phone, then paused, a wretched look on his face. "She's never going to get well."

"I know," I said, staring at her prone figure next to me. Her breath was slowing, and I could barely feel a pulse at all. "But you have to call the paramedics."

"I know," he said, ducking his head. He waited for another minute, then slowly made the call for the paramedics as Natasha's breath left her lungs forever.

I pushed myself to my feet, wincing. Every muscle hurt. We headed back to where Viktor was holding the child.

"How is she?" I asked, anxious. The syringe had been full and she hadn't given Eleanor the "medicine" yet from the way it had sounded.

"Asleep. I sang her a lullaby," Viktor said. "Dead?" He nodded toward the pier.

"Yeah, she OD'd." I moved to Viktor's side. "Can I hold her?" I wasn't much for kids, but the fragility of the little girl, and the realization that, had we decided to wait for tomorrow, Eleanor would probably be dead now, made me all too aware of how precious life was.

Viktor settled her in my arms and she woke up briefly. "Mama?" she whispered.

"We'll take you to your mother, Lani. We'll take you home." I kissed her forehead and rocked her gently. "I'm going to take her inside away from the rain." We were all soaked and the last thing she needed was to catch a cold.

"All right. Viktor, go with her. Direct the medics out

here."

Viktor and I headed back into the house. I slid into a kitchen chair, staring at the chaotic mess on the counters. It was just an outward symbol of the tempest that had been brewing inside Natasha. She had been in a whirlwind, caught up in a spiral that she couldn't break free from.

"I wonder…was she always messed up, or did the drugs do it?" I asked, looking over at Viktor.

"It's hard to tell. The drugs may have just set her off. She could have been primed to break down anyway. There's no way to tell. She was clean for ten years in prison, but she came out with full-blown psychosis." He pointed to Eleanor. "You ever want one of those?"

"They're so fragile, aren't they?" I shrugged. "I don't know. Definitely not now, maybe not ever. But it's too soon to tell. At least the Fae are fertile for far longer than humans, so I have a long time to decide."

The doorbell rang and Viktor moved to get it. The paramedics came trooping through.

"We've got a dead woman out back. She OD'd herself with crackalaine. And you need to check out this little girl."

"Her daughter?" one of the paramedics asked.

I shook my head. "No, but she's somebody else's daughter, and I think her mom needs to know that she's okay." I handed over Eleanor and one of the medics checked her out while the other headed out back. Herne walked him over to Natasha's body.

Viktor and I waited till the medic—his name was Jon—pronounced Eleanor fit and fine. She was hungry, but she checked out okay.

I called Angel. "Call Amanda. Tell her to get down to the Wild Hunt right away. Everybody needs to be there. We're bringing Eleanor home. Alive and well."

"Oh my gods, *you found her*? Alive?" Angel said, and I could hear her voice cracking.

"Yeah, but Natasha's dead. If we hadn't come by this evening, Eleanor probably would be too, but don't tell her mother that. We'll see you in an hour or so." I hung up, and turned just in time to see Herne coming through the door.

"The coroner will be here soon. I'll wait and talk to him. You two take Eleanor back to the agency and call her mother—"

"Already on it," I said, giving him a broad smile. "We won this one. Kind of."

"Yeah, kind of. But I doubt if Natasha would have ever pulled through, so maybe it's a good thing she didn't make it. How would you react if your head cleared and you found out that you had murdered three children? Four, including your own? Sometimes, being lost in your mind can be a blessing."

I nodded. Viktor called Erica and she said she was on her way, but for us to go ahead and take Lani to her mother. She would talk to Herne.

I poked my head into the Lexus on the way out and grabbed the car seat. Viktor helped me set it up and then we headed out, with Lani in my backseat. All the way back to the agency, all I could think about was Natasha's frantic pleas to be allowed to "medicate" her baby. That, and the fact that Lani was in my car kept me barely breathing until I made it safely back downtown.

As I carried Lani up the steps into the building, a froth

of emotions whipped inside me. Eleanor was awake now, and fussy, and by the time the elevator opened, I was looking forward to handing her over to her mother. I definitely wasn't ready for kids, that I could tell.

"Lani! Lani!" Amanda was standing at the counter, anxious, and when she turned and saw me carrying her daughter in, she burst into tears and held out her arms.

"Mama!" Lani started to cry and as I made the exchange, barely getting out of the way before being squished in a massive hug, I could smell the pheromones of relief wafting off Amanda. She was crying and laughing, and she buried her head in Eleanor's neck, kissing her again and again.

Angel guided her over to the sofa and helped her sit down while I headed toward the bathroom. By the time I came back, Angel handed me a hamburger and some fries, and a milkshake. Viktor had brought chairs out to the waiting room and we were all sitting around. Talia was talking to Amanda, and Yutani was doing something on his laptop.

"Herne should be back any time," I said.

"Who took her? Was it that woman?" Amanda asked.

"Yeah, it was. Herne will fill you in on the details," I started to say, but Yutani let out a yelp. I turned around. "What's happened now?"

He motioned for Viktor and me to join him. There, on one of the local news sites, was the headline, "COUNCILMAN WARRIS FOUND DEAD. LIGHT FAE COUNCILMAN BEATEN TO DEATH."

"Oh shit," I whispered. We may have solved one case, but we weren't out of the woods yet.

CHAPTER TWELVE

"We can't possibly deal with this tonight," Herne said when he returned to the office and found out about the councilman's death. We trooped into the break room.

"It feels like we live in this room lately," Viktor grumbled.

"I know. I asked Amanda to return tomorrow so we could settle up the case files." Herne tossed her file folder on the table. "At least we saved the day for a mother and her daughter. That's one thing we can be proud of tonight."

"I'm so tired," Angel said.

"Yeah, me too." I yawned. "I hurt, too. My body doesn't like running around right now. I feel like I could sleep for hours."

Herne smiled apologetically. "Well, the good news is that I called the cops and told them I'd be down to view the crime scene. The rest of you can go home. I'm not affected by lack of sleep as much, so off with you." He waved us toward the door. "Just be in tomorrow by nine. While we solved one problem today, we have a growing one on our hands and I'm not sure where to look next."

"By the way, Ember, you realize we missed the snowboard match?" Viktor said.

I frowned. "Great. Do you know who won?"

He shook his head. "No, but I DVR'd it. Want to come over for a watch party tomorrow night?"

I grinned. "You couldn't keep me away. Unless anything else earthshaking happens."

As we broke for the evening, I leaned down to lightly plant a kiss on Herne's lips. "I love you. See you tomorrow."

"Call me if you need me, for anything." His eyes were beautiful blue lakes, searching my face. Then he smiled and a veil of clouds over them seemed to part.

"Bye. Be good," I whispered, and then trooped toward the elevator with Angel.

I LEANED back against the sofa, yawning loudly. "I am so tired but I don't want to go to bed because that means tomorrow comes that much more quickly. I want a day off."

Angel returned from the kitchen, carrying a big bowl of parmesan popcorn and two cans of diet cola. "Here. We're not going to bed. Not until we've watched something giddy and goofy and fun." She picked up the remote and turned on the television just as a rerun of *Criminal Minds* started.

"Oh gods, no. Turn the channel. I've had enough of

serial killers to last me a long time." I scooted over as Mr. Rumblebutt bounced up on the cushion next to me. He let out a long yawn, purring at the end of it so that he sounded a little like a motorboat sputtering. He circled twice, then curled up next to me and closed his eyes. I stroked his back.

"Silly goober," Angel said, smiling at him. "I got a text from DJ today. He's apologizing all over the place for hacking into that computer. I told him that he needed to get his act together because I'm not going to bail him out of any punishment for crap like that, and neither is Cooper." She paused. "Also, Raven's birthday is coming up on the first."

"It would figure that she was born on Samhain," I said. "It's rather fitting. She having a party?"

"I don't think she was planning on it, but Rafé asked if we wanted to help him throw a surprise party on Friday night. I told him I thought we could manage." She paused, then said, "It's odd. I would think having him around would be painful, given he's a reminder of Ulstair. They looked so much alike. But I guess it gives her comfort."

Raven's fiancé had been murdered just a month ago. That's actually how we met her—when we took her on as a client to look for her missing boyfriend.

I glanced over at her, a piece of popcorn in my fingers. "You aren't jealous, by any chance, are you?"

She shrugged, then shook her head. "At first I was worried that he might go from comforting her, to…well… something more. But he talks about her like a sister so I guess he truly did mean that he would always be there as her brother."

"I don't think Raven's ready to date again, and I doubt

if she'd think of dating Rafé. You're safe on that score. But having him around must be like having a little part of Ulstair there. A reminder of the love they had. Raven's Ante-Fae. Remember, they aren't like us. They aren't like either humans or Fae." I popped the corn into my mouth and opened the cola.

Angel found a rerun of *Legally Blonde*, a movie we both loved, and we settled in to watch it. Before it was half over, we were both yawning. Finally I held up my hands.

"I give up. I'm too tired to finish this. My body hurts, I need some help medicating the cuts on my back, and I may sound old but I just want to go to bed."

Laughing, Angel turned off the TV. "I'll make sure the doors are locked. I fed Mr. Rumblebutt when I was popping the corn. You head upstairs and I'll meet you there."

As I dragged my sorry ass up the steps, once again I thanked the gods that Angel was my roommate. I seriously had my doubts if I'd ever be able to live with anybody else, and not end up wanting to kill them.

MORNING CAME TOO EARLY, even though Herne had given us permission to come in an hour later. We decided to drive in together. Angel didn't bother with cooking breakfast. Instead, she slapped together quick turkey sandwiches that we ate on the way in, and we stopped on the way for her tea and my coffee.

Herne was on the phone in his office as Yutani, Talia, and Viktor had all straggled in. We met in the break room, waiting for Herne. While we waited, Viktor cleared his throat.

"I have a personal problem and could use some female advice," he said.

Yutani snorted. "You think I can't give good advice?"

"On this, no. I think I'm better off asking the women." He set a box of pastries on the table and opened it. "I brought goodies."

"You brought *bribes*," I said, laughing as I reached for one of the chocolate glazed doughnuts with sprinkles on it.

"Can you blame me? I know how much you like your sugar and sprinkles." Viktor laughed and poured himself a mug of coffee. He poured cream in it, and two spoons of sugar.

"Speaking of sugar," Angel said, nodding at his cup.

"Yeah, yeah, I know. No stones for glass houses." The half-ogre settled down at the table, brushing his hand over his shorn head. "Okay, will you listen to my problem or not?"

"Of course we will," Talia said, picking up a maple bar. "What is it?"

Viktor sighed. "Well, here's the thing. You know Erica's my buddy on the force, right?"

"Right, she's an informant for us and a damned good one," I said.

"Well, Sheila's jealous. She's got it into her head that I'm knocking bits with Erica. I've told her time and again it's just a professional friendship, but Sheila's convinced we're doing the deed. I don't know how to convince her I'm not interested in Erica that way."

"First, truth. Are you?" Yutani asked.

Viktor tossed a rolled-up napkin at him, which Yutani deflected with a quick wave of the hand. "What did I just say?"

"Seriously. Are you and Erica doing anything you probably shouldn't be?"

"No. Erica's got a boyfriend. And…to be honest, even if she didn't, she's not my type. I'm not interested in damaging my relationship with Sheila." Viktor looked almost insulted.

"Have you used the L-word yet?" I asked.

Viktor shook his head. "No, though I've been tempted. I guess I've been afraid that she won't feel the same way."

"Dude, if she's worried you're screwing somebody else, then she obviously cares about you." I sighed. "I think you'd better talk to her about how you feel before she gets it in her head that you don't care enough to say the words. Lay it on the table."

"Agreed," Angel said. "If I was seeing someone for a while and things didn't seem to be progressing, and they hadn't told me that they loved me, I might be tempted to think they were getting some on the side. Just tell her how you really feel and go from there."

"What the girls said," Talia concurred.

Yutani laughed. "I think you have what is called a unanimous vote. Talk to your girlfriend. Clear the air. And maybe don't talk about Erica as much as you probably are. It can lead to all sorts of misunderstandings."

At that moment, Herne entered the room, carrying his tablet and a notebook. "Are we all here? Good." He paused to give me a quick kiss, then poured himself a cup of coffee and grabbed one of the glazed doughnuts from the box. "All right, everybody good to go?"

"Yes, though Viktor's mucking up his relationship," Yutani said with a grin.

"What?" Herne glanced over at Viktor, vaguely concerned.

"It's nothing. Don't worry about it. What did you find at the crime scene?" Viktor waved him off.

Herne cleared his throat, stopped to take a bite of his pastry and a long sip of coffee, then dove right in. "Councilman Warris was beaten to death by a gang of vigilantes. Apparently, Warris made the mistake of saying that he empathized with those who might be angered by some of the anti-Fae sentiments going around. He didn't *defend* the Tuathan Brotherhood or their actions, but I believe the general consensus was that he couched his comments in such a vague way that they could be misconstrued. And, apparently, the vigilantes either misunderstood him, or they were just looking for trouble."

"I hate to ask, but any idea of who did it?" Talia said.

"There were enough pheromones around—excitement level—that we know at least two different wolf shifters were involved. It's quite possible they just meant to rough him up and then mob mentality got out of hand, and *boom*." Herne sighed. "The cops are looking, but there weren't any witnesses, and the only blood at the crime scene was that of the victim's. No clear prints, either."

"So where does that leave us?" I wasn't sure what else we could do at this point.

"Nowhere, as far as the councilman is concerned. There's not much we can do about that, but we need to keep an eye out for updates." Herne shrugged. "The mayor is going to hold a press conference today to ask people to calm down, but we all know how likely that is to help."

"What have we found out about Dr. Nalcops? What do we know about him?" Angel asked. "He seems to be our primary point to enter this game."

Yutani pulled up a document. "He's from the Dark Court, originally. He was ousted by Saílle for experimenting with unsafe healing techniques that left some of his patients scarred, and worse. He's taken up private practice over in Port Gamble, and he seems to have an exclusive but small clientele from what I can see. There have been numerous complaints against him but they seem to have stopped about four months ago, and the outstanding complainants quietly settled their cases and withdrew their complaints."

"Who paid them off?" Talia asked.

"That is unknown. The documents were sealed by agreement of both parties." Yutani looked up from his screen. "Nalcops' website states he is no longer accepting new patients."

"Can you hack into his computer and see who's on his patient list?" Herne asked.

Yutani frowned, leaning forward to concentrate on whatever it was he was doing. After a moment, he shook his head. "I looked up the hosting service he's using and I've done a little digging. The front end of his site checks out. Hosted by InterStellar Hosting. But the back end? It's on the Dark Web. If I try to hack in, whoever is maintaining it will know and possibly trace it back to me. We're talking guys who rule the internet. However… here's something interesting."

I glanced at Angel. There was a weird buzzing in the room—I could feel it in the base of my neck. Angel was rubbing her head.

"Do you have a sudden headache?" I asked.

She nodded. "It just started a few minutes ago."

I turned to Yutani. "Whatever site you're on, it's sending out some pretty nasty energy. I know that sounds weird, but—"

"No, it doesn't. And you're right. Whoever is working the back end of this site is fluent in technomagic. There's an extremely strong magical energy interwoven through it. I'm not even sure if I haven't already triggered any alarms." He licked his lips, tapping another few keystrokes. "Come on, princess. Do this for me… There!" He hit a couple more keys and then closed the browser and brought up a file, opening a folder on it. "I found this little gem when I was poking around Dr. Nalcops' shadow site."

He turned the computer around and we found ourselves looking at the image of what appeared to be a poster. It was for the Tuathan Brotherhood. Under the large image of a hawk were the words, "JOIN THE TUATHAN BROTHERHOOD" in bold letters. And below that, a recruitment invitation.

JOIN THE TUATHAN BROTHERHOOD!

The Fae Courts have never before banded together, but now we must. There are numerous threats facing our joint races and culture in this modern world. We were once rulers of the countryside, and now we've been relegated to taking orders from not only shifters, humans, and vampires, but they have allowed an enemy to our people to join the ranks of government. An enemy who has already tried to strike against us, and no doubt will do so again as soon as they are afforded the chance.

Join with us, band together in arms, and be proud to work with others of our kind to bring the Fae Courts back to the strength and regality they once held.

Training will begin on December 17. To apply, visit UnderSurf and fill out one of the online enrollment forms. You must meet our guidelines or do not bother applying.

You must:

Be a Fae male, of either Court, under the age of 275.

Have a standing in your Court of at least "neutral" on the active rolls.

Be willing to join our recruitment camp for one week, and sign an NDA.

Be willing to put yourself on the line.

Strike a blow for Fae Solidarity and join the Tuathan Brotherhood today!

We stared at the poster for a moment.

"Well, they're no longer using the ruse of being a philanthropic organization. I guess that was just to get start-up members into the group." Herne shook his head. "This is bad."

"What the hell is 'UnderSurf'?" Talia asked.

Yutani shook his head. "UnderSurf is a site on the Dark Web where organizations can recruit individuals. A data collection site, and also a recruitment/sale site. It records your information and feeds it to the association in question. However, it's also used to…"

He paused, then let out a long breath. "UnderSurf is

used by human traffickers…not just human but Fae, shifter, whatever the case may be. It's a sales site where traffickers can record their 'property' for sale. In other words, UnderSurf is where the sex slavers and so forth go to list those whom they have for sale. Categories include by race, age, gender, ethnicity, hair color, build—whatever tickles the perv's fantasies."

"So it's like a warped eBay and SurveyDoll rolled into one," I said, trying to block out the mental images that were now running through my mind.

"Yeah, pretty much. There are similar sites where they sell explosives, uranium, guns and ammo, things of that nature. Also one for illicit items—endangered animals, stolen art and jewels, that sort of thing. I think the former is UnderShot, and the latter is UnderWyre. And then, there's UnderCast. It's an affiliate site where people can hire dark magicians, sorcerers, whatever they need. Sort of a magical hitman site." Yutani shrugged. "You can buy or sell just about anything online, including illegally harvested organs, blood, diseases like anthrax. Whatever you're looking for, it's out there."

My stomach turned a little. The thought of so many people willing to carry out such horrendous acts made me nauseated. Angel looked like she felt just about like I did. Nobody said anything for a few moments.

"So we have a recruitment for the Tuathan Brotherhood coming up," Herne finally said, breaking the silence. "We need to infiltrate them."

"We need a male Fae willing to go undercover," I said. "They only recruit men and they have to be fairly young, as far as the Fae go. They'll spot a shifter right away, and it's not safe to use a human—they'll be mincemeat."

"Unfortunately, you're right. And we don't have anyone here that fits our needs. I suppose I can talk to Cernunnos and Morgana to see if they can help us out." Herne shook his head. "I'd do it, but they'd know who I am."

"You're not Fae, either. Well, you've got Fae blood because of Morgana but I don't think that's going to fly." I let out a long sigh. "So, what do we do? Just wait for them? I can't help. I don't have any friends among the Fae."

Angel's voice shook as she said, "We know one of the Dark Fae who might help us."

I glanced at her, puzzled. "Who are you talking about?"

Her voice was so quiet I almost couldn't hear her. "Rafé."

I blinked. *Oh crap*, she was right. He was Dark Fae. The fact that he was her boyfriend and that suggesting him scared her spitless didn't escape my notice. I slowly turned to Herne, wanting to shake my head, to stop the suggestion before it went any further.

Herne caught my gaze. He, too, didn't look happy, but he let out a slow breath. "What do you think, Angel? Do you think he'd even consider the idea? I'm not about to push anybody into this who doesn't work for my agency. It's a dangerous proposition."

She leaned her elbows on the table, looking for all the world like she wished she had kept her mouth shut. "I don't know, to be honest. I don't like suggesting him, but if we're desperate…"

"What does he do? Is he busy right now, or can he come in to talk to us? I'm not saying we'll send him out, but we need to ask him if he'd be willing, then assess whether he's capable of handling the risk." Herne held up his hand as Talia started to speak. "Don't. Just don't. I wouldn't recruit a civilian if we weren't in deep shit. I'll go call Mother in a moment to ask if she has a better idea, but unless she's got a young man in her employ who could do the job, this may be the best way to go."

Angel cleared her throat. "Rafé's an actor and singer. He waits tables during the day so he can attend rehearsals and auditions during the evening." She glanced at the clock. "He's working right now at the Oak & Ash & Thorn—a Fae diner out in Woodinville. You want me to text him and see if he can come in after his shift? He gets off around three, because he works the breakfast rush."

"Would you?" Herne looked miserable. "I'm sorry, Angel. I'd rather not involve him in this, but unless Mother can think of something, we're up a creek."

"I know," she said dully. "Let me text him."

As she stepped out of the room, looking ready to cry, I leaned forward and hissed. "You just better make sure that he doesn't end up like Jasper or Menhir. If you break Angel's heart—"

"Hush," Herne said, frowning. "We'll do everything we can to keep him safe, if we even have to send him in. But you know as well as I do just how important this lead is. We can find out what's going on in there. And I'll ask Ferosyn to see if he can formulate something to keep the Ropynalahol from affecting him. If so, then Rafé will be able to remember everything he sees there."

"I hope you know what you're doing," I shot back at him, still not placated. Angel had made the suggestion without fully realizing the ramifications of where it might lead to, that much I was sure of, and now it was too late to back out.

Herne gave me a long look, then stood up. "I'll call Morgana." He moved to one side, as Angel returned to her seat.

"Rafé can be here around four P.M. I didn't tell him why, just that we had an important question for him." She picked up her tablet. "Do you need me anymore? I've got work to do at my desk."

Herne was on the phone. I nodded for her to go.

"Go ahead. If he complains, I'll take care of it."

As she left the room, softly shutting the door behind her, Viktor shook his head.

"I agree we need help, but this is not the way," he said. "But it's Herne's call."

Talia wasn't looking too happy, either, but she kept quiet. I turned to glance at Yutani, but he was completely immersed, studying something on his computer.

Herne returned to the table. "Where did Angel go?"

"Back to her desk, and if you're smart you'll leave her be. Rafé will be in at four to talk to us, by the way. What did your mother say?" I was hoping that Morgana would have interceded.

"She'll look through her staff, but she's mostly got women working for her right now. She'll get back to me as soon as possible. She recommended we contact Mielikki, over at Mielikki's Arrow, to see who's working on her staff right now."

"Send Kipa to ask her," Yutani said with a snort.

Herne rolled his eyes. "What a brilliant idea. Got any more, Wile E.?"

I couldn't resist a laugh at that. "Oh man, if Yutani's the coyote, who's the roadrunner?"

"Lately, everybody and their brother," Yutani said.

"I've been trying to contact the Great Coyote. If he's really my father, I want to talk to him and ask him why he's been tripping me into all the shit he has lately. And also to find out why the hell he hasn't told me that he's my father."

I wasn't sure what to say to that. It was a thorny subject, and not one that I felt comfortable teasing him about. When Yutani had discovered—quite by accident—that he was the son of the trickster god Coyote, he had come unglued for a bit and just about skipped town. But we had convinced him to come back. Whatever struggles he was dealing with had left him surly and irritable.

"I'll call Mielikki today," Herne said. "As far as Kipa is concerned, I've already called him and he's willing to work with us on this matter once he gets back, though what he can do, I'm not sure. Maybe I can have him go talk to the wolf shifter packs and calm down this vigilante crap."

"That's a good idea," Talia said. "In fact, can we hold several town meetings for both shifters and humans, asking them to please let us handle this and not take matters into their own hands? What about setting up a press conference with the news agencies?"

Herne thought over her suggestion for a moment, then nodded. "That's another good thought. You have a number of contacts in the press. How about setting up something for me? Today's Friday...make it for Monday, if you can. Or Tuesday. I think we're just going to have to accept that this isn't a problem we're going to solve in a couple of days. Once we infiltrate the Brotherhood, maybe we'll be able to stop it from there. But it's not going to be easy. I have a feeling we're facing a group of brilliant masterminds out to cause as much damage as they can."

"They're accomplishing it. They've got humans and shifters afraid of the Fae, and they've got the general Fae populace worrying about being targets of vigilante groups. Do you think that whoever is behind the group is out to start a civil war?" I hadn't thought about that before, but it seemed plausible.

"You could be right, Ember," Herne said. "All right, let's adjourn for now. We'll meet again when Rafé gets here. And regardless of what you think, Ember," he stared at me pointedly, "at this point, Rafé may be our only hope."

THE DAY PROGRESSED in a subdued manner. There was always the feeling of anticlimax after solving a case, and given we had taken care of Amanda's problem, now we only had a longer-term issue to dwell on. No doubt we'd have another case soon, but for now, it was back to paperwork and mulling over ideas.

Rafé showed up at four-ten, and we met in the break room again. Angel hung her head as Herne described what we were facing.

"I have to ask you to keep this quiet," Herne said after laying out what we were facing. "The public knows about the bombings and beatings, of course, but right now, we're trying to keep any speculation from running rampant."

Rafé nodded, his copper hair glinting under the lights. He was tall and lithe and matched Angel's body type perfectly. They made a striking couple. They were opposites and yet they complemented one another. Oddly enough, they made me think of a younger David Bowie—from his Ziggy Stardust red-haired days—and his wife, Iman. Rafé was dressed in black pants—the kind waiters often wear—and a long-sleeved, button-down white shirt.

"I'll be discreet," he said. "I can see the bind you're in. I have some questions. First, do you think I can pull this off? I'm a good actor, that's my calling. But if you're able to keep the Ropynalahol from affecting me, will you also be able to coach me in how I *should* act? And if the drug does manage to gain control over me, what guarantee do I have that I can be free of it? I'm willing to consider helping you, but not at the loss of my integrity or my life. And I won't risk losing Angel."

Herne sat back, eyeing him carefully. "I think we can do a good job of coaching you, so yes to the first question. If you're a decent actor, so much the better. Second—yes, I'm certain we can free you from the effects. There are drugs to counter the effects, and Ferosyn can administer a drug to sedate you until you're clear of the medication. However, there may be some side effects. I'll ask Ferosyn to present a clear picture of what you need to know before you make your final answer."

Rafé paused, the wheels turning in his brain. Angel was sitting next to him and she took one of his hands in hers, holding it tightly. He squeezed her hand, then leaned over to give her a kiss. Watching them together, I realized that—as much as Angel might think she was still just casually dating the man—there were some definite attachments forming between them.

Letting out a long sigh, Rafé said, "Give me a day to think it over. Have the list of potential long-term side effects waiting for me. I'm not willing to say yes, not just yet. But if I can, I'll help you. This is the best and most honest answer I can give you for now."

"I'd rather you think this over before agreeing, so I have no problem with your answer. We still have over a month before the recruitment camp begins. In that time, I'll also look into finding a professional spy to do the job, but if we can't, it would be nice to have a backup. I'll have Angel bring you a list of the side effects and potential dangers of the drug." Herne stood, shaking Rafé's hand.

"This would be the weirdest acting job I've ever had, tell you that." He paused, tugging on his collar. "This may sound mercenary, but I work a shit job to support my acting habit. I'd have to take at least a week off and…"

"We'll compensate you for your help. If you do end up helping us, I'll make sure that you are well paid." Herne smiled at him. "As for everybody else, that's it for today. Amanda settled her account, and we're closing that file. The police are in the process of notifying the other parents that their daughters' murderer has been caught. So that's all for the weekend unless something critical happens."

As Rafé and Angel headed out of the break room, followed by the others, I lingered behind. "You want to get together tonight?" I asked. I was still hurting, but I wanted to resolve the slightly scritchy energy between Herne and me. "I promised Viktor I'd go watch the snowboarding match at his place tonight, but I can reschedule."

He caught me in his arms. "Worried about arguing with me? Listen, we work together and we're bound to have a difference of opinion at times. That's the way of all relationships, love. And believe me, if I can figure out a way to keep from sending Rafé into that mess, I'll take it. I don't relish putting him in danger, especially since he and Angel are involved."

I leaned my head against his chest. "Thank you for saying that. I know this is your duty. I know that we're facing a serious problem. But…Angel is my heart, you know? She and I are soul mates. Once-in-a-lifetime friends. I won't let her be hurt, not if I can help it."

"I know. But remember, Angel's an adult," Herne whispered. "She's the one who suggested him. But I care about her too, and I don't want to see her hurt. We'll figure it out. Now kiss me."

I pressed my lips to his, warming in the glow that spread through my body. He lazily cupped my ass and I let out a little moan, though it wasn't for pleasure.

"I have cuts from the glass there, too. Sitting's bad enough, but no squeezing the goods, dude. Not till they heal." I laughed softly, even through the haze of pain. Sitting was rough enough, but getting pinched on the slashes across my backside? Not so much fun.

"I'm sorry. I think you should rest tonight. I want to go talk to Cernunnos and Morgana about all this, so I think I'll head to Annwn for the evening. You go over to Viktor's and watch the match. Then go home, make yourself a drink, play with the Rumblebutt, and eat all the junk you love to eat." He kissed me again, holding me gently as his lips crushed against mine.

As we headed toward the front of the office, he slid his arm around my waist. I was growing more comfortable with our relationship in front of the others, and they seemed to accept it as a matter of fact. I glanced up at Herne, feeling a sudden swell of joy.

"Dude, you know how much I love you, right?"

He nodded. "Yeah, I do. And ditto."

I told Angel that Viktor would give me a ride home after we finished watching the games.

As Viktor and I headed out into the growing darkness, I tried to clear my mind, but they were a jumble of bombs and killers, of my love for a godling, and for the coming Cruharach. Caught in the tempest of thoughts, I quietly stared out the window as Viktor pulled out of the parking garage.

CHAPTER THIRTEEN

When I woke up, Mr. Rumblebutt was batting my face. He leaned over, sniffed my lips, then meowed loudly.

"All right, all right, I'm up." I groaned as I pushed myself up against the headboard and grabbed his fuzzy butt, cuddling him to me. "What's the matter? Didn't Angel feed you?" I glanced at the clock. It was already nine, though outside it looked stormy as all get out. Viktor had brought me home right after the match, stopping along the way so I could buy some takeout for dinner with the money I'd won off of him. Given Angel had a date with Rafé, I opted for one of my favorite foods —a bucket of heavily breaded fried chicken. I had carried the chicken bucket up to my bed and curled up with Mr. R. to watch a movie until we both fell asleep. I squinted now, staring at my bed. I had forgotten to move the chicken, and the pieces that had been left were scattered across my comforter, with cat-sized tooth marks in them.

"Nice going, trash panda. Good job." I eased out from

under the covers and shoved all the remains of the bird into the bucket, then set it on my dresser. After that, I stripped the cover off my bed and piled it by the laundry basket in the corner. I'd be doing laundry later today, that was for sure. After making the bed fresh, I jumped in the shower, grimacing as the water beat a staccato tattoo on my back, pelting the sores. But they didn't hurt as much as they had the day before, so that was a win.

I got dressed, choosing a comfortable pair of low-riding blue jeans and a blue turtleneck sweater, hoping they wouldn't irritate my cuts. Luckily, the cuts had scabbed over enough that the material wasn't rubbing against them. I threaded a black leather belt through the loops and fastened my dagger to it. I was coming to learn the hard way that it was better to go armed than not. Pulling on a pair of pointy-toed ankle boots in black leather, I zipped up the sides. Then, after putting on my makeup, I brushed my hair out, letting it fall over my shoulders, and slid on a black headband to keep it out of my face.

As I headed downstairs, Mr. Rumblebutt on my heels, I heard Angel in the kitchen. I darted around the staircase and into the kitchen, stopping short when I saw Rafé at the table, wearing one of Angel's pink robes. He glanced up, grinning at me as I entered the room.

"Well, good morning to you, twinkletoes. You look comfortable," I said, sticking my tongue out at him. "I see you just got up."

Angel was wearing a long sleep shirt, and she was in the process of making waffles. "Morning, honeybee," she said, a wide smile on her face. Her eyes were twinkling and she looked way more relaxed than she had the day before. I had a feeling Rafé was directly responsible for that, but decided to let it drop.

But Rafé, apparently, didn't have my sensibilities. "We didn't keep you awake, did we? You were nowhere to be seen when we came in."

I coughed. "I was probably asleep. I ate in bed and fell asleep before I could even finish my chicken." I plunked the chicken bucket into the garbage. "Rumblebutt woke me up. Did you feed him yet?" I glanced at his dish. It was abundantly full. "Dude," I said, catching him up and holding him up so I was staring at him. "You lied to me. You have food."

He purped and I let him down. He promptly raced over to his dish and began to devour his breakfast. I stared at him, shaking my head, then turned to Angel.

"You have a waffle for me?"

"Sure. You sure one will do?" She snickered.

"You know when I say one, or 'a,' I mean two or three." I fired up the espresso machine and pulled four shots, then frothed some milk and added chocolate syrup, stirring it into the foam. "So what are you two up to today?"

Angel handed me a plate with two waffles on it. "I'm making more, don't worry."

I carried my plate and mug back to the table, sitting opposite Rafé. He pushed the butter and syrup across the table to me and I loaded up, drowning my waffles.

"We're thinking about taking the ferry over to Bainbridge Island for the morning," Rafé said.

I glanced up at Angel. "You aren't thinking of dropping in on Nalcops, are you?"

She blinked, shaking her head. "Are you kidding? No. We're just going to drive around the island for a while."

Pausing, her voice dropped. "Rafé is probably going to say yes to helping us." The words came out strained and I realized how hard it was for her to say them.

"Are you sure you want to do this?" I turned back to Rafé. "You don't have to."

He shrugged, cutting his waffle into tidy squares. "I know. But this is important. And I've never had the chance to make a big difference in life, to be honest. I can contribute something here—and my brother would have done it, if he'd been asked. I trust Herne, and the rest of you."

I peeked over at Angel. She was focused on the waffle iron, her lips pressed thin. The tension between them had gone from zero to a hundred in ten seconds flat. Deciding it was better to step gently out of the water, I cleared my throat.

"I'm headed over to Marilee's this morning. It's my last prep session before the Cruharach. She said it's going to be a simple deep meditation, so I should be fine for tonight."

Rafé took his clue from me. "What's tonight?"

"Girls' night at Raven's," I said, grinning. "So no boys allowed."

Angel let out a long sigh. "Quit trying to pretend this isn't an issue with me. I wish I'd never opened my mouth in the first place, but I did. I'm just going to have to woman up and accept that this job comes complete with danger for those we care about. At least DJ's out of the target zone. Now I understand why it was important to let him go."

"He's also learning things about his heritage that he never could have with you. You did a very unselfish thing by letting Coo—the family take him. They're treating him right, and he's having fun. Well, when he's not getting grounded." I slipped out of my chair and joined her at the counter. There were five waffles on the plate. "You've got plenty here. You never eat more than one, so just stop and sit down and eat your breakfast. I'll make you some more tea."

Before she could protest, I picked up her cup and carried it over to the sink, where I rinsed it out. Then, placing a fresh tea bag in it, I checked the electric kettle we had recently bought and, finding the water still hot, I filled her cup and carried it to the table. Angel brought over the stack of waffles and took her place beside Rafé. I speared a waffle and dropped it on her plate, then snagged another.

"You mother me," she said. "I kind of like it."

"We mother each other, and I think that we deserve it, given we're both sans mothers at this point." I handed her the syrup and butter.

The rest of breakfast passed in peace, and by the time I drained my mocha, Rafé and Angel were headed upstairs to dress. I cleared the table and rinsed the dishes, putting them in the dishwasher, and then—making certain Mr. Rumblebutt had plenty of dry food—I gave him a smooch on the forehead, grabbed my jacket and purse, and headed over to Marilee's.

MARILEE LIVED in a gorgeous house on Boyer Avenue, near the arboretum. The preserve was filled with trees and plants both exotic and endemic to the area. The gardens spread across the entire two hundred acres, and "enchanting" was the only way to describe them. The staff were mostly Fae and the magic they infused into the grounds had created a wonderland. Trails threaded through the thickets and gardens. I liked coming here to wander when I was in an introverted mood. The green magic that riddled the arboretum always lifted my spirits and spread out in a ripple effect through the entire neighborhood.

Marilee's house was enchanting as well. With a roof that reminded me of a pagoda, and gardens that were tended with care, her home was inviting and cozy. An air of protection spread over the entire lot.

I dashed up the steps. Marilee must have been watching out the window, because she opened the door seconds after I rang the bell. She was five-four, athletic and trim, with a long silver braid. She looked human, though I wasn't actually sure and I had never asked. Whatever else she might be, she was first and foremost a priestess of Morgana.

Marilee wasn't wearing her robes today, but jeans and a peasant shirt with delicate embroidery around the neck. She looked older, but again, just how old—I didn't know. She might be seventy, or she might be seven hundred.

She welcomed me in. "I'm glad you could make it this morning. How are you feeling?" Concern filled her eyes, but her voice was steady. Marilee was compassionate, but she was also one of those people who was good at pushing me to knuckle under and deal with the things life threw at me. I had learned a lot since she had undertaken my training, and was grateful that Morgana had assigned me to her.

"I'm all right. A bit stiff, and a little sore, but I'm alive and walking and that's better than a lot of people who were in the path of that bomb." I dropped my purse on the table, then followed her into the ritual room.

"Good way of looking at it," Marilee said.

"Herne's offered me access to one of Ferosyn's counselors," I added.

"Do you think you need counseling?" Marilee opened the door and led me in. There was no circle drawn on the floor today, but merely a yoga mat with a pillow and a blanket. "Sit down there."

I obeyed, settling myself in a cross-legged position on the mat.

"Honestly? I don't know. I do find myself flashing back, but I don't feel traumatized per se. I just feel…angry."

"Angry about what?"

I thought for a moment, then said, "That so many people were injured, that people died. I was listening to the news on the way over and five of the most critically injured have died. Four more bodies of the missing were found."

"Anger is a natural response, and one that I would expect more from you than PTSD. Especially with your lineage. If you feel you need counseling, accept it. If not, then don't worry about it. All right, are you ready for the last session?" She squatted down beside me.

I took a long breath and let it out slowly. "I suppose." Pausing, I stared at the mat for a moment before adding, "Do you think I'm ready? I have this ominous feeling building up inside me. What if I'm not prepared for the Cruharach? What if…"

"What if you fail? Then we cope with that when it happens. You can't run away from this, Ember. There's no escaping it and let's face it, the Cruharach will come to you. In fact, it's barreling right toward you. I can feel it in your aura. It creates that ominous feeling you're worried about. The Cruharach is shadowing over you like a massive cloud, ready to burst. So the best we can do is hope that we've prepared you enough. You'll either come through it or you won't. Those are the only two options."

"What if I don't?" The thought of going mad was scarier than the thought of dying. "Promise me, Marilee, if something happens to me…if I don't come through… you'll help Angel with whatever she needs?"

Marilee took my hand. "I promise," she said gently. "But I think you'll manage it. I can't guarantee anything, but you've come a long way in your training."

"What will happen if I pass through?" I glanced at her. "Will I still be me?"

"You've asked that a dozen times. And each time, what have I said?"

Once again, I caught my breath. "That I'll still be me, only more so. My magic will have its direction, and so will my innate abilities." I swallowed my fear, bringing my focus firmly into the room. The crystals amplified feelings, and I didn't want them to amplify my fear and doubt. "All right. Let's get this show on the road. What's on the agenda today?"

"Today is simple. I want you to lie down, close your eyes, and sleep. I'm going to give you a tincture that will work on your subconscious while you're asleep. You won't feel it, you won't dream, but it will prepare your body for next week."

I didn't ask any questions. I trusted Marilee with my life. Morgana would never have given me over into the care of someone who was a danger to me.

"All right. Let's do this."

As she dropped three drops of a vile-tasting tincture on my tongue, it occurred to me that I still had no idea exactly what the Cruharach would be like. But I also knew that if I asked, there would be no answer.

Marilee had been right. I had no memory of what had taken place in my sleep, but I did have the sense that my body had shifted. Almost…lighter. The wounds were less painful, and I felt like something inside was shifting and changing, though I couldn't pinpoint how.

As I scheduled the ritual for Monday night—Samhain Eve—on my phone, I felt a shudder of apprehension. Squelching it the best I could, I bid Marilee farewell until then.

One thing Mama J.—Angel's mother—had kept telling us over and over: *Don't borrow trouble. You never know what's going to happen. So if you worry too much about what's coming, you're wasting precious time. You could walk out your door and get hit by a bus in five minutes, so take each moment as a blessing and don't waste your life fretting.*

As I headed to my car, I felt a spring in my step and realized that a lot of my tension and aches and pains had vanished. Whatever was in that tincture worked wonders. It occurred to me to ask Ferosyn if he could create a sleeping potion similar to it, for nights when sleep came hard.

I glanced at the clock. The meditation, as she called it, had taken three hours. It was almost two, and we were due at Raven's at around six. Since Angel and Rafé were off to Bainbridge Island, I decided to go shopping. I still had to replace my leather jacket. But first, I brought up my lawyer's site on my phone and used the e-scheduling app to make an appointment for Monday. I needed to take care of something before I went into the Cruharach on Monday night.

Two hours later, I was not only wearing a new black leather jacket, complete with chains and studs, but I had bought a new purse that matched, a pair of leather gloves, and a new corset. I stopped at the corner market to pick up a dozen roses for the house, and a dozen to take over to Raven's, as well as a box of chocolates. Angel was always on me because I loved sweets, but since she had moved in, at least my diet had improved thanks to her love of—and skill in—cooking. By the time I got home it was almost four-thirty, and Angel had texted me that she was home. Rafé's car was nowhere in sight. He must have taken off for the evening.

"Honey, I'm home!" I opened the door, carrying my packages into the house.

"In the kitchen," Angel called, laughing.

I carried my packages in, handing her one of the bouquets. "I left the other in my car, for Raven."

Angel brought the flowers to her nose, inhaling deeply. "Lovely scent. They must have thorns," she said, laughing.

"The best scented flowers do," I said, setting my bags on the counter. I pulled out the chocolates. "And...a little pre-dinner celebration."

She stared at the box. "And what are we celebrating?"

"My last session with Marilee. Next week, I undergo the Cruharach. So don't even mention the amount of sugar in these." I held her gaze. "I need to say something now, and I don't want you to try to avoid the subject or tell me to stop."

"This sounds serious," Angel said, carrying a vase and the flowers over to the table, where she began to cut their stems and arrange them. "So, what is it?"

I bit my lip, then decided just to come out with it. "I made an appointment with my lawyer for Monday. I'm going to appoint you the beneficiary of the house and everything I have, except for my dagger—that goes to Herne—just in case I don't come out of the Cruharach. I'm also giving you power of attorney in case something goes wrong."

She slowly placed the rose she was holding on the table and put down the scissors. "Nothing is going to go wrong."

"There's a chance, Angel. I don't want to think about it either, but there's a chance. I could go mad. I could die. I could…change. I just want to know things are in order."

"I said, nothing is going to go wrong." She looked up at me. "*I* need to believe that you'll be all right. I understand you need to do all this, and thank you for telling me. But nothing will go wrong. *Do you hear me?*" Her voice was so low I could barely hear it, but I recognized the look in her eyes. This was Angel's line in the sand.

Nodding, I leaned back in my chair. "I hear you. Nothing will happen. But I still need you to go in with me, to sign off on the POA. Will you do that?"

She picked up the rose again. "Yes. But turnabout fair

play. If I get to be your POA, then you get to be mine. Deal?"

"Deal." And that was all we said on the matter.

Raven BoneTalker's house was over on the Eastside, on 61st Place NE. She lived at the edge of UnderLake Park, a dangerous park that had a long history of murder and hauntings. It was a beautiful, feral place, hiding dark secrets as well as the bodies of those who had vanished on its paths.

As Angel and I parked behind Raven's Toyota sedan, I noticed that Raven had put up a new railing along the walkway, and the stepping-stones leading to the house were new. The house itself was hidden behind a hedgerow, though the trees in front were bare-branched. The ground was littered with sodden leaves, and a feeling of heavy magic cloaked the entire lot.

As we swung around the walkway onto the path behind the hedgerow that led to her door, we saw Raj. He perked up when he saw us and let out a low grunt. Raj was a gargoyle, and he had been with Raven for some time now. She had saved him from a demon who had clipped his wings. Raven wiped the gargoyle's memory to help him forget the loss and the pain, and now he was like a massive puppy-dog, his gray leathery skin well oiled.

Raj walked on his knuckles and his back feet, looking very much like an orangutan. He was guarded against strangers, but Angel and I were now on his friends list. We were greeted with a slobbery kiss as he first licked my face, then hers. He reserved his growls for strangers. Raj spent a lot of his time in his little house by the sidewalk, guarding the door, though Raven let him in whenever he wanted.

"Hey Raj, how you doing, buddy?" Angel said, pulling a piece of jerky out of her pocket. Raj loved beef jerky and we always brought him treats when we visited.

"*Ruff*." Raj snorted as he saw the jerky, his eyes lighting up. He delicately plucked it from Angel's hand and chewed happily away.

I patted him on the head as we moved past him, stopping at the door where I rang the bell. Angel was holding the bouquet, as well as a bottle of wine.

As Raven let us in, I could smell spaghetti cooking in the background. My stomach rumbled. I hadn't had lunch, just a bag of pretzels after I left Marilee's, and the chocolates back at the house.

"I'm so hungry, and that smells so good."

"I'm glad. I made enough for an army." Raven Bone-Talker was one of the Ante-Fae, and it showed in every move and in the timbre of her voice. Like the Fae, who were descendants from the Ante-Fae, Raven had an otherworldly look about her. Curvy and buxom, she was more padded than I was, but I wouldn't bet winning in a fight against her. She had hair the color of deep espresso streaked with plum, but the color was natural. It cascaded down to her waist, coiling in waves. Her eyes were the same rich brown as her hair, and she was pale to the point of looking almost like a porcelain doll.

Raven was wearing a long lace skirt with an asymmetrical hem. Higher in front than in back, it flowed easily off her hips. Over the skirt, she wore a plum-colored corset, and she had on black witchy boots, calf-high with silver laces. A magnetic aura surrounded her, and she crackled with energy. Her smile was both crafty and yet infectious.

"Thank you! I love roses!" Her voice was sultry, and she gathered the flowers in her arms, spinning around as she breathed in the rich, dusky scent. "Let's put these in water." She carried them into the kitchen and we followed after shedding our coats and purses.

"How goes it?" she asked, searching for a vase in the cupboard.

Angel leaned over the pot of sauce simmering on the stove, waving the steam toward her nose. "Oh, this smells so good. What's your secret?" Given how good of a cook Angel was, when she thought something was good, it had to be excellent.

"I grow my own herbs, and I use a mixture of ground venison and ground pork for the meat." Raven handed me the vase. "Water, please. Angel, can you get out the plates?"

We moved in unison. We had only known each other for about a month, but in that time the three of us had bonded. Raven could be a little scary in how intense she was about certain subjects. The fact that she was Ante-Fae helped in the "don't mess with me" attitude that she wore like a cloak. But she had a wicked sense of humor, and was a natural leader when it came to getting into mischief and causing havoc.

I clipped the stems of the roses and arranged them in the vase as Raven stirred the sauce and drained the spaghetti. Angel set the table and placed the roses in the center.

Raven's home was minimalist—all clean lines, and neutral grays and blues and whites. It almost had a windswept ocean feel to it, and I could easily see it transported to a cliff overlooking the ocean. The floor was striking—a checkerboard of black and white. The table was in the kitchen nook, looking out through sliding glass doors onto the backyard.

Raven's dishes were black and white as well, with silver trim. She poured the sauce over the spaghetti and thoroughly mixed it, then carried the steaming tureen to the table.

"There's bread in the oven, and a salad in the fridge if you could grab it." She settled the tureen on the table as Angel moved to get the bread and salad. I walked over to stare out the sliding glass door at her backyard, which was a tangle of roses and herbs and lilacs.

"I go through the Cruharach on Samhain Eve," I said.

Raven paused, turning to me. "So it's come."

"Yeah, it has. Do the Ante-Fae have anything like that?" I didn't know much about her people, especially since they were all unique, and there weren't really any generic traits that seemed to belong to all of the Ante-Fae.

She walked over to stand beside me. Goosebumps raised along my arm as the magic surrounding her crackled against my own. We weren't all that dissimilar, but hers was far more potent. Raven was a bone witch, and she dealt heavily in death magic and the spirit world.

"Are you afraid?" she asked softly.

"Shouldn't I be? There's a chance I could go mad during the ritual. Or die. It's not that I expect those things to happen, but I'm tired of people telling me they won't. I want to face the reality that there is a chance—however slight—that I won't come through this." I spoke softly, so that Angel couldn't hear.

Raven nodded. "You want your fear acknowledged.

This is a serious ritual, and I understand that. But how many actually do go mad, though? Or die? Only a small percentage, right?"

"Yes," I conceded. "I guess I'm mostly afraid that I won't be *me* anymore. One side of my parentage will take the dominant position, and whatever powers I'm to inherit from both will settle in and make themselves known. I'm worried that…I won't be *Ember* anymore, but some cunning hybrid predator." And there was my *real* fear. The fear that I'd end up worse than dead—that I'd end up someone whom I'd hate.

"You will be Ember, regardless of what happens. And you *will* change. No Fae can go through the Cruharach and come through untouched. This is the way of your people. If your parents were alive, they would have prepared you for it."

"I suppose so." I stared out at the darkness. "I suppose I need to just quit worrying about it. I'm like a dog with a bone."

"Or Raj, with his jerky. By the way, thank you for remembering him. He's such a sweetheart, and he's taken with you two. Do you mind if I let him in during dinner? You'd be surprised how many people object. Of course, they never find themselves invited over again, so there's that." She arched her eyebrows and winked at me.

"We love Raj. He's welcome as long as he doesn't try to steal my food." I laughed, pushing away my thoughts. Raven's matter-of-factness comforted me. She had a way of making my shadow thoughts almost seem amusing.

We settled down at the table, and Raven poured the wine. It was rich and robust, with undernotes of plum and cinnamon, and honey behind that. As we fell to our dinner, we kept the conversation light. Once we finished—even Angel had eaten two servings of the spaghetti—we carried our glasses and a fresh bottle into the living room, leaving the cleanup till later.

"I have a quandary that I want your input on, ladies," Raven said, sitting in one of the recliners and folding one leg beneath her.

"What's up?" I asked, pouring myself another glass of wine, and topping off Angel's.

"It concerns a friend of yours, so I'm hesitant to say anything," Raven said. "But I'm at my wits' end. I mean, I could cast a whammy on him and make him stop, but my hexes have a way of doing more damage than I plan and I don't really want to hurt him."

Angel and I gave each other a long look.

"It's not Ray, is it?" If Ray was targeting my friends now, I was going to have to pay a little visit to him.

"No, it's actually Yutani. He's been calling me, asking me out. And while I like him, there are two problems. One—I'm in no way ready to date again. I'm still in mourning for Ulstair. And two—Yutani's not my type. He's cute, but I don't think we'd play well together, if you know what I mean. I wouldn't mind having him for a friend, but that's it." She frowned. "He's called me four times in the past two weeks, and each time I've told him, thank you, no, I'm not interested in dating. So either he's not listening, or he thinks he can wear me down."

I cleared my throat, taking a big swallow of wine. "Yutani's a very private person. It surprises me he's still pushing. But then again, he's also impulsive as hell." I glanced at Angel. "You don't think he could be drink—" I stopped. I hadn't told Angel what Yutani had told me.

"Drink? Yutani drinks too much?" Angel said.

I shook my head. "Not anymore. I shouldn't have said anything. It's his secret to tell. But yeah, now that I've let the cat out of the bag, he has a history of drinking to escape. Don't say anything to him, please? Either one of you? I don't want him knowing that I let his secret out."

"Don't worry, I'm not looking to engage him in conversation," Raven said. "As I said, I like the guy, but if he won't take no for an answer, he's going to get a buttload of 'No means no' shoved down his throat."

"Have you tried being blunt? As in, 'Don't call me again' blunt?" Angel asked.

Raven shook her head. "Not quite so direct, but by now he should figure it out. I've been pretty blunt. I don't hand out mixed messages. I really don't want to be rude, but he's pushing the boundaries."

"He's dealing with some serious issues. That's not an excuse, but it could be the reason he's not really listening. He recently found out that Coyote is his father." I set my glass down and took off my boots, curling my feet beneath me on the sofa.

"That's pretty hard core," Raven said. "But regardless, it's *so* not my problem. Anyway, I wanted to get your advice on how to approach this. I'm not going to ask you to talk to him for me—that's my job—but do you think I should just go full-tilt rude on him?"

"You may have to. He's blunt enough with everybody else. He should be able to accept it from others." I shook my head. "I never thought Yutani would be *that* guy, but then again, I didn't expect my ex-boyfriend to become a stalker either. Though to be fair, my glamour had something to do with it. Now, he's just being an asshole."

"And a good one at that," Angel muttered. "Okay, enough about men. What are we going to do tonight? And before anybody suggests anything, I'm *not* game for trying to summon up another dead rock star. That didn't go so well."

I snorted. "You can say that again." Our recent drunken adventure in trying to conjure up Jim Morrison had gone so far south that we had vowed to keep it between the three of us forever.

Raven rolled her eyes. "You have no sense of adventure. Granted, it was rude of us, but he didn't have to throw that big of a tantrum, either. It took me two days to wash all the ectoplasm off my walls, and even longer to convince the ferrets that it was safe to come out. I thought we might get a song out of him, but really, Jim could have just said 'Leave me alone' and I would have canceled the spell. But you have to admit, at least the evening wasn't boring."

"Boring? Definitely not. Fun? That's another matter. But seriously, what should we do tonight?" Angel topped off our glasses. "I could use something fun to distract me."

"I just bought a whole lot of new makeup, and I raided the Vanity Vintage store. I've got a bunch of gorgeous clothes. Why don't we dress up and hit the Burlesque A Go-Go? It's a great new nightclub out near TirNaNog." Raven clapped her hands. "A friend of mine opened it recently."

"Sounds good to me," I said.

Angel agreed. We headed toward Raven's bedroom, which was almost the opposite style of the living room. Done up in purples, greens, and black, her bedroom was a lush boudoir, with the king-size bed piled high with velvet throw pillows. She brought out an armful of clothing, and we played dress up.

I tried on a short blue lamé mini dress that barely covered the tops of my thighs. Raven and I were almost the same bra band, though her boobs were fuller than mine, and she tucked me into a push-up bra, adding just enough extra cushioning so the cups fit right. The dress was low cut and I felt like sex on legs.

"All I need is a pair of go-go boots," I said, staring at myself in the mirror.

"Wrong era. Here, try on these." She dangled a pair of strappy heels with five-inch stilettos on them.

"I can't walk in these." I shook my head, holding up the sparkling silver shoes.

"Yes, you can. They're platforms. They may be five-inch heels, but they feel like three-inch ones and I've seen you manage those perfectly fine." She shoved me on the bed and dropped the shoes next to me. "We'll do your hair next."

Then she turned her attention on Angel. "For you, I have this." She brought out a flowing caftan in gold lamé. "Belt this with a black belt. I've got a five-inch wide stretchy one that might be small enough to fit you. Wear the same boots you've got on, and it will be gorgeous."

Angel looked skeptical but she tried on the dress. It was a little short, but it worked with the black patent leather boots she was wearing, and the belt cinched it in so that she looked like she was right out of the 1970s.

As Raven changed into a black tulle mini-skirt, a pair of fishnets, and a silver corset, I admired the tattoos normally hiding under her clothes. She was heavily inked with intricate patterns across her back and down each leg.

Raven fastened a silver chain around her neck and then pulled on opera-length fingerless gloves. Finally, she slipped into ankle boots that were a mile high and studded with metal spikes. Both the heels and the spikes looked like they could put your eye out.

"All right. Hair." She pointed for Angel to sit on the vanity bench, but she shook her head.

"Nope. I've got this. You chose the outfits, I get to do hair, and Ember gets to choose our makeup." Angel cackled. "By the way, we probably shouldn't be driving tonight."

"No problem. I'll call a LUD. And if you aren't sober enough to drive home, you can just take one back to your place and come get your car tomorrow." Raven put in a call. "They'll be here in forty-five minutes."

We primped and powdered and by the time we were ready to leave, we looked like we were heading off to Studio 54 back in its heyday. Laughing, half-drunk already, we squeezed into the LUD, and we were off for a night of partying.

CHAPTER FOURTEEN

The Burlesque A Go-Go was in the basement of a dark building in Old Town, a small, gritty suburb squeezed between Redmond and Woodinville. It had built up as Navane and TirNaNog stretched out to take over the area, and it was haven to some of the shadier types. Mostly Fae, but some vampires as well.

The streets were wide, the buildings grungy, and half the street lamps were constantly broken. The LUD driver parked in front of the Shaft, a store catering to kink, and Angel and I looked at each other. This was an unfamiliar area for both of us, but Raven hopped out of the cab, looking perfectly at home. She motioned for us to follow her and, with a shrug, I fell in behind her.

"So who owns the club?" I asked, trying to keep my voice casual.

"It belongs to one of my friends, Vixen. Vixen's one of the Ante-Fae, though the club caters to Fae and human as well. Not so much shifters. They're uncomfortable with the amount of magical energy." Her eyes were sparkling, and I could feel the excitement wafting off of her. "I work hard and I play harder. And I'm so perplexed by this current case I'm on that I really need to just forget about it and cut loose."

She strode around to the side, walking effortlessly in the stiletto death-boots. We followed her into the shadows, only to stop in front of a man in a black and white pinstripe zoot suit, leaning against the railing of a stairwell that led to a door below ground. He tipped his fedora as we approached.

"Miss Raven, good to see you again." His voice was husky, and his eyes sparkled as he looked us over. He wasn't Fae, but I couldn't put my finger directly on what he *was*. Not human, that much I was sure of.

"Zylo, love. I've brought friends of mine to play. May we go in?" Raven reached out and with one long black nail, stroked his cheek, leaving a welt as she ran her nail down to his chin.

He shivered, but just nodded. "Yes ma'am, you may. Have fun."

"Is Vixen in tonight?" Raven asked as she started toward the stairs.

"Yes, and tonight Vixen's a woman and would prefer to be referred to as 'she.' I suggest paying your respects." Again, the slow tip of the fedora as Zylo nodded.

I was beginning to feel like Angel and I might be out of our depths, but I trusted Raven. She wouldn't take us somewhere too dangerous. Or at least, not dangerous to us…I hoped.

I cautiously descended the steps. The heels weren't too bad, given they were platforms, but I felt oddly exposed and vulnerable. Angel navigated in heels better than I did, but she also looked mildly apprehensive.

As Raven neared the plain steel door, it opened, and we faced yet another bouncer in yet another zoot suit. He said nothing, just stood back, holding the door as we passed by. Raven gave him a short nod as we entered the club.

The first thing that hit me was the luminous quality of the nightclub. It was almost as though a black light filled the entire room, with all brighter colors standing out in a blaze of neon. I glanced down. The blue sparkles of my dress were almost blinding, and they shifted as I moved.

There was a long bar to the left, with a dim light behind the counter that cut through the haze of black light so that the bartenders could see what they were doing. A line of bar stools bordered the bar, half of them filled. Around the edges of the massive room were small tables for two to four people, and about half of them were also filled.

The center of the room appeared to be a dance floor—that much we could tell by the couples who were shimmying to the music. The smell of marijuana filled the room, and in one corner, I spied a table with a large hookah sitting on it. The music was hypnotic, heavy on percussion with a beat that made my body want to flow into it and move. The magic here was so strong that I could feel it prickling on my arms, on the back of my neck. I wasn't sure if it was in the decor, or if it was coming from any one person in particular.

At that moment, Angel poked me in the ribs and nodded to the far corner of the bar. There, at a table, sat the source of the magic. Or at least *one* of the sources—power emanated from the woman in waves.

"Who's that?" I leaned over to Raven and nodded toward the figure.

"That's Vixen. Tonight she's a she. They're a powerful Ante-Fae, who's gender fluid in the truest sense of the word. They've settled into their feminine form tonight. Vixen prefers we use the pronouns for their gender of choice at any given time, so refer to them as 'she/her' tonight. Come, I'll introduce you."

Before we could say anything, she was dragging us toward the Ante-Fae. As we approached the table, we got a better look at Vixen, who stood, bowing gracefully. Vixen was wearing a shimmering silver gown that flowed down to her calves, and it billowed gracefully out from her body, almost as though she was wearing a light full-body petticoat beneath it. Vixen's hair was shoulder length and also silver, and her eyes were a pale hazel that seemed to shift into green tones as we neared. Her features seemed smooth, and there were no wrinkles or lines on her face.

Raven circled around the table and curtseyed, taking Vixen's hand as she held it out.

"Your Grace," she said, pressing her lips to a massive diamond ring on Vixen's finger. Then she rose and stepped back beside us.

"My love, Raven. It's good to see you back. And these are friends of yours?" The Ante-Fae turned her gaze to us and I suddenly felt naked, as though she could see through me. All Ante-Fae had unique abilities, and I had no idea what powers Vixen possessed, but whatever they were, the magic around her was thick and lush.

"Yes, may I present Ember Kearney, and Angel Jackson. They're from the Wild Hunt Agency. This is Vixen, the Mistress of Mayhem. She owns the Burlesque A Go-Go."

"Well, well, a couple of Herne's chickens in my coop. Welcome, dearies, mind your manners, and we'll all have fun." Vixen stared at us without blinking so long that she made me think of an owl. "We play hard in this club, but everything's on the up and up. The only scenes allowed are those of which I approve."

As if on cue, the dancers vacated the floor.

"The show's about to begin. I suggest you order your drinks and find a table." Vixen motioned for us to leave and Raven, again curtseying, turned and led us to the bar.

"Their specialty here is Rasabella mead. I highly suggest it." She ordered a bottle, along with a plate of assorted appetizers, and led us to a table on the edge of the dance floor.

"What kind of show is this?" Angel started to ask, as a slow beat began. A line of drummers entered the room. They were carrying various drums, and two of them had instruments that looked like flying saucers.

"Those are handpans," Raven said. "I own one and play it. I use mine for my magic, but they're beautiful instruments."

As the drummers settled themselves in a circle around the edge of the stage, they began to play. True to what Raven had said, the handpan players began to tap out a rhythm on their instruments and the sound reminded me of some ancient song, metallic and melodic and melancholy all at the same time. They interwove their song with the beating of the drums as the lights narrowed to a single golden spotlight on the main floor. A dancer appeared.

He was gloriously beautiful, his skin had a golden hue, and his long hair flowed over his shoulders. He was muscled but not overly so, and his body rivaled that of the statue of David. He was wearing a pair of ivory harem pants, so sheer that we could see the golden bikini below. A circlet of golden bells surrounded his ankle, and he began to dance, his body flowing in ways that no normal body should be able to. He was breathtaking to watch, beautiful, like a ray of sunlight dancing against the ground.

I caught my breath, realizing that I wanted him, and yet there was a feeling that he was an illusion—too beautiful to be real, too ethereal to touch. He made my heart stand still as he wove his way around the floor. I managed to pull my gaze away to look at Angel. She, too, looked transfixed.

The music flowed around us, the handpans echoing through the club, their notes airy and almost impossible to capture, yet they reverberated through me, speaking to the core of my heart, inviting me to join the unearthly dance.

I wasn't sure how long the dancer wove his dance, but after a time, he slowly lowered himself to the floor, folding down into a delicate ball, his arms stretched forward in a plea of supplication, his forehead touching the ground. For a long moment, nobody moved, then as the last note faded away, there was uproarious applause, and I found myself joining in.

"He's... I've never seen anything quite like it," I said, turning to Raven. "Who is he?"

"His name is Apollo, the Weaver of Wings. He's Vixen's Golden Boy. He's Ante-Fae as well. Wait till you see the next one."

I took a long drink of my Rasabella mead. It went straight to my head and was far stronger than I expected it to be. I shivered as the glow spread through my body, and found myself sinking into our surroundings. Visions of Apollo danced through my mind, but then the spotlight shifted from warm to an icy glow as three women appeared. They looked similar enough to be sisters, and they were obviously Ante-Fae. Their hair was long and caught into dreads, a caramel color streaked with black and white, and their skin bore an olive undertone.

As they looked around the audience, their eyes gleamed with a green light, like sunlight shining through summer leaves. They were muscular and curvy, and taller than most women I knew. Dressed in black PVC short shorts that started well below their belly buttons and barely covered their butt cheeks, their shorts had long strings of fringe. They were wearing shiny black boots with platforms a good six inches thick, studded with hardware and chains, and on their heads, they were wearing deadman's hats, with long red and green feathers streaming off them.

The beat picked up, strident, demanding, and the women began to dance, their movements precise and angular, turning belly dance into something entirely new. As I watched, their fringe became feathers, and the dancers became vulture-like, cautiously interweaving with each other. Then they spread out toward the audience, hunting, their eyes glinting with hunger.

Angel clutched my arm and I took her hand. They

were on the prowl, looking for prey. I glanced over at Raven, who was staring at them with delight. There was no fear in her face but an odd joy, as the dancers circled the room, beautiful and deadly.

As much as Apollo had entranced me, these dancers made me shutter up. I wasn't afraid, but wary. I felt a wave of emotion swelling within, and suddenly realized that my Leannan Sidhe side didn't like them. These creatures were beyond my control, and that didn't sit well with my mother's blood. I was about ready to excuse myself when the dance ended. The lights came up as the dancers exited the room and a round of applause rang out. I leaned over to Raven.

"What the hell are *they*?"

"They're the Vulture Sisters. They live out in Snoqualmie, away from the city. They dance every month or so and they fetch a good fee, enough to hold them over until the next time. But…" She paused. "You don't want to cross them. And they don't make good friends. I found out the hard way. But at least when you tell them to fuck off, they usually do so."

I almost spit out my mead. "You were involved with them?"

Raven shrugged. "They looked like they might be fun to hang out with. But…not so much. I love watching them dance, but yeah, that friendship ended quickly."

Angel poured another round of mead, emptying the bottle. "Well, they about knocked me over. They feel like actual birds of prey, but not like some shitfaced serial killer."

She was slurring her words a little and I could tell she

was tipsy. For that matter, so was I. Raven ordered another bottle of mead as the drummers left the floor and a blast of techno started up. She grabbed my hand and pulled me onto the dance floor. Angel joined us and we began to dance to Mai Lan's "Pumper" as the lights began to shift and sparkle. I turned around and found myself dancing with Apollo. I almost dropped my glass, which was still in my hand, but as we swayed to the music, I felt my inhibitions slip away. The night flowed on, and so did the mead, all awash in a haze of sparkling lights and magic as the music drove us on.

By the time the LUD poured us out at our doorstep, Angel and I were carrying our shoes. We hadn't bothered to go back to Raven's house. We were too wasted, so we told her we'd be back the next day to pick up everything and return our party clothes. We were all drunk off our asses, including Raven.

"I can't see to get to the door," Angel said, weaving toward the fence.

"That's because it's four in the morning." I squinted, trying to make out anything in the dark. I was carrying my shoes because I couldn't walk in them. "Ew, I think I just stepped on a slug! Ick! Hey, do you have your keys?"

"Keys? Of course I've got my keys. They're in my bag." Angel stopped, turning to the side to throw up. "Oh gods, I'm going to have the hangover from hell," she said, managing to find the handle of the screen door and opening it. "Where's my bag?"

I groaned. "I don't know. I've got my keys right here.

Can you use the flashlight on your phone so I can see the keyhole?"

After a few minutes, Angel managed to turn on the flashlight and I went about trying to fit the key into the lock. After a second attempt, I giggled.

"Boy, I'm sure glad Herne can find his way around me better than this."

"His key fits in your lock just fine, does it?" Angel said, snorting.

"Well, there's not much spare room, but he gets in there pretty good." I leaned my head against the doorjamb. "Oh, my stomach's fighting a war with itself. All right, let's try again."

This time, I managed to get the key into the lock and opened the door, but Angel and I were pressing against it and we went sprawling through into the foyer, a tangle of shoes and coats and limbs. Angel's bag was on her wrist and she held it up.

"Oh, look what I found. And *ow*, I think that hurt," she said, rolling over onto her hands and knees.

"I think my pride hurts more than anything, though I'll let you know in the morning. Well, later this morning."

I crawled over to the wall and used it to balance as I struggled to my feet. I flipped on the light, which brought another stunning round of pain. Squinting, I lifted my foot to stare at the bottom. A blotch of slime and fir needles were stuck to my sole.

"Crap, I did step on a slug."

"Don't track it onto the carpet. Let's go in the kitchen and I'll help you clean it off."

She motioned for me to follow her and, making sure

the door was locked, I limped down the hall, keeping my right foot on tiptoe so I didn't muck up the floors.

"Sit down," she said, once we were in the kitchen.

I did so, gratefully. She carried over a bunch of paper towels and the spray cleaner.

"You're cleaning my foot with *that*?" I pointed to the bottle.

"Shut up. It will work." She plopped down on the floor and I held out my foot. She sprayed it with the cleaner—which was a natural blend and, I hoped, non-toxic—and began to scrub at my foot. After a while, she dried it off. "There. That should do. How does it feel?"

"Like you just stripped off all the natural oils." I crossed my leg over my knee to look at the bottom of my foot. It was relatively clean. At least the slug juice was all gone. "We should go to bed. Thank the gods we don't have to go anywhere today."

Mr. Rumblebutt appeared, glaring at us.

"I know, I know. We're late. And you need your…shit, we forgot his dinner." I turned to Angel. "Grab a dish and I'll get his food." After feeding Mr. Rumblebutt and apologizing with a thorough petting, we headed up the stairs.

I entered my bedroom and stripped off my clothes, thinking that sometimes being friends with one of the Ante-Fae could be hard work. I liked Raven a lot, but I was grateful that I didn't live in her world all the time.

"Coffee." Wearing a pair of sweats and a tank top, and a pair of old sneakers, I blurrily entered the kitchen. I had taken a shower, but the water had barely skimmed the edges of my hangover.

Angel was sitting at the table, hunched over what looked like a double-strength cup of tea, eating toast and eggs. "I didn't make you any because I wasn't sure when you were going to get up. I did feed His Highness, though. He's still miffed."

"Of course he is. He's a cat." I headed over to the espresso machine and pulled five shots, pouring them into a tall mug. I frothed the milk and then added it, along with some chocolate syrup. As I stirred my mocha, I stared lethargically at the stove. "Angel...will you make my eggs?"

She shot me a nasty glance, but pushed herself to her feet and nodded. "Yes, but you get them out for me, along with some cheese. You can toast your own bread."

We worked silently together, and five minutes later, I joined her at the table. "My head feels so foggy I can barely think."

"Yours and mine both. I think I drank less than you and Raven, but man, every move is a struggle. How do you think Ulstair kept up with her?" Angel finished off her eggs and leaned back in her chair, staring at me with bloodshot eyes.

"I don't even want to know. But man, she has some freaky friends. That dude Apollo, though..." I suddenly flashed back on dancing with him. "Oh gods, I didn't do anything I'll regret, did I? I remember dancing with Apollo."

"You danced with him. Raven danced with him. I danced with him. But I think I saw him sitting on Vixen's lap. I get the feeling he belongs to her, so I think we're safe. By the way, just who is Vixen? Is she royalty?"

"I have no idea. I don't know how the hierarchy works with the Ante-Fae. I have to admit, even though I got so hammered that my stomach feels like it's on permanent protest, I did have fun. Did you?" I glanced at Angel, hoping she hadn't regretted the evening.

"Yeah, I did. But you know what? How about tonight we just curl up with a movie and popcorn, and make it an early evening?" She winked at me. "Ow, even my eyelids hurt."

"I think that sounds wonderful." I went back to my breakfast as the caffeine began to work on my hangover headache.

I WAS out in the garden. The afternoon was clear, though chilly. It was one of those rare autumn days in Seattle where the clouds had parted and the sun shone down, the rays barely breaking the chill. I walked over to one of the rose bushes. We had pruned and snipped and finally things were set for spring. All the garden needed was to sleep through the winter.

Angel was taking a nap. I thought I was alone, but then, my crow necklace warmed against my throat and I felt a shift. Someone was nearby.

"Thinking?" The voice was low and sultry.

I whirled, almost making myself dizzy. There, in all her beauty and power, stood Morgana. She was shrouded in a long indigo cloak, fastened at the neck with a Celtic triskelion. Her raven hair was hidden beneath the hood, but she was staring at me, a smile on her face.

"I suppose," I said, crossing my arms for warmth. The temperature felt like it had dropped several degrees. "What can I do for you, milady?" I wondered whether I should offer her a seat, or something to eat or drink. As far as I knew, there wasn't a Miss Manners to consult when it came to dealing with the gods.

"Oh, I just came to talk to you. Tomorrow night is the ritual of the Cruharach. I thought you might like to chat." She moved past me, the smell of ocean brine following her. Overhead, the crows circled, as though they were guarding us.

I nodded, following her over to the nearest garden bench. As we settled on it, I was aware of a wave of warmth that flowed around us. The smell of warm sand filled my nostrils, and I caught the images of sea green water and exotic flowers floating atop the ocean.

"I'm nervous." I looked up at her. Morgana shifted height every time I saw her. I had begun to realize that the gods could change shape at will. Or at least work with glamour.

"I know you are. I won't tell you not to be. That would do no good. But you will find your way through it. Of that I'm sure." She paused, holding out one hand. One of the crows landed on it for a moment before flying away. "Most of the Fae have varying lineages, but seldom does a mix like yours come along. They do spar for dominance, you know. Usually, one heritage will be submissive to the other, or both parents will come from the same branch. That's how it seems to work. But the Leannan Sidhe and the Autumn Stalkers…neither likes to give up control."

"Will that affect how the Cruharach changes me?"

After a pause, she said, "Yes. But how you react to it is more important. Did Marilee warn you to go in with an open mind? Don't take sides, Ember. Don't hope for one over the other. You must let whatever happens, happen. Only through surrender will you discover the mastery you hope for." She leaned down and picked up one of the fallen leaves. "What you did to your grandfather was a necessity. It doesn't mean the Leannan Sidhe side of you has to be a killer. You instinctively reached for the power that would help save your life at that moment."

"I know that. But he was my grandfather. I hated him, but I feel so conflicted about what I did to him. Will *that* ever go away? Could I have done something different that would have saved his life and yet saved mine, as well?" Even though everybody kept saying "Don't feel guilty," I couldn't help it. I did feel guilty. I had murdered him.

"There's never a way to know for sure. But Ember, if you hadn't protected yourself, you'd be dead now. Or worse. The ritual that he wanted to put you through strips more than one bloodline from a person. It's forbidden because it changes the very psyche. It permanently damages the ego. He was insisting you go through a rite that would have destroyed who you are."

"And the Cruharach won't do that?"

"No. It will merge your bloodlines into the best possible form, as long as everything goes right. It's a natural metamorphosis, unlike what your grandfather sought for you." Without warning, she took my hand in hers. "Close your eyes."

I closed my eyes. The pulsing grew louder, and it felt as though I was in the middle of the ocean as it shifted and turned, waves growing in the storm. They roared past, silver tides churning as they threatened to drag me under. Their fury was bathed in ice and frost, and their glory was in the morning sun, climbing into the sky over lazy waters beneath which turtles swam and dolphins danced.

And then I was in the water, swimming with the dolphins, letting them pull me along as I hung onto their fins. We raced through the waves, the foam churning from our wake, and joy filled my heart as I opened myself to the power of the Ocean Mother. And then, under the moon, the dolphins beached on the shore, letting me go before the waves reclaimed them, and I ran toward the tree line, darting up the trail, where I blended into the undergrowth, all my hunter's instincts coming to play.

A moment later, I pulled out of the vision and shook my head.

"Are you telling me it doesn't have to be one or the other?"

"The word 'merge' does not indicate exclusivity." Morgana stroked my cheek. "Do not fear losing part of yourself. The whole is stronger than the sum of the parts. And now, my dear, I will see you tomorrow night. You will not work tomorrow, but spend the day in quiet meditation. Go to Marilee's around five tomorrow night. She will know what to do next."

As quickly as she had appeared, Morgana vanished, and with her the warmth that had cloaked me. Exhausted and feeling exposed, I headed back to the house to take a nap before dinner. All my thoughts were on the Cruharach, and I just wanted to get it over with, regardless of the outcome.

CHAPTER FIFTEEN

*M*onday, on Samhain Eve, I met with my lawyer, dragging Angel along with me After the meeting, I had done as Marilee asked. I had spent the day in quiet mediation, but a growing nervousness had taken hold. I had spent a lot of time out in the garden, trying to calm the butterflies in my stomach. I tried not to think about what could happen, but my mind kept straying toward the darker outcomes and finally I gave up and watched the House and Garden TV network, choosing shows that were calming.

Both Angel and I had recovered from our hangovers, and she went to work while I stayed home. Herne had called me, making sure I could get to Marilee's without a problem. I wondered if he'd be there for the ritual, but decided not to ask. I didn't think I'd get a straight answer, anyway.

Monday evening I arrived at Marilee's at five P.M., promptly. I was carrying my ritual gear in a duffle bag.When I knocked on the door, Marilee opened it, but she wasn't dressed in ritual robes. No, she was wearing a pair of jeans and a shirt, and a jacket.

I frowned, suddenly wondering if I had gotten my wires crossed. "It's tonight, right? The ritual?"

"Yes, but it won't be held here. Come along. Follow me." She led me down to her car. "Put your bag in the backseat. I'm going to blindfold you so that you won't see where we're going."

I stared at her, then cleared my throat. "Okay, then."

I tossed my bag in the backseat and allowed her to fit the blindfold over my eyes. As the shade lowered over my eyes, my stomach shifted again. I couldn't see a thing. She helped me in to the car, and I could tell that I was sitting in the backseat as she fastened my seatbelt.

"Open your mouth and stick out your tongue. I need to give you the tincture that's required to guide you into the Cruharach." The compassion had drained out of her voice and she sounded gruff, almost irritated.

The realization that I had already lost control of the situation hit me. I was about to ask if it was safe, but then stopped. I already knew what she would tell me. *Nothing was guaranteed*. Obediently, I stuck out my tongue as she dropped three drops of a grassy-tasting liquid on my tongue. It was absorbed before I could even swallow.

The car shifted.

"All right, we're ready to go." Her voice came from in front of me, and I knew she was in the driver's seat. "Ember, I want to say something. I have every confidence you can pull through this and I'm looking forward to seeing what happens once you're on the other side. I won't be able to help you. No one will. But you have the skills to handle this, and you've met both sides of yourself.

Go in without expectations. What's meant to be, will happen. I want you to remain silent during the ride. Focus on your core and your breathing."

The car started then and we were moving. I could feel the car making turns, though I soon lost track of which way we were turning. I had no idea where we were going. After a time, we eased to a stop and I prepared myself for whatever was to come next, but then I heard one of the car doors open—it seemed to be the passenger door up front by the way the wind whipped in, and somebody settled themselves there. Whoever it was kept silent, but I recognized the smell. Herne.

The little kid in me wanted to shout, "I know who you are," but I stopped myself. This wasn't the place for games or for acting like a smartass. I kept my mouth shut and tried to do as Marilee asked. I focused on my breathing, keeping it even and rhythmic.

The car continued for quite some time until we pulled to a stop. The back door opened and someone—I smelled Marilee's perfume—took hold of my arm and gently guided me out of the car, holding my head down so I wouldn't hit it on the door. Then another hand took my other arm—I was sure it was Herne—and the two of them began leading me across a rocky patch of either grass or dirt. I suspected it was grass, given the feel under my boots.

Finally, about five minutes later, we came to a stop.

Marilee whispered, "Good luck. Do not remove your blindfold until you are given permission."

I stood there, unsure of what to do. The longer the blindfold was on, the more helpless I felt and any residue of my snarkiness vanished, leaving behind a quietly growing fear. My stomach shifted, and I was grateful I had obeyed the instructions and not eaten or drunk anything after noon. I was thirsty and hungry, but at least I didn't need to go to the bathroom.

"You know I'm here, don't you?" Herne's voice whispered in my ear.

I nodded, still not certain if I was allowed to talk.

"You can speak now."

"Where are we?"

"I'm here to lead you through the gates. You will find yourself in Annwn, in the forest. There are trails there. It's your task to reach the other end of the trail alive. I cannot come with you, my love, but I will be there in spirit."

He slowly removed the blindfold and I found myself staring at a large pair of oak trees. They were half-bare of leaves, and those that were still holding on had turned color and were waiting for one good wind to blow them aloft. The light was dim and I didn't recognize where we were, but it appeared to be an abandoned field of some sort. The oaks were smack in the middle, and along the edges there appeared to be a thicket of trees.

"What do I do?" I asked, my fear rising. I had only been to Annwn a couple of times, and then, only to Cernunnos's palace and Morgana's island. The otherworld of the Celts was a vast and dangerous place, from what Herne had told me.

"Here. Take these." He handed me first a backpack, then a pair of leather gloves.

I stared at them. "What's this?"

"You're wearing your jacket, and jeans and boots, so you're set that way. But you'll need the gloves. The pack contains food, a blanket, water, and a few first-aid supplies."

Growing more nervous with every minute, I took them, slinging the pack over my back, then tugging on the gloves. "What next?"

He handed me my dagger, along with a second one, and then a pistol grip crossbow and quiver of bolts. "There will be options along the path for you to take a different route. There is no correct answer as to which one to take. Listen to your intuition. Let your instinct guide you. Don't try to think your way through this."

I slowly took the weapons, strapping one dagger sheath around my left thigh and the other around my right. I slung the quiver over one shoulder and gripped the bow in my right hand. I felt in my pocket and found a bandana, which I folded into a long rectangle and tied around my head to keep my hair back.

"I heard you and Angel had quite a party with Raven the other night," Herne said. "Angel told us about it today." He leaned down, his lips near mine. "Get through this, Ember. I love you. I'd come with you if I could, but that would only muck up things. You get through this and come back to me. You understand? I'll be waiting on the other side for you. All paths lead to the same end—they're just roundabout ways."

I wanted to kiss him, but it felt wrong in this case. I could feel his breath on my face, and I inhaled sharply, memorizing his scent.

"I love you," was all I could say. I couldn't speak of my doubts, or even think about them. I could feel them squirming in the back of my mind, but to give them voice was to give them power, and the last thing I wanted was for my worries to follow me into the woods.

Herne seemed to understand what I was thinking, because he held my gaze for a moment longer, possessing me with his look, and then he stood back and pointed to the oaks.

"Walk between them. They'll take you directly where you need to go. Stay alert. Keep ever watchful. Annwn awaits."

Blowing him a kiss, I turned and walked between the oaks and into the heart of the Cruharach.

One blink, and the world was shifting. Two blinks and my body stretched and flew and scattered and then fell back together again, stardust drifting and then condensing into form. Three blinks, and I was on terra firma again, in the heart of the forest.

The woodland was deep and dark, illuminated only by the moonlight above. I could feel the heart of autumn on the wind. Tonight was the night of the dead. The night of the ancestors. The night when the veils were thinnest and the ghosts of those long past walked the world again. Tonight was Samhain Eve, when the Lord of Fire and the Lady of Ice scoured the land, hunting for the souls of those who were ready to pass over.

All around me, the trees rose like silent watchmen, massive and dark. This forest reminded me of home—of the woodlands around Seattle. Fir trees—tall timber—towered over the rest, hundreds of feet high. Cedars bushed out, massive and shaggy, and I recognized huckleberry thickets crowding around their trunks amidst the waist-high ferns. But unlike home, the firs here were interspersed with ancient oaks creaking in the wind, and occasional maple and birch whose dry leaves mirrored the susurration of the wind. It was an unlikely forest, but it felt *right*. The whispering gusts that rustled through the branches played a haunting tune, and I felt like everywhere around me, I was being watched.

The trail was distinct—there was no chance of losing track of it, and I slowly began making my way along the compacted dirt path. Eyes peeked from the forest, the reds and yellows gleaming in the night, and I held my breath, hoping they were friendly, whatever they were.

"Stop," a voice in my head told me. "You haven't done your preparation."

I froze, wondering what I had forgotten.

"Breathe." The word echoed in my thoughts and I realized that by holding my breath, I was running on fear. I slowly let out my breath and focused on trying to relax. Whatever shadows waited in this woodland, would be best met if I was alert but calm. I shook out my shoulders and began moving forward again.

Before long, my stomach rumbled and I remembered I was thirsty. I glanced around for a place to sit, and found a fallen log near the side of the trail. Cautiously, I lowered myself to the tree trunk and shrugged off my pack. As I opened it, a beam of moonlight shimmered down to reveal the contents.

Herne had packed a half-dozen sandwiches for me,

and there were cookies, an apple, some toilet paper, a small first-aid kit, a microfiber blanket rolled up tight, some matches in a plastic box, and several water bottles.

"How long does he expect me to be out here?" I muttered, unwrapping a sandwich at random and biting into it. The flavor of roast beef hit my tongue, and my stomach rumbled to attention. I devoured the sandwich, along with several cookies, and then cracked open a water bottle and drank half of the contents. The food helped ground me, and I yawned. Even though I had done nothing all day, I still felt weary. I thought about unrolling the blanket to use as a poncho, but I didn't want to delay the ritual any longer, so I left it in the pack and fastened the buckles again.

As I stood, my knees cracked, and I stretched out my arms, yawning. The oxygen quickened my blood, and I picked up the crossbow. A glance at the sky revealed a panorama of stars. I paused, squinting.

To the north—I wasn't sure how I knew the direction, but my instinct said it was north so I trusted myself—there was a faint outline in the sky of a silver castle, centered in a wheel of stars. Something about the sight chilled me to the core. There was an air of power to the castle, as though whoever lived there could reach down out of the heavens and scoop me up, carrying me off into the depths of space.

I slowly pulled my gaze away. The feeling of being watched had increased.

Taking a deep breath, I turned back to the trail and began walking. I wasn't sure how fast time passed here. Annwn wasn't the same as home; things worked differently. As I continued along, I could hear rustles in the bushes, the sounds of huffing and low growls. I had to stop several times to calm my breathing.

Finally, I stood in the center of the path, closing my eyes. As I lowered my consciousness into trance, I began to feel the buzz and crackle of the forest.

Like all woodlands, the forests of Annwn were alive. The forest had a sentience to it, created by the sum of all its inhabitants, both flora and fauna. I tried to key in on the central hub—the core of the forest—to understand its energy. I dug through the layers, slowly prying away the barriers of briar and thorn, edging my way toward the center. After a while, I felt the resistance give way and there it was...*the heart of the forest, bathed in shades of deep hunter green and vibrant streaks of both gold and rust.*

"Hello," I whispered, and to my surprise, the forest whispered back.

Welcome. But the welcome wasn't totally clear—there were hidden threads attached, snares for the unwary and the unwise, and dark secrets hiding behind the leaves and branches that watched over the land.

I dug deeper, burrowing like a worm to the core of the apple.

The sound of water in the distance caught my attention, the flowing of rivers into ponds and lakes, and beyond that, the faint rush of ocean waves crashing against the shore. From another direction, winter lurked, creeping forward, quietly absorbing the land. And yet, in another direction, I could feel the melancholy fires of autumn, crackling at the edges. Beyond that, a whispered hope of spring caressed the breezes. All of these belonged to the forests of Annwn, all in their time and place.

Another layer lower and I could hear the rustle of

bobcats and lynx as they padded along through the treetops, and a red fox who darted through the trees. Overhead, the screech of an owl echoed through the forest, and behind that, the cawing of crows. A wolf howled from a distant mountain, and the moon shook and the forest reverberated, echoing the howl back to the alpha.

Still lower into trance, I felt the snuffling of skunk, and the slither of an adder moving smoothly through the undergrowth. The ferns whispered as it passed by, and the bracken and ivy picked up the chorus, magnifying it so that all who walked the trails of the woodland might know that danger lurked in the darker corners.

As I slowly merged into the feeling, a heady intoxication began to take hold, and I leaned my head back, laughing for the sheer joy of understanding the language of the land. I opened my eyes and began to stride ahead, ready for whatever lie in my path.

I rounded a bend in the trail and paused. The trail ahead ended in a Y-fork. I could go either left or right. Pausing, I started to think through which way I should take, but Herne's words echoed in my ears.

Listen to your intuition. Let your instinct guide you. Don't try to think your way through this.

I let out my breath and closed my eyes, asking, "Which way?"

"Left," my gut replied, and so I turned onto the left fork and before I could hesitate, headed off to the side.

The trail began to descend and to my left, the embankment fell away into a deep ravine. I could hear water coming from below. Pushed from some inner urge, I sped up, jogging along with only the moon's light to guide me. The trail kept curving as the embankment to the right grew higher beside me. I was headed downhill.

The scent of water flooded my nostrils and I could feel the elementals nearby. They were playing, and joyful, and I wanted to join them. I hastened my pace, sure on my feet, until I came around a final bend to the left and out onto a wide shoreline. I was facing what seemed to be an ocean, with the water dark as pitch and cresting waves, splashing seafoam against the rocky beach.

I slowed to a walk, stepping out to greet the water. In the waves, I could see elementals rising up to play catch with massive driftwood logs. I watched them for a moment, marveling in their strength, then began walking along the shore. Up ahead was a figure, and I felt compelled to see who it was. I followed the shoreline, the water's spray misting over me, until I came to a man sitting on a log. He was staring out at the water, and I could feel the sadness that floated around him, cloaking him like a blanket.

"What's wrong?" I asked.

"I've lost my fire," he whispered.

As I stood there, wondering what to say, I could feel hunger rising up, only it wasn't for food. It was for him, for his energy. I blinked, trying to force the insatiable need back, but it broke loose, flooding over me, and I strode forward, dropping the crossbow in the sand as I pushed him back off the log onto the sand and straddled him.

"Want me," I whispered, holding his gaze with mine. "Long for me."

He blinked, staring into my eyes like a drowning man spying a glass of water. "Muse…beautiful muse…"

"Need me." I was quickly losing my senses in the spiral of lust and hunger that rushed through me. *"Beg for me."*

As though in a trance, he nodded. "Please...I've been so lost."

I leaned down and ripped open his shirt, licking his chest. And it was a fine chest. He was a gorgeous hunk of pining, aching manhood, desperate for a spark to light his muse, and I was the fire. The torch that could bring him back to life. But there was a price, and that price would be his soul. I would feed him and nurture him, and then, when he was ripe and healthy, I would feed.

"Wait. Who are you?" A flicker of fear crept into his eyes as I bared my teeth, snarling.

"I'm your muse. I'm your passion. I'm your everything." I tilted my head, and from the back of my mind, I flashed back to the Vulture Sisters. They were soul eaters like me. They hunted like I did, and they gave no mercy to their quarry.

"Don't hurt me," the man whispered, licking his lips. I could feel his arousal through his pants, but his desire was mingled with fear, and the fear only stoked my hunger.

A crash of waves splashed over us, soaking us through. I laughed, shaking my hair as the water strengthened me. But as I glanced up at the embankment, in the distance I caught sight of a glimpse of silver. A stag was watching me from above, and something about it seemed familiar. I tried to pinpoint what it could be, both irritated and oddly relieved that it had interrupted my feeding cycle. As I stared at the creature, it reared, and its bellowing echoed all the way down to the shore.

"*Herne*," I whispered, and a shudder ran through me as I looked down at the man below me. He was half-drowned from the waves, and he was staring at me, terrified and yet longing. He would hand himself over to me if I forced him.

"No…no…" My thoughts broke through the wall of hunger and I rolled off of him, coming up to one knee, forcing the hunger to retreat. "No. I can control this."

At that moment, I glanced up to see a mirror image of myself running toward me. She was eyeing the man on the ground and I could read her thoughts. She was going to drain him dry. I leapt up, jumping in front of him, my arms wide as she came at me.

"If you won't feed, then let me."

"No. I don't need to feed and neither do you. Back off." I gave her a shove, pushing her back.

"You stupid bitch. You never know where your next meal's coming from. Get out of my way." She launched herself at me.

I grappled her to the ground, turning to glance at the man. "Run! Get out of here."

He scrambled up, racing along the shore as I wrestled with my twin. She was as strong as me, but she was fighting out of desperation and hunger, and I had self-control on my side. She lashed out, scoring my face with her nails. I grabbed her hand, feeling the blood pour down my cheek, and managed to get hold of her other wrist as well. I pressed her arms back over her head as she struggled below me.

"I can't let you go, can I? I can't just send you away."

I stared down at her, suddenly realizing what I had to do. She would haunt me forever unless I took her inside of me. We had met before, and I had embraced her powers. But now I had to embrace her shadows as well, because I could control them if I accepted them as part of myself. I didn't want to—I didn't like this side, the grasping, cunning, nature of the Leannan Sidhe, but once I had opened my heart to her, I'd be able to manage her.

I leaned down, staring at her. "I don't want to hurt you. But you can't run wild."

"But I am wild—how can you lock up a tiger?"

"You can't, but you can learn to work with them instead of against them."

Leaning down, I pressed my lips to hers and began drawing her breath into me. I could feel the stream of her life ebbing, even as a glorious sense of well-being sent me reeling like a bottle of fine brandy. She tasted of sex and passion, of power and control, of creative energy unfettered, and of the heady dance of blood flowing through veins.

As I drained the life out of her, she continued to struggle, but then I opened my heart to her, welcoming her in, and she began to quiet down. A moment later and her body was still, devoid of breath. I stumbled to the side, panting as I struggled to stand up. I turned toward the ocean, tears streaking down my cheeks. I didn't know why I was crying—she had been wild and feral and untamed and dangerous.

That's why you cry, fluttered through my thoughts. *You tamed the untamed spirit...and there's always sorrow in that.*

Mourning, I reached down and arranged her arms to cross over her chest. Then, picking up my crossbow, I turned to the ocean. A massive wave was rolling in, so huge that I knew it would swallow the beach. I took a step back, then turned to race back to the trail. I scrambled up to a safe height, then turned back just in time to see the wave cover the body, along with the rest of the sand, and when it withdrew, it took her with it out to sea, home to the ocean forever.

THE PATH LED UP AGAIN, away from the shore. I paused, feeling hungry again—not for energy, though I could feel my Leannan Sidhe blood churning, interweaving with my own. I didn't feel remorse like I had with my grandfather, or guilt, but I could feel a sense of cunning and stealth creeping into the corners, seeking its new home.

I felt stronger in spirit, and when I closed my eyes, I could see how to call up the ability to drain the life out of someone. But it was limited—I wasn't sure just how, but the urge to feed wasn't as free as it had been at first.

My head suddenly began to hurt and my stomach rumbled. I sat down on the side of the path and pulled out another sandwich and the rest of the cookies. I drained another bottle of water as I ate, and then, finished, crept behind a bush to pee. After rinsing my hands with the remains of the first water bottle, I zipped up my jeans and started out again.

The stars overhead were whirling, and I could still see the silver castle high in the air, looming over the land. There was a strong sense of familiarity about it, but I couldn't pinpoint why. I returned my gaze to the path and, as I broke through a patch of ferns overgrowing the trail, I found myself back on the main trail.

I began to walk faster now that I was on level ground. I had fallen in tune with the forest, and soon I found myself moving at a blur through the thicket. I wasn't sure why I felt the need to hurry, but I did, and so I jogged steadily along until I came to another fork in the road. Only this time, the trail continued straight.

I considered the three paths, shaking away my conscious thoughts.

"Which way?" I closed my eyes, listening as the wind raced past. It motioned me to the right. I started to question myself, but pushed it aside.

Go on instinct. Don't question yourself.

I turned to the right, expecting another descent, but this time the path stayed level. I slowed my pace. The forest felt different here, and there were no sounds of water save for raindrops dripping off the boughs. The night was clear, but it had rained here recently. The ground was muddy, but the mud was covered with a layer of autumn leaves.

As I crept along, the feeling of being watched intensified yet again. Acting on instinct, I reached back to the quiver, catching hold of a bolt that I fit into the crossbow. Keeping my finger off the trigger, I held it ready as I began to zigzag along the path, certain a glowing target was emblazoned on my back.

Crap. I'm being hunted.

A snarl rose up in my throat. *Nobody* hunted me.

I slowed, eyeing the sides of the path. I could feel it… right…*there*…over behind one of the giant cedars to my right. Something was watching me from behind the tree. Ducking into the woods on my left, I vanished behind a stand of fir.

There, I found an oak that had the perfect setup of boughs. I sprang up to catch the lowest and pulled myself up, swinging to loop my feet over the branch.

As I pivoted, crawling toward the trunk, I stood, gazing up at the tangle of limbs. More quickly than I thought possible, I began to climb, leveraging myself two-thirds of the way up the trunk. From there, I found a branch that led over the path.

The branch was about five inches in diameter and sturdy.

I crouched on the branch and slowly began to move forward, creeping along, somehow managing to keep my balance as I crossed over the path to the other side. Grabbing a branch from the cedar on the other side, I swung myself onto the tree, cautiously making my way through the tangle, brushing my way through massive spider webs.

I paused, stretching out on the limb to stare down into the gloom.

And there he was.

He was Fae, that much I could tell, and he was carrying a bow. He was craning his neck, looking toward the path.

Oh no, I thought. *You don't get off that easy.*

I was about to jump down but then froze. There was another one, a little farther back in the trees. How many were there in this hunting party?

I propped back against the trunk and closed my eyes, conjuring the spirit of the forest again. I needed eyes. I needed to see. I sought the crows but they were all asleep. Well, I'd have to pick somebody else. I sought for another spirit, and found that of a white fox, hiding in a burrow.

I need your help.

My thoughts seemed to take the shape of an arrow and I aimed them toward the fox, then let go. They sprang forward and suddenly, the fox awoke and stood, shaking its head.

What do you want, milady?

Ah, so you are a forest spirit and not just a fox.

As you guessed, yes, I am.

I need you to tell me how many hunters are in the forest below me.

The fox paused, then I felt it grin. *I am kitsune. What will you offer in exchange for my help?*

I thought for a moment. *Are you hungry? I have a sandwich.*

Two. And a promise to never harm my kind unnecessarily. My fox brothers.

I thought for a moment. The sandwiches were no problem, but I had to think over the other demand, for I knew any vow I took this night would be binding.

As long as I don't have to—as long as they aren't hurting others or attacking me, I can give you that promise. I'll never hunt your fox brothers without good reason, and never in greed or hunger for their fur.

Then I accept. Wait.

I waited, staying as still as I could so I didn't make any noise. It felt like an eternity passed, during which time I had to keep from shouting as a massive orb weaver crawled across my face, then scuttled off onto the tree. Finally, though, the kitsune returned.

There are three. They are Autumn's Bane. They seek you, and will not rest until you are dead. Now, my reward?

As soon as I take care of them, I'll give you your sandwiches. My promise to you stands from this moment. I paused, then asked, *Will I have to kill them?*

If you do not, they will continue to hunt you, no matter where you go.

That made my mind up. They'd prevent me from

reaching the end of the Cruharach. I wasn't sure if they were actual hunters, or simply a test spinning out in my mind, but either way, I couldn't let them win. *Where is the third?*

Behind the oak, two trees over.

I knew that I could pick off the first two from up in the cedar, but that would leave the third to fight hand-to-hand. There was no help for it—I had a battle on my hands.

I lowered myself to a branch from where I could easily see the first hunter.

The second was farther away, but I thought I could pick him off from here, too. I slowly brought up my crossbow, feeling oddly reluctant. I didn't like taking life, even though I had done my share of killing. I never wanted to *get* used to it, either. But tonight was all or nothing.

I aimed at the first hunter, slowly letting out my breath as I pulled the trigger. The bolt shot true, whistling through the air. The hunter jerked his head up as he heard the quarrel streaming toward him, but before he could do anything, it landed square in his heart and he let out a shout as he fell to his knees, and then to the ground.

The other hunter spun around, glancing at his companion. The next thing I knew, an arrow came zinging through the tree, barely missing me. I forced myself to stay still, fitting another bolt in my bow. But this one was harder, since he was now on his guard. He had darted behind a bush, but he'd have to come out in order to fight me. If he shouted to alert his remaining comrade, he'd give his presence away.

I waited for a moment, once again seeking the wisdom

of the forest. I sought for the feeling of fear. A sudden whisper on the wind turned me in the direction of a large patch of juniper. I brought the bow up and, going on instinct, let the bolt fly. It sung through the air, and I heard a sudden shout as the hunter staggered out. I'd hit him in the side.

I fit another bolt and again let it fly. Before he could attempt to notch his arrow, the bolt hit his chest. As he fell, he shouted a warning, and I dropped my way through the tree, coming to rest on the ground by its trunk. I dropped the crossbow as the third hunter came darting out, long dagger ready. There was no room to draw a sword in the undergrowth.

I flipped the snaps on both daggers and pulled them, circling toward him. His eyes were glinting—he was enjoying the challenge, that rang clear as a bell.

"You want me? Come get me," I said, feeling my own blood rise in response.

He lunged toward me, springing off the ground as he flipped over my head. Startled, I whipped around, daggers up and ready. He rolled, aiming for my calves, and I jumped over his blade. As I landed, I spun, bringing both daggers overhead, spreading my arms to balance myself. He was coming out of his crouch and I managed to land one dagger in the back of his shoulder. Instead of pulling away, I shoved it hard into the muscle and brought my other arm around to his side, driving the other dagger deep into his ribs.

He let out a gurgling sound as I withdrew my blades. I stood back, staring at him. He was still kneeling in front of me, and I slowly placed my foot on his back, pushing him over, feeling an odd thrill as I did so.

The bush in front of me rustled and I looked up. *Oh crap.* My Autumn Stalker twin stepped out. She was holding the same daggers as I was, and she twirled them in her hands.

"Are you ready?" she said. "You know the rules. You know the score."

A shiver ran down my back. As good as I was, she was better. She was of my father's blood, pure and strong. And I could feel her craving for the fight rise up. She'd fight me till one of us was done. And if she won…she'd take over.

How could I win against someone who was stronger than I was? But then, I knew what I had to do, and I blessed my luck that I'd chosen the other path first. I straightened and turned my gaze toward her. Summoning the hunger, I let it swell within my heart and rebound out to swirl in my aura.

This is how my mother won my father over. I knew it sure as I knew my own name.

"Want me," I whispered.

My opponent jerked as I forced all my will into my words. She tried to pull her gaze away.

"You want me. You need me. You crave me." I stepped forward, summoning up the ocean waves with their beckoning call. *"You hunger for me."*

She lifted her blades. "Stop." But her voice was shaking and she gave away her fear as she pulled back a step.

I set my gaze on hers, holding her captive as I summoned the strength of the water into my movements, surrounding myself with a cloak of foaming waves.

"Hear my voice. Listen to me. You hunger for something that you never knew you needed. You know that together, our

strength will multiply. My inspiration will light your path. You need me, Ember." The words rolled off my tongue, sweeping forward on a cresting wave. All around us, the darkened forest responded to my song.

And then, as though her hands were tired, she dropped her blades. "Who are you?"

"I am you. Join me and together we can be stronger than you imagine." I sheathed my blades and slowly held out my arms. "What is your creed?"

"Yield to no one, save those stronger. Die in battle if I cannot succeed." Her voice was so low I could barely hear it.

"I am stronger and you know this. Give yourself to me. You will die a glorious death and be reborn in my heart." The energy swirled around me, so strong that I could barely breathe. I needed her. I wanted her. She would be mine. And together, we would prevail.

Fear crept into her eyes and she started to turn.

"Stop. You are no coward and you know it." I moved toward her, one step at a time. Overhead the stars began to spin, whirling around the castle in the sky, and a loud percussive beat began rippling through the forest.

She froze, her eyes wide. "I do not yield. I do not yield…"

"Yet you will." I held out my arms. "Come to me, child. Come to me."

She stiffened, but began to stagger toward me, as though she were being drawn by chains. The drums grew louder and I grabbed hold of the energy, weaving it around her like a web. She lurched forward, fear clouding her face.

"This will not hurt. I promise you."

And I kept my promise. I summoned every ounce of passion into my touch as I caught her shoulders and pulled her toward me. She began to relax as the drums quickened. I pressed my lips to hers as I began draining her the same way I had drained the other. Her strength and will flowed into my veins, and the magic of the hunt streamed out on her breath.

I drank deep, her life becoming mine, her courage shoring me up.

As the energy transferred from her to me, I felt it begin to merge with that of my Leannan Sidhe heritage, forming a new force, a hybrid that the Cruharach strengthened. As the last wisps of breath left her body, I caught them up, swallowed them down, and then let her fall, standing back as tendrils from deep in the ground reached through the leaves to wrap around her. They trussed her up and pulled her beneath the leaves, deep into the soil, to return to the Mother.

Silently, I turned. I picked up my bow and opened my pack, tossing two sandwiches for the kitsune, who dashed out from beneath a bush to swallow them whole. I added a third.

Thank you.

Who are you? he asked.

I don't even know if I have an answer to that.

And with that, I returned to the path as a mist rose around me. Up ahead, I could see the path merging back with the original trail and beyond that, I saw the end of the road. And there, waiting, stood the silver stag. As the fog rolled around my legs, rising to my knees, I began to run toward Herne, and my future.

CHAPTER SIXTEEN

Five days later...

"Here she comes!" Herne's voice echoed as I came down the stairs. I was wearing a long plum-colored gown that cinched at the waist and flowed out. It had an asymmetrical hem, with the front four inches above my knees, and the skirt tea length in back. The sweetheart bodice ended in halter ties behind my neck. I was also wearing a pair of kitten-heel knee boots, and I had gathered my hair up into a chignon. Talia had tucked roses in the bun, and had lent me a pair of crystal earrings. At my throat was Morgana's necklace.

"Woohoo!" Angel shouted as I appeared.

A sudden swirl of confetti sparkled down over me from all directions.

Yutani was playing DJ, and techno was pouring out of the speakers.

Everybody from the office was there, including Charlie, as well as Sheila, Raven, Rafé, and Marilee. And so were Morgana and Cernunnos. We were ostensibly taking a break from the stress over the Tuathan Brotherhood, but I knew the party had been Talia's idea to celebrate me making it through the Cruharach.

The caterer was serving up suckling pig and roast lamb, and the tables were filled with trays of shrimp and crab, lobster and dinner rolls, salads and fruit tarts and a cake that was three tiers high. A bartender was mixing drinks behind the wet bar. All in all, the place was a mansion. I wasn't sure who owned it, but the log cabin reminded me of a rustic yet fancy ski lodge. A fire crackled in the oversize fireplace.

I took Herne's hand and he spun me into his arms. "The lady of the evening! May I present Ember Kearney, who has passed through the Cruharach intact, and now is…a mystery to unfold." He pulled me to him. "May I have this dance?" He was dressed in a tux and tails, with a top hat, and I couldn't resist.

"She Bangs" came on and we broke into a modified salsa, given I only knew some of the moves. As we spun and pranced our way around the floor, Viktor held out his hand to Sheila and she gave him a rueful smile and let him pull her onto the dance floor. I was glad to see their argument seemed to have ended. Rafé grabbed Angel's hand and they too joined in.

At that point, Cernunnos moved forward, holding Morgana's waist, and they went for it. Everybody else stopped, backing off the floor to watch them. Seeing the gods not only salsa but put their own spin of magic into it wasn't something you saw every day.

As I watched Cernunnos, I saw where Herne got his moves. His father was sultry, the heat of the dark woods in summer. Morgana was wearing a sparkling mini-dress that acted like a sequined kaleidoscope every time she moved. As they danced, the passion between them seemed to flame higher and I couldn't look away. Cernunnos's long dreads spun as he sailed across the dance floor, Morgana keeping up with them.

"Your parents are incredible," I whispered.

Herne nodded. "Yes, I know. When they're good, they're great. When they argue, it's best that they have their own houses. Come on, let's get a drink."

He steered me over to the bar and I accepted a glass of mead. As we walked away from the dancing, I felt oddly distanced. I had come through the Cruharach intact, but it had definitely changed me, and I was only beginning to sort out how.

I felt older, more confident. I also could feel the aging process drastically slowing. It was as though an internal clock had suddenly stopped ticking, slowing down to milliseconds instead of seconds. Deep inside me, both sides of my heritage coiled together, no longer separate but integrated into my psyche.

"Who owns this place?"

Herne shrugged. "A friend of a friend. Leave it at that." He paused, then asked, "How are you? *Seriously*. We haven't had much chance to talk in private since before the ritual." He gazed down at me, his eyes piercing my heart.

"I'm good." I looked up at him. "You saved me, during the Cruharach. You came to me on the shore and kept me from making a terrible mistake."

"I couldn't help you. I wasn't allowed." His gaze gave away nothing. "I was on the other side, but I couldn't be present during the actual ritual. Father forbade it."

I shook my head. "I *know* you were there. I saw the silver stag up on the embankment."

Herne took my glass and set it aside, along with his. "I mean it, Ember. They wouldn't let me help you."

"Then who did I see?" I knew what I had seen.

"You were born with the mark of the silver stag. Maybe there's a greater force involved. Whatever the case, I'm so glad you're here with me." He pulled me toward him, his hands on my waist. "We can't predict the future, but right now, right at this moment, I can't imagine my life without you in it."

Leaning down, he gathered me in his arms and pressed his lips to mine. The kiss was hot, so hot it made me melt. I wanted to drag him aside, find a private place and screw his brains out, but tonight wasn't just for me. It was for all of my friends who had been worried about me.

"Excuse me." The voice was so deep it could only be Cernunnos.

We spun around.

"Father, is something wrong?" Herne asked.

Cernunnos shook his head. "Your mother requests you attend her for a moment, son. I'll keep Ember company."

I swallowed hard as Herne nodded, then turned to go find Morgana. Once he was gone, I cleared my throat and turned to Cernunnos. As approachable as Herne was, Cernunnos was the opposite. He was every inch a god, and he made me feel about the size of an ant whenever I was near him.

"So, you have passed through the awakening. Welcome to your true nature," Cernunnos said.

I struggled to answer. "Thank you, milord."

"Your father was worried that you wouldn't manage it—he asked me to help at one point. He and your mother knew they weren't likely to live long enough to see you grow up. But I knew you could do it. Morgana and I would have stepped in if fate hadn't brought you to us first." He paused, then in a husky voice, he said, "Don't ever fear your powers. Fear will kill you faster than anything else."

"I got that impression during the Cruharach." Then, gazing into his eyes, I saw a glint of silver and I gasped. "It was *you*. You were the silver stag on the embankment."

Cernunnos let a slip of a smile show.

"Like son, like father," he said, then turned away. But before he returned to Morgana, he glanced over his shoulder. "Ember, make certain you listen to your heart. My son might be a god, but he has feelings. And I may chastise him for many things, but I do not take betrayal easily. For myself, my wife, *or my son*. Do you understand?"

He held my gaze.

Inside, I was terrified, but I didn't want him to see that. "I love your son. If that changes, I'll be honest and upfront. I only ask the same in return."

"Well, then. So we understand each other." He turned back to the party.

I picked up my glass and drained it. If Cernunnos was warning me not to betray his son, then perhaps Herne was more serious than I thought. And just what did

Cernunnos consider betrayal? Was it dancing with Apollo? Talking to Viktor? Or something more questionable?

As Herne walked back toward me, I realized that I wasn't sure if I was happy, or scared shitless. But for now, I decided on happy. Herne held out his arms and I went running into his embrace, as—for the first time in my life—I felt a sense of belonging like I had never before experienced.

Deep in the forest, the soft sound of chanting fell silent. At this altitude, a light snow was falling. From between the snowflakes, a vapor began to appear—a silver mist that spread across the clearing. The figure who had been chanting suddenly stopped as the mist enveloped her, and a moment later, she lay silent in the snow. The mist coiled into tendrils and began to surround the body, wrapping around the woman's limbs. As the snow continued to fall, the mist seeped into her open mouth. Another moment, and the chanter sat up, looking around. She knew where she had to go, and what she had to do. And so, she began the long trek out of the deep, dark woodland.

IF YOU ENJOYED this book and haven't read the first four books of the Wild Hunt Series, check out THE SILVER STAG, OAK & THORNS, IRON BONES, and A SHADOW OF CROWS. You can preorder book 6—THE SILVER MIST—now.

Meanwhile, I invite you to visit Fury's world. Bound to Hecate, Fury is a minor goddess, taking care of the Abominations who come off the World Tree. Books 1 to 5 are available now in the Fury Unbound Series : FURY RISING, FURY'S MAGIC, FURY AWAKENED, FURY CALLING, and FURY'S MANTLE.

For a dark, gritty, steamy series, try my world of the Indigo Court, where the long winter has come, and the Vampiric Fae are on the rise. NIGHT MYST, NIGHT VEIL, NIGHT SEEKER, NIGHT VISION, NIGHT'S END, and NIGHT SHIVERS are all available now.

If you prefer a lighter-hearted paranormal romance, meet the wild and magical residents of Bedlam in my Bewitching Bedlam Series. Fun-loving witch Maddy Gallowglass, her smoking-hot vampire lover Aegis, and their crazed cjinn Bubba (part djinn, all cat) rock it out in Bedlam, a magical town on a magical island. BLOOD MUSIC, BEWITCHING BEDLAM, MAUDLIN'S MAYHEM, SIREN'S SONG, WITCHES WILD, CASTING CURSES, BLOOD VENGEANCE, TIGER TAILS, and Bubba's origin story—THE WISH FACTOR—are available.

If you like cozies with an edge, try my Chintz 'n China paranormal mysteries. The series is complete with: GHOST OF A CHANCE, LEGEND OF THE JADE DRAGON, MURDER UNDER A MYSTIC MOON, A HARVEST OF BONES, ONE HEX OF A WEDDING, and a wrap-up novella: HOLIDAY SPIRITS.

The last Otherworld book—BLOOD BONDS—will be available in April 2019.

For all of my work, both published and upcoming

releases, see the Bibliography at the end of this book, or check out my website at Galenorn.com and be sure and sign up for my newsletter to receive news about all my new releases.

CAST OF CHARACTERS

The Wild Hunt & Family:

- **Angel Jackson:** Ember's best friend, a human empath. Angel is the newest member of the Wild Hunt. A whiz in both the office and the kitchen, and loyal to the core, Angel is an integral part of Ember's life, and a vital member of the team.
- **Charlie Darren:** A vampire who was turned at 19. Math major, baker, and all-around Wild Hunt gofer.
- **Ember Kearney:** Caught between the world of Light and Dark Fae, and pledged to Morgana, goddess of the Fae and the Sea, Ember Kearney was born with the mark of the Silver Stag. Rejected by both her bloodlines, she now works for the Wild Hunt as an investigator.
- **Herne the Hunter:** Herne is the son of the Lord of the Hunt, Cernunnos, and Morgana, goddess

of the Fae and the Sea. A demigod—given his mother's mortal beginnings—he's a lusty, protective god and one hell of a good boss. Owner of the Wild Hunt Agency, he helps keep the squabbles between the worlds of Light and Dark Fae from spilling over into the mortal realms.
- **Talia:** A harpy who long ago lost her powers, Talia is a top-notch researcher for the agency, and a long-term friend of Herne's.
- **Viktor:** Viktor is half-ogre, half-human. Rejected by his father's people (the ogres), he came to work for Herne some decades back.
- **Yutani:** A coyote shifter who is dogged by the Great Coyote, Yutani was driven out of his village over two hundred years before. He walks in the shadow of the trickster, and is the IT specialist for the company.

The Gods, the Elemental Spirits, & Their Courts:

- **Cerridwen:** Goddess of the Cauldron of Rebirth. Dark harvest mother goddess.
- **Cernunnos:** Lord of the Hunt, god of the Forest, and King Stag of the Woods. Together with Morgana, Cernunnos originated the Wild Hunt and negotiated the covenant treaty with both the Light and the Dark Fae. Herne's father.
- **Coyote (also: Great Coyote):** Native American trickster spirit/god.
- **Danu:** Mother of the Pantheon. Leader of the Tuatha de Dannan.

CAST OF CHARACTERS

- **Ferosyn:** Chief healer in Cernunnos's Court
- **Herne:** (see The Wild Hunt)
- **Kuippana (also: Kipa):** Lord of the Wolves. Elemental forest spirit; Herne's distant cousin. Trickster.
- **Morgana:** Goddess of the Fae and the Sea, she was originally human but Cernunnos lifted her to deityhood. She agreed to watch over the Fae who did not return across the Great Sea. Torn by her loyalty to her people, and her loyalty to Cernunnos, she at times finds herself conflicted about the Wild Hunt. Herne's mother.
- **The Morrígan:** Goddess of Death and Phantoms. Goddess of the battlefield.

The Fae Courts:

- **Navane:** The court of the Light Fae, both across the Great Sea and on the eastside of Seattle, the latter ruled by **Névé**.
- **TirNaNog:** The court of the Dark Fae, both across the Great Sea and on the eastside of Seattle, the latter ruled by **Saílle**.

The Ante-Fae:
Creatures predating the Fae. The wellspring from which all Fae descended. Unique beings who rule their own realms. All Ante-Fae are dangerous, but some are more deadly than others.

- **Apollo:** The Golden Boy. Vixen's boy toy. Weaver of Wings. Dancer.

CAST OF CHARACTERS

- **Blackthorn, the King of Thorns:** Ruler of the blackthorn trees and all thorn-bearing plants. Cunning and wily, he feeds on pain and desire.
- **Raven, the Daughter of Bones:** (also: Raven BoneTalker) A bone witch, Raven is young, as far as the Ante-Fae go, and she works with the dead. She's also a fortune-teller, and a necromancer.
- **Straff:** Blackthorn's son, who suffers from a wasting disease requiring him to feed off others' life energies and blood.
- **Vixen:** The Mistress/Master of Mayhem. Gender-fluid Ante-Fae who owns the Burlesque A Go-Go nightclub.
- **The Vulture Sisters:** Triplet sisters, predatory.

The Force Majeure:

A group of legendary magicians, sorcerers, and witches. They are not human, but magic-born. There are twenty-one at any given time and the only way into the group is to be hand chosen, and the only exit from the group is death.

- **Merlin:** Morgana's father. Magician of ancient Celtic fame.
- **Taliesin:** The first Celtic bard. Son of Cerridwen, originally a servant who underwent magical transformation and finally was reborn through Cerridwen as the first bard.
- **Ranna:** Powerful sorceress. Elatha's mistress.
- **Rasputin:** The Russian sorcerer and mystic.
- **Väinämöinen:** The most famous Finnish bard.

CAST OF CHARACTERS

Friends, Family, & Enemies:

- **Aoife:** A priestess of Morgana who guards the Seattle portal to the goddess's realm.
- **Celia:** Yutani's aunt.
- **Danielle:** Herne's daughter, born to an Amazon named Myrna.
- **DJ Jackson:** Angel's little stepbrother, DJ is half Wulfine—wolf shifter. He now lives with a foster family for his own protection.
- **Erica:** A Dark Fae police officer, friend of Viktor's.
- **Elatha:** Fomorian King; enemy of the Fae race.
- **Ginty McClintlock:** A dwarf. Owner of Ginty's Waystation Bar & Grill.
- **Marilee:** A priestess of Morgana, Ember's mentor. Possibly Human—unknown.
- **Myrna:** An Amazon who had a fling with Herne many years back, which resulted in their daughter Danielle.
- **Rafé:** Brother to Ulstair, Raven's late fiancé; Angel's boyfriend. Actor/fast-food worker. Dark Fae.
- **Sheila:** Viktor's girlfriend. A kitchen witch; one of the magic-born. Geology teacher who volunteers at the Chapel Hill Homeless Shelter.

PLAYLIST

I often write to music, and THE HALLOWED HUNT was no exception. Here's the playlist I used for this book.

- **AJ Roach:** Devil May Dance
- **Air:** Napalm Love; Playground Love
- **Android Lust:** Here and Now
- **Arch Leaves:** Nowhere to Go
- **AWOLnation:** Sail
- **Band of Skulls:** I Know What I Am
- **The Black Angels:** Currency; Half Believing; Comanche Moon; Hunt Me Down; Grab as Much (As You Can); Death March; Young Men Dead
- **Black Mountain:** Queens Will Play
- **Black Rebel Motorcycle Club:** Feel It Now
- **Broken Bells:** The Ghost Inside
- **Camouflage Nights:** (It Could Be) Love
- **Clannad:** Newgrange
- **Cobra Verde:** Play with Fire

PLAYLIST

- **Colin Foulke:** Emergence
- **Crazy Town:** Butterfly
- **Creedence Clearwater Revival:** Green River; Run Through the Jungle; Susie-Q
- **Damh the Bard:** The Cauldron Born; Obsession; Cloak of Feathers; Morrígan; The Wicker Man
- **Dizzi:** Dizzi Jig; Dance of the Unicorns
- **Eastern Sun:** Beautiful Being (Original Edit)
- **Eivør:** Trøllbundin
- **Faun:** Hymn to Pan
- **FC Kahuna:** Hayling
- **Gabrielle Roth:** The Calling; Raven; Mother Night; Rest Your Tears Here
- **Gary Numan:** Ghost Nation; My Name is Ruin; Hybrid; Petals; I Am Dust
- **The Gospel Whiskey Runners:** Muddy Waters
- **Gotye:** Hearts A Mess; Somebody That I Used To Know
- **Gypsy Soul:** Who?
- **The Hang Drum Project:** Shaken Oak; St.Chartier
- **In Strict Confidence:** Silver Bullets; Wintermoon; Snow White; Forbidden Fruit
- **John Fogerty:** The Old Man Down the Road
- **The Kills:** Nail in My Coffin; You Don't Own The Road; Dead Road 7; Cheap and Cheerful; Sour Cherry
- **King Black Acid:** Rolling Under
- **Lorde:** Yellow Flicker Beat; Royals
- **Loreena McKennitt:** The Mummers' Dance; All Souls Night

PLAYLIST

- **Low with Tom and Andy:** Half Light
- **Mai Lan:** Pumper
- **Marconi Union**: First Light; Alone Together; Flying (In Crimson Skies); Time Lapse; On Reflection; Broken Colours; We Travel; Weightless; Weightless, Pt. 2; Weightless, Pt. 3; Weightless, Pt. 4; Weightless, Pt. 5; Weightless, Pt. 6
- **Matt Corby:** Breathe
- **Motherdrum:** Big Stomp; Ceremony; Instant Success
- **Nirvana:** Come As You Are; Lake of Fire; Something in the Way; Heart Shaped Box; Plateau
- **The Notwist:** Hands on Us
- **Orgy:** Social Enemies; Blue Monday
- **A Pale Horse Named Death:** Meet the Wolf
- **The Pierces:** Secret
- **Rachel Diggs:** Hands of Time
- **Ricky Martin:** She Bangs
- **Ricky Nelson:** Garden Party
- **Robin Schulz:** Sugar
- **S. J. Tucker:** Hymn to Herne
- **Sharon Knight:** Ravaged Ruins; Bewitched; 13 Knots; Let the Waters Rise; Star of the Sea; Siren Moon
- **Shriekback:** Over the Wire; Dust and a Shadow; Underwaterboys; This Big Hush; Now These Days Are Gone; The King in the Tree; And The Rain; Shovelheads; Wriggle and Drone
- **Snow Patrol:** The Lightning Strike; What If

PLAYLIST

This Storm Ends; Disaster Button; Lifeboats; If There's a Rocket, Tie Me To It
- **Stevie Wonder**: I Wish
- **Supertramp:** Gone Hollywood; Take the Long Way Home; The Logical Song; Breakfast in America
- **Sweet Talk Radio:** We All Fall Down
- **Thievery Corporation:** Water Under the Bridge; Voyage Libre; History
- **Tom Petty:** Mary Jane's Last Dance
- **Tori Amos:** Caught a Lite Sneeze; Blood Roses; Mohammad My Friend
- **Traffic:** Rainmaker; The Low Spark of High Heeled Boys
- **Transplants:** Diamonds and Guns
- **Tuatha Dea:** Wisp of A Thing (Part 1); The Hum and the Shiver; Long Black Curl
- **Wendy Rule:** Let the Wind Blow; Elemental Chant; The Circle Song
- **The Who:** Behind Blue Eyes
- **Woodland:** Blood of the Moon; The Grove; Witch's Cross; First Melt; The Dragon; Secrets Told
- **Zero 7:** In the Waiting Line

BIOGRAPHY

New York Times, *Publishers Weekly*, and *USA Today* bestselling author Yasmine Galenorn writes urban fantasy and paranormal romance, and is the author of more than sixty-five books, including the Wild Hunt Series, the Fury Unbound Series, the Bewitching Bedlam Series, the Indigo Court Series, and the Otherworld Series, among others. She's also written nonfiction metaphysical books. She is the 2011 Career Achievement Award Winner in Urban Fantasy, given by RT Magazine.

Yasmine has been in the Craft since 1980, is a shamanic witch and High Priestess. She describes her life as a blend of teacups and tattoos. She lives in Kirkland, WA, with her husband Samwise and their cats. Yasmine can be reached via her website at Galenorn.com.

Indie Releases Currently Available:

The Wild Hunt Series:

The Silver Stag
Oak & Thorns
Iron Bones
A Shadow of Crows
The Hallowed Hunt
The Silver Mist

Bewitching Bedlam Series:
Bewitching Bedlam
Maudlin's Mayhem
Siren's Song
Witches Wild
Casting Curses
Blood Music
Blood Vengeance
Tiger Tails
The Wish Factor

Fury Unbound Series:
Fury Rising
Fury's Magic
Fury Awakened
Fury Calling
Fury's Mantle

Indigo Court Series:
Night Myst
Night Veil
Night Seeker
Night Vision
Night's End

Night Shivers

Otherworld Series:
Moon Shimmers
Harvest Song
Blood Bonds
Earthbound
Knight Magic
Otherworld Tales: Volume One
Tales From Otherworld: Collection One
Men of Otherworld: Collection One
Men of Otherworld: Collection Two
Moon Swept: Otherworld Tales of First Love
For the rest of the Otherworld Series, see website at Galenorn.com.

Chintz 'n China Series:
Ghost of a Chance
Legend of the Jade Dragon
Murder Under a Mystic Moon
A Harvest of Bones
One Hex of a Wedding
Holiday Spirits

Bath and Body Series (originally under the name India Ink):
Scent to Her Grave
A Blush With Death
Glossed and Found

Misc. Short Stories/Anthologies:

The Longest Night: A Starwood Novella
Mist and Shadows: Tales From Dark Haunts
Once Upon a Kiss (short story: Princess Charming)
Once Upon a Curse (short story: Bones)

Magickal Nonfiction:
Embracing the Moon
Tarot Journeys

CPSIA information can be obtained
at www.ICGtesting.com
Printed in the USA
LVHW041551270619
622553LV00004B/573

9 781798 043806